W9-BPJ-238

TIME TRAPPED

Also by Richard Ungar

RICHARD UNGAR

TIME TRAPPED

G. P. PUTNAM'S SONS
An Imprint of Penguin Group (USA) Inc.

G. P. PUTNAM'S SONS
An imprint of Penguin Young Readers Group
Published by The Penguin Group
Penguin Group (USA) Inc., 375 Hudson Street, New York, NY 10014, USA

USA | Canada | UK | Ireland | Australia | New Zealand | India | South Africa | China
Penguin Books Ltd, Registered Offices: 80 Strand, London WC2R 0RL, England
For more information about the Penguin Group, visit penguin.com

Library of Congress Cataloging-in-Publication Data
Ungar, Richard (Richard Glenn)
Time trapped / Richard Ungar.
pages cm
Sequel to: Time snatchers.
Summary: "Caleb must train a group of young time-snatching recruits and
thwart his dangerous rival"—Provided by publisher.
[1. Time travel—Fiction.   2. Adventure and adventurers—Fiction.
3. Orphans—Fiction. 4. Crime—Fiction.   5. Science fiction.]   I. Title.
PZ7.U425Tk 2013
[Fic]—dc23
2013001812

Published simultaneously in Canada. Printed in the United States of America.
ISBN 978-0-399-25486-4
1   3   5   7   9   10   8   6   4   2

Design by Annie Ericsson.
Text set in Minion.

For Dayna

Fists are pummeling me.

But the part of my brain that's on duty tells me that I have nothing to worry about, that these small fists aren't likely to inflict any lasting damage. Still, the annoyance factor is enough to make me roll over.

"Get up, Caleb!"

The voice said my name. But that doesn't mean I have to listen, does it? Not when I have more important things to do, like sleep.

I snuggle deeper into the blankets. As an extra precaution, I bury my head under a pillow.

But it's no use. My attacker is relentless. He throws off my blankets and grabs at my arms.

"C'mon. You've got to make me breakfast. I don't want to be late for school. It's show-and-tell today, and I'm gonna bring the toy soldier you got me for my birthday."

Something doesn't compute. I manage to open one eye and fumble around on the night table for my wristwatch.

Through the haze of sleep, I can see that Mickey's big hand is near the three, which doesn't overly concern me. But his little hand makes me groan: it's on the four.

"Zach, it's way too early. Go back to sleep."

"I can't. I'm too 'cited."

1

"Fine. But let me sleep," I say.

"But I don't wanna be late."

"Trust me. You won't be." I turn onto my side and try to get back to sleep.

But it's no use. By four thirty, Zach has me up, dressed and eating Cheerios with him.

By the time we all leave the house, I'm ready for a nap. Not Zach, though. He's all fired up, bouncing down the steps as if he has springs for legs.

Which makes me wonder why I'm not even the smallest bit excited. After all, it's my first day of regular school. The school I went to before this one, the one for special kids, was okay, but after a while, I found it was too easy. Maybe it was because the accident didn't affect my ability to do schoolwork as much as Diane and Jim thought it would.

The accident. I still don't know what happened on that day in July. I don't even know for sure that I was in an accident. That's just what everyone says. What I do know is that along with not remembering the accident, I don't remember anything that happened before it. And none of the therapies and other stuff they tried with me at that other school made it any better.

Acute amnesia. That's what the doctors call it. But I call it having all my life's memories flushed down the toilet. Every once in a while, though, from someplace deep inside my brain, a piece of a forgotten memory surfaces just long enough to torture me.

Right now, the memory flashes are coming in fast and furious: a snake wrapped around an hourglass, a twirling umbrella, a pie tin spinning through the air.

I pull out the memory notebook that Dr. Winton gave me and jot them all down. He said that writing about the flashes might help me remember. But so far that hasn't happened. If anything, it's made me even more confused.

We arrive at Zach's school first. He runs to catch up with one of his friends in the yard.

Diane smiles and says, "You go ahead, Caleb. I'll wait until he goes in."

"Why don't I wait here too?" I say. "I can keep you company."

But there's no fooling Diane. She can spot a procrastinator at twenty paces. She narrows her eyes at me and says, "Get going, mister."

I walk as slowly as I can. But it's no use. Seven minutes later, I'm standing in front of the wide stone steps at the entrance to Jefferson Junior High School.

A bell sounds, and I get pulled along with a wave of students through the front door.

I can sense the excitement of the other kids, but I don't feel part of it. It's almost like I'm watching everything from inside my own little bubble. This amnesia thing wouldn't be so bad if at least I knew what caused it—preferably something respectable like hitting my head while rescuing a drowning boy or diving off of a cliff in Mexico. But all I know is what Jim and Diane told me—that one night I showed up at their doorstep with their son, Zach, and when I woke up the next morning, I had no idea who I was. The only reason they kept me is that I was the one who found Zach after he was kidnapped. That and the fact that Zach swore up and down that it was me who saved him from the kidnappers.

This place smells like lemons. I climb the well-worn stairs to the third floor, find room 301 and make my way to the back of the class. The seats fill up quickly.

Mr. Tepper, the world history teacher, doesn't waste any time. Even before the last student is seated, he's already stroking his mustache, telling us all about the hunting patterns of prehistoric man.

I suppose some people might find it interesting, but not me. Instead I keep busy counting the little squares on his red and green bowtie, which is tougher than it sounds, because Mr. Tepper moves around a lot while he talks.

I'm up to twenty-three little squares when I see her. Two rows over.

Long auburn hair. Gorgeous emerald eyes. Wearing a pleated navy skirt and ruby red sweater. Amazingly, she turns her head and looks at me. I mean *right* at me. For a moment, I can't turn away. My eyes are locked on hers. Her lips are curving up slightly in a smile.

The weird thing is she's looking at me as though she knows me. But I honestly can't say I know her.

I look away. My cheeks are burning. Real smooth, Caleb. I try to keep my eyes straight ahead, but it's impossible. Every few seconds, I find myself snatching glances at her.

For the next half hour, Mr. Tepper drones on and on about ancient man, but I tune him out. Who cares about what Cro-Magnon man ate for breakfast forty-five thousand years ago?

Finally, after what seems like forever, the bell rings. I take my time gathering up my stuff, all the while watching her out of the corner of my eye. When she leaves the classroom without a single look my way, I feel a tinge of disappointment.

Maybe I imagined it all. Maybe she was looking at a boy next to me and I only thought she was smiling at me. I look over my shoulder, and sure enough, a guy with curly blond hair and a Jefferson basketball shirt rises from his seat. Nice, Caleb. You totally embarrassed yourself. She's probably having a good laugh with her friends right now, telling them how the dorky-looking guy with the mousy brown hair was giving her goo-goo eyes.

I sigh, stand up and leave the classroom.

The hall is noisy with kids shouting and lockers clanging. I walk over to mine, fish out my combination and start turning the dial.

I'm halfway through when a voice says, "Hi. It looks like we're neighbors."

I turn and almost faint. It's her!

I should say something. Something really witty that will blow her socks off. But when I open my mouth, all that comes out is a squeaky "hi."

She smiles.

We both fumble around in our lockers for a minute. I desperately want to say something else, but my tongue seems to have gone into hiding.

"I guess they like to put the lockers for the new kids together," she says, brushing a lone strand of hair away from her eyes.

"Are you new too?" I say. I can't believe I just said that. The girl tells you she's new and then you ask her if she is. Brilliant.

"Yeah. I'm here on an exchange. The family I'm staying with lives on Somerset."

I'm rewarded with a flash of those amazing green eyes. But then panic sets in. It's my turn to talk, and I've got absolutely no idea what to say. If I don't say anything, she'll think I'm boring and walk away. Or if I say something lame, she'll think I'm a total idiot.

I make a move to grab my math binder from my locker. Three notebooks and my memory book go flying off the top shelf and land on the floor between us.

I bend down to pick everything up, but she's already got my memory book in her hands.

"What subject is this?" she asks.

"No subject. It's just a book where I write stuff down," I say.

"What kind of stuff?"

Something about the way she says it makes me want to tell her.

"Things that come into my head," I say. "And questions that I don't know the answers to."

"Can I take a look?"

"Sure. But it probably won't make any sense to you."

Great. I insulted her intelligence. Now she's going to hand the book back to me and say "see you around," and it will be true—we will see each other during the next two years of junior high—but she won't talk to me because I have now blown everything with one stupid remark and for the rest of my miserable existence on this planet, I'll think of what could have been if only I had said something else to the girl with the amazing emerald—

But incredibly, she's not handing me the book back. She's opening it.

"'Turtle jaws ripping my flesh'?" She looks up at me, eyebrows arched.

"Yeah, I know. You want to hear something even crazier? When I wrote that, I swear I had the taste of a black jelly bean in my mouth . . . and I wasn't eating anything."

"I hate the black ones," she says.

"Me too."

"Did you do this sketch?" she asks.

I look over her shoulder. She smells like mangos. The memory book is open to the page where I made a drawing of the warrior girl.

I nod.

"She's pretty. Is she anyone you know?"

"Maybe. I'm not sure," I say.

She looks up, smiles and hands me the book back. As she does, our fingers touch and I feel a warm shiver.

"Thanks for showing me," she says. "Listen, I've got to get going, or I'll be late for French."

That's it. I scared her off. What an idiot I am, showing her my memory book. Now she thinks I'm a total nutcase. I open my mouth to say something, but my throat closes up.

"Maybe I'll . . . see you around," I finally manage.

"Yeah. That would be nice," she says.

Nice! She said it would be nice to see me again. Does that mean she also thinks that *I'm* nice? It must. I mean, a person wouldn't say that it would be nice to see another person again if she didn't think that other person was nice . . . would she?

I watch her turn and begin to walk away.

"Hey," I call after her. "I'm . . . Caleb."

"I know." She laughs over her shoulder.

She knows? How does she know?

"Wait! What's your name?" I call after her.

She's going to disappear into the crowd. The beautiful girl with no name. And I'll be left wondering . . . Or worse, she'll say her name and I won't hear it. Because the noise level in the hall is increasing and a hundred inane conversations are going on around me and despite strict orders from my brain, my ears are picking up random words like *belch* and *freight train,* and *pumpkin,* and I'm afraid that when she finally says her name, I'm going to hear *mustard* instead and then what will I do—

"It's Abbie!" she calls out.

Abbie. I've got it. Abbie. Abbie. Abbie. Three times should do it. Just in case, I whip open my memory book to jot it down. A scrap of paper flutters out.

I pick it up and gaze at the big loopy letters. She gave me a note! I can't believe it. I unfold the paper.

Meet me in the park at 4:00 P.M. We need to talk in private.

We do? A beautiful girl needs to talk to me. And not only does she want to talk to me, but in private too. My dreams are coming true. This is incredible. It can take years to get a note like this from a girl, and I've done it in just over thirty minutes. A school record. Heck, maybe even a state record. My picture is going to be in *Sports Illustrated*. Right next to the girl who shot three holes in one during her sophomore year.

I look up to see if I can spot her. But Abbie is gone.

When the last bell rings, I'm already jogging down the hall, dodging other students. Once I'm outside, I sprint all the way to the park.

I arrive with seven minutes to spare and lean back against the monkey bars, facing the park entrance.

A man wearing earmuffs and a young girl in a yellow snowsuit are about to pass by when the girl says, "I want to go on the monkey bars, Daddy."

"Are you sure, sweetheart?" the father says. "Those bars look really cold. Don't you want to go on the swings first?"

The girl shakes her head vigorously and says, "Monkey bars."

I stick my hands in my pockets and stamp my feet to stay warm. I wish I had that guy's earmuffs, or even better, the girl's snowsuit. I still don't see any sign of Abbie, but that's okay. I mean, someone has to be the first to arrive, and someone has to be the second. And I'm glad that I'm the first, because if anyone's going to have to wait, I'd rather it be me than her.

I hope she didn't forget.

"Look at me, Daddy," the little girl shouts from near the top of the monkey bars. "I'm the king of the castle, and you're the dirty rascal!"

The words *king* and *rascal* echo in my brain, spurring a flood of new images: a freshly baked blackberry pie, a person dressed in the

9

yellow robes of a Chinese emperor and a vast desert. I pull out my memory book and write it all down.

I glance at my watch. Twenty minutes after four. She's not coming. All my excitement evaporates. Where is she? Something must have happened. Maybe the family she's staying with needed her home right away. Or maybe she was abducted by aliens who were collecting humans with red hair.

I can't stick around here all night. But what if she comes right after I leave? I make a deal with myself. If she's not here by five o'clock, I'm out of here.

At five thirty, I take one more look around. No sign of her anywhere. I sigh and head out of the park. Rustling comes from some tall bushes nearby.

"Abbie?" I call out, but there's no answer.

I continue walking, this time with my senses on full alert. There's a cracking sound, like ice breaking under someone's shoe. I whirl around but don't see anybody. I stand still for a moment, listening.

Nothing.

Maybe I imagined it. But how do you imagine a feeling? And this feeling is as strong as they come: Someone is following me. Watching me.

I pick up my pace. My feet are itching to run, to get out of here as fast as I can, but my brain is telling me to stay calm. It's a close contest, and I'm certain that if I hear one more noise coming from the shrubs, my feet are going to win.

As soon as I reach the edge of the park, I allow myself to slowly exhale. I watch the vapor from my breath rise and then fade away.

The farther I get from the park, the more I'm convinced I imagined everything and that no one was actually following me. Well, I must have one heck of an imagination then, because it felt so real.

Now if only my memory was as good as my imagination, I could really get things done.

After ten more minutes, I arrive home and let myself in.

"Caleb, is that you?" says Diane's voice from the kitchen.

"Yes," I answer.

"Where were you? We were starting to get a little worried," she says.

It's 5:50 P.M. Was I really in the park for almost two hours?

"I, uhh, went to the park after school to meet a . . . friend," I say.

"Well," says Diane, "if you're going to be home late, you should let either Jim or me know, honey."

"Sorry," I say, and I am. Sorry I didn't mention it to Diane but even more sorry that I went at all.

I go to my room, close the door and pull out my memory book. Most of my scribbles from today make no sense at all. As my eyes scan the page, I stop suddenly.

Near the bottom of the page are the words *Uncle who?* that I wrote this morning. Except now there are some next to those that make my breath catch in my throat. They say *He's just "Uncle" . . . he doesn't have a last name.* But here's the thing. I didn't write that.

I peer at the words and think hard. Except for Zach, Diane, Jim and Dr. Winton, I've never shown my memory book to anyone . . . until today, that is.

I dump the contents of my backpack on the bed. It's not here! Where is it? I know! I reach into my jeans pocket and feel the scrap of paper.

Meet me in the park at 4:00 P.M., says the note. I hold it up next to the message in my memory book. The loopy letters are the same!

I read the message again. *He's just "Uncle" . . . he doesn't have a last name.*

Abbie knows who he is!

Which means he's not only in my imagination. But how does she know about this guy?

And what else does she know?

My bedroom door creaking open interrupts my thoughts. Zach wanders in and flops down on the bed.

"What'sa matter, Caleb?" he asks.

"Do you think something's the matter?" I say.

Zach nods.

"You're right." I say, turning to face him. "Sometimes I get frustrated about things. Do you know what *frustrated* means?"

"Yes," he says. "Mom says she gets frustrated when Daddy doesn't put the toilet seat back down."

"Yeah, that's it exactly," I say. "Sometimes I get frustrated because I can't remember things. And sometimes I get frustrated about being frustrated. If you know what I mean."

"Yes, I understand," he says in his best grown-up voice.

"Zach, what do you remember about the time before I brought you home from the park?" I say.

His features cloud over for a moment. "You mean, the other place?"

"Yes," I say.

"I 'member it was big. Way bigger than this room. And there were other kids there too."

"And what else?"

"I 'member the bad man. And the bad boy. And being scared in the elevator."

"Anything else?" I hate pushing him like this, but I've got to know.

"He made us call him Uncle," Zach says in a hushed voice, as if he's afraid of being overheard.

A shiver goes through me as I remember the words Abbie wrote in my memory book.

"It's all right, Zach," I say. "The bad man can't get you here."

But even as I say those words, I wonder if they are really true.

III

I sit down on a bench and lace up my skates. There's some fog out on the Charles, but the weather doesn't matter much. In fact, unless there was a raging blizzard, I would have come anyway. I've got a lot to think about. And I do my best thinking on the river.

I take a few steps over to the riverbank and push away. The ice feels choppy under my skates. Farther out, it's smoother. As I glide along, the cold air on my face feels good. There are only a few other skaters out, but they're far enough away that if I close my eyes to slits, I won't see them. Looking toward the Esplanade through the mist, I glimpse snow sculptures near the Hatch Shell: a crouching tiger and a crusader's castle.

Push and glide. Push and glide. Squinting, I imagine that it's not 1968 but sometime in the distant past. It's not hard to do, since rivers don't change very much. It could be a hundred years ago, and this place would still look the same. I don't know why, but it's comforting for me to know that.

Something interrupts my thoughts: the sound of skate blades swishing across the ice. I look over my shoulder, and there's a big man skating in my direction, maybe ten yards behind me. And twenty or so yards behind him is another guy who might be even bigger. That's strange—I could swear they weren't there a minute ago.

I pick up my pace and sneak another glance back. Only the

14

closest big guy is still there. The other one is nowhere to be seen, which is quite a trick, considering the ice is too thick to fall through and there's no other way he could have disappeared from view that fast. But I don't give it a second thought because the big guy who's left is moving fast. He's closed the gap to seven yards now.

I've got to stay calm. After all, I don't own the river. He's probably here for the exercise, same as everyone. So why is my throat dry, and why are warning signals going off in my head?

Shards of thoughts (memories?) flood into my brain: a man holding my wrist and plunging my hand down into frigid water.

I look around for other skaters. I only see two, and they're about fifty yards away, skating nearer to the shore. I pick up my speed and head for them.

My legs move like pistons as I swing my arms back and forth.

Heavy breathing right behind me. How did he catch up so fast? I dare not look back.

Come on, legs! Sprinting all-out now.

Lungs screaming for air. Legs cramping. I can't keep this up. Then a hand on the back of my jacket. I zig, breaking his grip.

But a second later, he grabs me again. I try to scream, but only a strangled cry comes out.

I swipe at him, but he doesn't let go. In a single motion, I unzip my jacket and squirm out of it. As I do, something hits my legs and I go flying.

My body slams down on the ice, and pain shoots through my right hip. The giant lands on top of me, and for an instant, I'm sure that he is going to crush me completely. I smell his sour breath and breathe in the damp wool of his jacket. I'm going to suffocate unless I can get him off me. But he's not getting up. He's got my wrist now.

I open my mouth to scream, but his huge hand clamps down on it.

"Say good-bye to 1968," he says.

I try to wrap my mind around what he just said, but before I can, I'm hit by a wave of dizziness. Then, a sensation of fading away, vanishing. But that's impossible, isn't it? Unless this is what death feels like.

And then blackness.

IV

When I open my eyes, the river is gone. I'm sprawled on a sidewalk and surrounded by towers of granite and steel that soar into the sky.

Where am I? How did I get here? I have no idea. I must have been drugged. But why? By whom?

It's warm here. What happened to the winter?

The buildings are taller than any I've ever seen. And there are street signs that have moving words and pictures on them.

The cars on the street look sleek. Nothing like Jim's boxy station wagon. And the people are talking into miniature walkie-talkies or gazing at screens the size of cigarette lighters.

This has got to be some big joke. Either that or I'm on a movie set for a new science-fiction flick. Yes, that's it. Any second now, the director is going to announce a coffee break for all of us extras.

The thing is, I don't see any film cameras or movie trucks.

But if this isn't a movie set, then there can be only one other logical explanation: I must be asleep and dreaming.

The big man who tackled me is leaning against the side of a building having a smoke. At the curb, a taxi is parked with its engine running. It all looks so real. But sometimes dreams can have an incredible level of detail too.

I try to scramble to my feet but can't move my arms or my legs.

17

Aha, I know. This is what they call dream paralysis—which just proves my theory.

"Get up," says the big guy. "We have an appointment."

"You're only part of my dream, so I don't have to listen to you," I tell him.

He laughs and grabs me by the arm. His grip feels so real.

"Let go," I say, but he doesn't loosen his hold.

"Look, I have orders to bring you to Frank," the goon says. "You can either cooperate, or we do things the hard way. Your choice."

Did he say my choice?

"I pick . . . the hard way!"

I shake off his arm and sprint for the taxi. As soon as I'm in, I slam the door shut and yell, "Drive!"

"To where?" says the driver.

"It doesn't matter! Just get out of—"

The door swings open, and large hands are pulling me from the taxi. I reach for the headrest and wrap my arms tight around it. But I'm no match for him. He yanks me out, kicking and screaming.

"Someone help me! I'm being kidnapped!"

By now, there's a small crowd watching, but no one steps forward.

The goon pushes me up against the side of a building. There's a dull thud as my head hits the brick.

"Don't try that again," he says.

Then he's dragging me along the sidewalk. He pulls me up the steps of a brownstone building.

As we enter the foyer, I gaze at the whitewashed walls. Something is familiar about this place. Stepping onto the elevator, the feeling is even stronger.

"Well, look who crawled out from under a rock," says a voice.

I look up. There's a television screen on the wall of the elevator, showing a woman doing her laundry. There must be thirty cats in the room with her, pouncing and leaping or just lounging. The woman on the screen pauses, holds up a cake with pink frosting and says, "I got this for you, Caleb. It was on special. I know you can't see the writing on it from there, but it says, 'Happy Retirement, Sharon.' It was either that or 'Rest in Pieces, Morris,' which I didn't think you would like."

I could swear the television set is talking to me. Best that I ignore it. Even if this is a dream, I need to keep my wits about me.

"Bring us up to four, Phoebe," the big man says.

"The place has gone downhill since you left," whispers Phoebe, ignoring him. "None of these new guys have a sense of humor. Hey, you're looking a little white around the gills. I hope Luca Palooka hasn't been mistreating you."

She really is talking to me. What does she mean, since I left? I've never been here before in my life.

"That's enough," says the man she called Luca. "Bring us up to four, now."

"See what I mean? 'Bring us up to five, now.'" She imitates his deep voice. "No personality whatsoever."

This is all so unreal.

The elevator finally starts to go up. When it stops and the doors open, Luca and I step into a reception area. The crooked sign on the wall says NEW BEIJING EXPORT COMPANY. The room smells of mold, and the stuffing is threatening to burst out of the arm of the only piece of furniture: a sad-looking white sofa.

He bends down and presses a button on the side of the sofa. The wall opposite us slides open and we step through into a different room, one that's a whole lot nicer and cleaner. A sign floating in the air (how does it do that?) says TIMELESS TREASURES.

Luca pushes me ahead of him down the hall. At the end there's a door emblazoned with the design of an hourglass with a snake coiled around it. My heart skips a beat. I've seen that logo before.

He stops at a door halfway down the hall and presses his thumb against a pad on the wall. The door slides open.

I stumble into the room, and the first thing I notice is that it's chilly, a good five or ten degrees colder than the hall. The walls and ceiling are white, and in the center of the room is what looks like an operating table surrounded by various machines that I can't identify. My stomach clenches. Why did they bring me here?

A boy about my age stands by the bed. His head is a mess of black wavy hair, and he's wearing a green silk bathrobe with a dragon design on the front.

"Hello, Caleb," he says, smiling.

How is it that everyone around here knows my name?

"I'm sure this is all a bit of a shock to your system," he says, "coming home after such a long time away. But you'll find that not much has changed, really."

"I don't know who you are and what you're talking about." I struggle to keep my voice even. "And this isn't my home!"

He smiles again. His teeth are brilliantly white. "My apologies. I really should have introduced myself first. My name is Frank. You and I go way back. And this *is* your home. But of course you have forgotten all of that. It appears that someone has wiped your memory. I am vaguely curious about who did that. But don't you worry. A little brain surgery, and you'll be as good as new."

He laughs and runs his fingers through his hair, sweeping it back. That's when I see the top of his right ear is missing.

This is a crazy house, and I've just met the chief crazy. I turn and make a beeline for the door. But Luca blocks it with his massive bulk.

"Relax," says Frank. "No one is going to hurt you."

There are those teeth again. Nobody's got teeth that white. If I had a pocket mirror, I bet I could blind him with the reflection. They must be false. Why am I even thinking about his stupid teeth? I need to figure out how to escape before Dr. Frankenstein here gets to work.

"Luca, will you kindly prep the patient for surgery," Frank says.

Luca grabs my arms with his meaty paws. He throws me down onto the operating table and begins strapping my arms and legs.

"This is kidnapping!" I yell. "If you don't let me out of here this instant, I'm going to call the police."

Frank chuckles, nods to Luca and the big man places a mask over my nose and mouth. He's not kidding. They are really going to do this. I tug at the bands holding me down, but it's no use.

Breathing in something sweet now. Getting drowsy. No. Got to fight it.

"It will go easier for you if you relax and breathe normally," says Frank. "He'll be here in a moment and then the procedure will begin."

He? Who is he?

Lungs bursting. I take a breath in. Everything is fuzzy. Waves of thick wool cloud my thoughts. Drowning them. Can't move my arms. No power. Someone has come into the room. The others step back.

The new guy leans over me, icy-blue eyes, a green surgeon's mask.

"Has he been prepped?" he says, and somewhere in my muddled mind there's a spark of recognition. I know that voice.

"Yes, Uncle," says Frank. A shudder goes up my spine. I sense that my life is in danger.

Too late. Can't fight it anymore. Eyes closing. Then sweet thickness rolls over me, taking me away.

V

October 4, 2061, 11:34 A.M.
Doune Castle, Scotland

I'm lying facedown on a mattress on the floor, and my head is pounding. But that's not the worst of my pain. Not by a long shot. That particular honor belongs to my right wrist. It feels like someone has ripped it open and is using it for archery practice.

Grunting, I push myself up onto my left side for a better look. Through the dim light I can make out a rough-looking bandage. I brace myself and peel back a corner. My wrist is purple, and there's a long incision running from the base of my palm to almost halfway up my forearm. I gaze at it for a moment, then cover it up again.

My hand goes to my head next. There's a bandage there too, right near my hairline.

I sit up. There's not much to see. It's only me, four rough-hewn rock walls and a sturdy-looking wooden door with a thin slit.

I suppose I should be thankful for the slit, since without it, it would be pitch black in here.

The place reeks of mildew and sweat and piss. My hand brushes a wall and comes away covered in dark slime. Things have died in here, I'm sure of it.

Where am I?

There are gouges on the wall beside me: small vertical slashes in the stone in neat rows that seem to go on and on. Too many to count.

And on another wall, a crude drawing of a twin-masted sailing ship, etched right into the rock.

It reminds me of the ship I timeleaped to when I was going after the Xuande vase. That one had massive, billowing sails; that is, until it came under attack and caught on fire moments after I landed on it.

Wait.

I remember!

And that's not all.

I, Caleb, am a time snatcher working for a ruthless boss named Uncle. Or I was until I rescued Zach from the Compound and Uncle's clutches. I escaped with Zach and Nassim to Boston in 1967. My first night in 1967 I took two memory wipe pills because I wanted a fresh start to my new life with Zach and Jim and Diane. I stayed with them for about five months before being dragged away by Uncle's new goon.

It's all there. My memories are back!

I stand up slowly and make my way over to the door. The slit is at the level of my knees so I have to crouch down to look through it.

Nothing. Just more bare stone on the other side of the door.

I stand back up and pace the small room. I'm getting a bad feeling about all of this. The only places I know that have this much stone are castles.

And the only person I know who has a castle is Uncle. That must be it. He's brought me to his castle in Scotland, locked me up in a dungeon and is leaving me to rot. Now that I have my memories back, I can truly appreciate how miserable my situation is. How's that for irony?

My hand strays to my wrist. I prod it lightly with my fingers. There. Beneath the skin. My time-travel patch! It's back.

A memory flickers. Uncle dressed in green surgeon's scrubs, scalpel in hand. He had taken out my patch before sending me to the Barrens. But now it's back. Why? And why the bandage on my head too?

Who cares why? The fact is I've got my time-travel patch, and I'm going to use it right now to break out of this rocky prison.

Gently, I place my fingers on my wrist and begin tapping.

"Leaving so soon?" says a voice.

I whip around. Frank is standing by the open door, hands on his hips, with his usual smug expression. "How are you feeling, Caleb?" he asks, his eyes full of mock concern.

"Peachy," I lie.

"Did you have a nice holiday in Boston?" he asks.

"It wasn't a holiday, and you know it," I blurt out. "How did you find me?"

"Ahh, so the little operation to restore your memory was a success," he says, ignoring my question.

Frank's expression is downright depressing. But the next second, my depression is washed away by something even stronger: fear. Because if I'm where I think I am, the next friendly face I see is bound to be Uncle's. Except he won't be smiling when he sees me, unless of course he's deciding what kind of torture to inflict on me. I don't think he took too kindly to me escaping from the Compound with Zach and Nassim. And unless he's mellowed a lot since I've been gone, I'm easily looking at a long stint in the Barrens as punishment.

"You will find that your new patch is very similar to your old one but with a few improvements," he says. "One is that the patch can be remotely disabled. All senior time snatchers have been upgraded to the new patches."

He calls remote disabling an improvement? Maybe for Uncle but certainly not for me. It means that no matter where or when I am, Uncle can pull the plug and leave me stranded in the past.

"Because you haven't had a patch for a while," Frank continues, "it will take a little getting used to, but I'm sure you'll get the hang of it soon."

The only thing I'd like to hang is standing across from me, smirking. How did he find me? I was sure I had covered my tracks. Abbie and I had been over everything. Abbie! Maybe she's here too—I've got to speak with her.

"There is one thing, though," Frank says with a coy smile.

"And what is that?" I ask, trying to keep the anger out of my voice.

"Your access to certain time periods and places has been blocked."

"What are you talking about?"

"Well, it's really just a small sliver of time and space, so you don't have to worry," he says.

"Spit it out, Frank."

He laughs. "You are denied access to Montreal and Boston in the 1960s and 1970s."

I keep my expression neutral, but my head is swimming. Zach!

He's bluffing. Just saying that to get me angry. But why would he bluff? Well, even if he isn't lying and he's really blocked my access, there's another way I can get back. Abbie can take me. Abbie . . . now I've got to find her more than ever.

"Nice of you to drop by for a visit, Frank," I say, my voice shakier than I'd like. "But if you don't mind, I'm feeling a little sleepy. I think I'll take a nap now."

There's that chuckle again. "Good idea," he says. "I'm sure it's been a long day for you. I'll see you soon." Frank turns and heads out the door.

I stare at the door for a moment. He closed it, but not completely. It's still open a crack.

This is a trick. I'll bet anything he's standing on the other side, and as soon as he hears me go for it, he's going to slam it shut and slide the bolt home.

Why give him the satisfaction? Now that I have my patch, I can go anywhere and anytime. First, let's see if he's bluffing or telling the truth about my access to the '60s and '70s.

As I reach for my wrist, the door swings open.

The girl standing there is dressed in lemon chiffon, cinched tight at the waist but with a big bustle. Her auburn hair is piled high on her head, giving her the appearance of someone much taller.

"Ab—"

"Bie," she finishes for me. "What's the matter, Cale? Catacombs got your tongue?"

VI

October 4, 2061, 11:58 A.M.
Doune Castle, Scotland

Abbie!"

In two steps I'm across the room, and we're hugging.

"Hey, be careful of my bustle," she says, laughing and gently letting go.

I stand there for a second, gazing at her. Just then, something clicks, and I'm plunged back into the here and now.

"Quick," I say, grabbing her wrist and closing the door. "Take me back." My voice is high, panicky.

"Whoa," she says, "slow down."

"Abbie, there's no time. As soon as Uncle finds out I'm awake, he's going to come in here and dish out my punishment."

"I think you'd better sit down, Cale."

"I don't want to sit. I want . . ."

She takes my hand in hers and for a split second, I think she's going to whisk me away from this place. But instead she passes me a slip of paper.

We can't speak openly here, it says. *Not even over our mindpatches. He's listening and watching. Keep it light.*

Light? I don't do light. Only heavy. Speaking of heavy, I wouldn't put it past Uncle to have a Scottish maiden lying around here somewhere—a tall wooden contraption with a weighted blade that chops off your head in a single blow. At least it would be a quick way to go. Much better than slowly dying of thirst in the Barrens.

"Uhh, what year is this?" I say.

"2061," says Abbie.

"Are you sure?" I say. "It looks more like 1361."

She laughs. "I'm glad to see you still have your sense of humor."

"Are we where I think we are?" I say.

Abbie nods. "Yup. This is Uncle's castle in Scotland."

"Why?" I ask.

"Didn't Frank tell you? Uncle has planned a special day for all the senior time snatchers. He's taking us on a grand outing. Just like the good old days. This is the kickoff."

It takes a moment for her words to sink in. My brain functions slowly at the best of times, and this certainly isn't the best of times. In fact, as recently as a minute ago, it was the worst of times.

When Abbie's words finally register, I still don't understand. Why would Uncle include me in any special day? Time snatchers who go AWOL aren't supposed to be welcomed back with open arms. Or even with arms, for that matter. What game is Uncle playing at?

I sit down on the mattress and close my eyes. I've already given up on this being a dream, but there's still a chance that I'm hallucinating all of this. I read somewhere that the brain is an incredible organ, capable of constructing hallucinations so lifelike that it's impossible to tell what's fake and what's real—that is until the hallucination goes poof and disappears.

But when I open my eyes again, Abbie is still there. She sits down beside me, and for a moment, our knees touch. It feels so real. But like I said, the brain is capable of amazing things.

"Uncle thought you might need some more time to rest after

your operation. So he brought you here early. The rest of us arrived a few minutes ago."

"That was considerate of him," I say. Now that I'm leaning toward none of this being real, my side of the conversation is beginning to flow much easier.

The only part of the hallucination that's letting me down so far is this room. It's got zero personality. Would it have been too much for my brain to conjure up a view, or better yet, a minibar?

I lean back against the rough stone wall and take a deep breath.

"Don't get too comfortable," Abbie says. "It's time for lunch. I've been asked to bring you. Here, let me help you."

I take her hand and stand up. As I do, I get a whiff of mango. My calm of a moment ago is shattered. No hallucination can be this detailed.

"This is all . . . really happening, isn't it?" I croak.

She nods slowly. "I'm afraid so."

"All right," I say, taking a deep breath. "Lead on."

I follow her from the room and through a narrow passageway.

"Go slow on the stairs," she says. "They're a bit tricky."

No kidding. Whoever designed this place forgot the handrails. I brace my left hand against the stone wall and slowly follow her up the narrow winding steps.

"Keep looking ahead so you don't get dizzy," she says after a minute.

"Too late," I say. But that's okay, because dizzy is working for me. It's keeping my mind off of other things. Like the pain in my head and my throbbing wrist and the fact that I can't go back to check on Zach on my own or even talk to Abbie about it because Uncle's watching and listening.

We must be getting somewhere, because it's warmer now. And the smells are better too.

Huffing and puffing, I step out onto a landing. Abbie leads me through a narrow hallway with a ceiling so low that I've got to keep my head down. The hall twists right, then left.

"Here we are," she says finally. "The Great Hall."

I follow her into a large room. The vaulted ceiling reminds me of a church sanctuary. But judging from the display of swords, dirks and other assorted blades ringing the walls of the room, this is no church.

The only furniture in sight is a long table and chairs. At the far end of the room, just past a stone archway, a huge pig is turning on a spit in a massive fireplace.

Luca is turning the crank of the spit.

Frank, Lydia and Raoul are standing near the fireplace, talking. Or rather, Frank is doing the talking and the others are listening.

As I approach, Raoul says, "Hi, Caleb. I'm glad you're back."

"Thanks, Raoul," I say. I suppose I could have added, "It's good to be back," for the benefit of Uncle's listening devices, but there's probably no point, since the more modern ones have an app that can tell if you're lying.

Lydia barely glances my way before whispering something to Frank. I can pretty much guess what's going through her mind—that I'm a fool for having tried to escape and that I'm going to get punished big-time and that she doesn't want to be anywhere near me when that happens because sometimes punishment has a way of spilling over onto anyone who happens to be close by.

Just then, a horn blares. Three long bursts.

Everyone stops what they're doing. A moment later, I hear footsteps approaching.

"He's coming," whispers Raoul, and suddenly I have an idea for a new game show. It will be called *You Don't Say!* The way it works is all the contestants try to outdo each other by saying things that are not only obvious but *painfully* obvious. With that gem, Raoul would easily make it to the semifinals.

Seconds later, Uncle enters the room. He's wearing a shirt made of finely woven iron rings over a sky blue tunic. His open-faced helmet is shiny, pointed and draped with iron mail. In his left hand, he carries a stout shield of dark oak emblazoned with a blue lion. In his right, he holds a great battle-ax with a wicked-looking curve.

I wonder which one it's going to be? The shield or the ax? One good bop on the head from that shield, and I'll be out like a light. But that would be too quick for Uncle's taste. He's probably more likely to slice and dice me with the ax—carve me up like that pig roasting on the spit.

When he gets to within a few feet of us, he stops, clears his throat and recites,

"Scots, wha hae wi' Wallace bled,
Scots, wham Bruce has aften led!
Welcome to your gory bed,
Or to victorie.

"Now's the day an' now's the hour;
See the front of battle lour—
See approach proud Edward's power,
Chains and slaverie!

"Wha will be a traitor knave?
Wha will fill a coward's grave?
Wha sae base as be a slave?
Let him turn and flee!"

He pauses and wipes away a tear, which is a chancy thing to do when you're holding a battle-ax.

"That, my friends," says Uncle, "is part of the 'Scots Wha Hae,' the song that is the unofficial national anthem of Scotland. It was penned by one of the greatest poets in history, Robert Burns. It is even more beautiful in Gaelic. The poem is an ode to another Robert, one who is dear to my heart: the incomparable Robert the Bruce, king of Scotland, savior of the Scottish people, warrior and statesman."

A sound catches my attention. Raoul is tapping his boot on the stone floor.

"On this very day, seven hundred and forty-seven years ago, a great battle was fought only a few miles from here, at Bannockburn. At stake was Stirling Castle, the last of the great castles not yet taken by the English. Robert the Bruce himself was in the thick of things, riding and wielding his battle-ax. You see, my friends, he was a leader who didn't skulk behind stone walls while his soldiers got bloodied on the battlefield—he led his men from the front.

"On that fateful day in 1314, Sir Henry de Bohun, a knight of the enemy, rode in full gallop toward Robert with lance extended. Do you know what Robert did?" Uncle pauses a moment for dramatic effect. "He lifted his ax, and with a single mighty downward blow, clove Sir Henry's helmet and the head within in two."

Too much information.

"You may ask what all of this has to do with you. Why would your dear Uncle bring you to this place and bore you with tales of kings and battles that history has long forgotten?"

He's right. That was one of my questions. But my main one is: what is going to happen after he stops talking? Is he going to propose a toast to my homecoming? Yes, that's exactly what he's going to do. And mine will be the only cup with that little something extra in it:

hemlock, the poison of choice for the royal set during the Middle Ages. On the plus side, not counting a short interlude where I'll feel a cold sensation creeping up from my toes, it's supposed to be a mostly painless death.

"The reason I have brought you here," says Uncle, "is to remind you that history is not the static, dead thing found in dusty tomes. It is very much alive. And because of the special advantage we have, history is even more alive for us than for others.

"Robert the Bruce is more than just a historical figure. He was the greatest leader of the Scottish people. And on this, the anniversary of the most important battle in the history of Scotland, I pledge that I will follow the example of Robert the Bruce. I will lead you from the front. I will not waver from our cause. Together we will weather defeat and rejoice in triumph. I will be your statesman, your king and your hero."

As I listen to Uncle, it occurs to me that I haven't heard him mention the Great Friendship or the emperors of ancient China once. And this from a guy who wouldn't be caught dead wearing anything other than a *hanfu* with dragons up and down the arms. But then again, I suppose there's not that much difference between calling yourself a king or an emperor.

"Now, without further ado," continues Uncle, "I will leave you to enjoy your lunch. After you have eaten, Luca will direct you to the first stop on today's special outing, where I will join you. *Chi mi a dh'aithghearr sibh!* See you soon!"

With a flourish and the clanking of his chain mail, Uncle spins on his booted heel and departs the Great Hall.

Wait. What just happened here? I was certain he was going to punish me.

I should feel relieved, but instead there's a sick feeling in my stomach. He must have something in store for me. Otherwise, why bother sending his brute all the way to 1968 to yank me back?

But I've got to put all of that out of my mind right now and concentrate on the one thing that matters most: getting out of here and back to Zach.

VII

October 4, 2061, 12:42 P.M.
Doune Castle, Scotland

You heard Uncle," Frank says. "It's time for lunch. Luca, cut me a hunk of that roast meat."

I glance over at Luca, expecting him to say something like "cut your own bloody piece," but amazingly, he doesn't say anything—just begins hacking at the pig.

"What else is on the menu?" asks Lydia boldly.

"Porridge, haggis and blood pudding," says Luca in a flat voice. "Sit down if you want some."

"I'm afraid I can't have blood pudding," she says. "It makes me break out in hives."

Baloney. She's only saying that because she doesn't want to have it. Mind you, if that line works for her, I might try the same one.

"I will be reporting to Uncle who has eaten what," says Luca dully.

"In that case, I think I can manage a smidge," she says. "But not too much, please. I'd like to save some room for the haggis. It's my absolute favorite."

Liar. I bet she doesn't even know that haggis is sheep guts.

Luca begins ladling bowls of steaming porridge from a large pot. "It's hot," he says as he hands us our bowls, and in my mind, I have him advancing to the next round of *You Don't Say!* With any luck, Raoul will demolish him in the final.

As we wait for the porridge to cool, Luca dishes out the haggis.

"You're a lucky guy, Caleb," says Frank with his mouth full. "I've been after Uncle for years to give me a couple of weeks of vacation. And out of nowhere, he gives you five months off. I guess your case was different, though. It was obvious that you were getting burned out and needed a rest."

"Leave it alone, Frank," says Abbie before I can say anything.

He smirks but says nothing.

I ignore him and take a bite of roast pig. Pretty good. Then I try the haggis and almost spit it out.

Luca is checking out who has what left on their plates. Quickly, I stab the haggis with my fork and plunk it deep down out of sight under my porridge. There's still a bit of haggis showing, so I spoon some porridge from Raoul's bowl into mine and patch the hole.

"Where are we going first?" asks Lydia, all bright and cheery. Her plate is clean, which means she must have emptied it under the table when Luca wasn't looking.

"New York City in 1912," Luca answers. "Details are being uploaded to your patches."

Lydia stands and is about to leave the table when Frank puts a hand on her arm. "Not right away. I want to make a toast."

She sits back down.

"To Uncle," Frank says, lifting his cup. "For taking us on today's grand adventure. May the winds of Loch Leven always be at his back."

And may the Monster of Loch Ness rise up and bite you in the ass, Frank.

"We will all meet, fully changed, in the courtyard in ten minutes," Luca says. "Packets of period-appropriate clothes with your names on them are by the archway, along with anti-time-fog pills and directions as to when to take them. Uncle has also authorized for each of you a special one-time fifty-dollar advance against your allowance, which you may use for any personal items you purchase or you may save for later use." Then he strides out of the room with Frank.

Anti-time-fog pills? A fifty-buck advance? Wow. Things have certainly changed since I've been away. The pills definitely make sense. If you can stay in the past for a whole day without getting time fog, it means you can do more complicated snatches. I sure could have used that when I was snatching the Xuande vase.

And fifty dollars is way more money than I can remember Uncle ever giving us at one time. Still, I'm not about to complain.

"C'mon, Cale. I want to show you a bit of the castle," Abbie says, standing up.

"Don't you think we should change first?" I ask.

Now, why did I say that? Here's the one person I've been desperate to speak to ever since I got yanked from the twentieth century, and when my chance finally comes, I say "no thanks." Sometimes I really wonder at the things that come out of my mouth.

"Nah," she says. "There's oodles of time to change. C'mon."

I follow her into a small alcove. She looks all around and takes my hand. "Hold on."

The familiar sensation of the timeleap washes over me—two parts dizzy, two parts excited and one part nauseous.

When I land, I can't move a finger. But I can see for miles and miles. Lush green hills and vales. And sheep—lots and lots of sheep. Some of them have blue or red slashes on their sides. In the distance, a thin tendril of gray smoke spirals up from the chimney of a stone cottage.

"Where are we?"

"Top of the tower," Abbie says. "This is still Uncle's castle. Only it's a week earlier. No one is here yet."

I stand silently next to her for a moment, wondering where to start. "Abbie, you were supposed to meet me in 1967 . . . What happened?"

"I did come. You got my note, didn't you?"

"Yeah . . . but it said you'd come back and you didn't."

"I wanted to . . . but I couldn't." She turns toward me. "I went back to tie up a loose end."

"What loose end?"

"Nassim," she says. "When you escaped to 1967 with him and Zach, Nassim's timeleap was recorded."

I stare at her. "That's impossible. His file was erased, remember? We were there when Phoebe did it."

"I thought so too," she says. "But it wasn't enough. I remembered that the central database records all timeleaps, too. I went back and convinced Phoebe to erase the leap that Nassim took with you from the elevator . . . but I was too late. Frank had already seen it.

"Once I found out that Frank knew, there was no way I could go back to 1967 again. If I had, Uncle and Frank would have known that I helped you and Zach escape. Luckily, Phoebe erased all of my trips there before anyone saw them—from every database."

I kick at a stone, and it skitters across the rocky floor. So it's true then. Uncle knew all along that I was living in the past with Zach and his family. He could have brought me back at any time.

"Why did he wait so long before he snatched me back?" I ask.

Abbie shrugs. "I don't know. Maybe he thought as long as you thought you were safe, you weren't going anywhere. And with time travel, they could come bring you back whenever they wanted."

Everything she's saying sounds logical. But there's one piece of the puzzle that's still missing.

"That was you, wasn't it? In Mr. Tepper's class?"

She nods.

"Why did you take the chance? If they found you there, like you said, they'd know you were in on the escape plan with me."

She looks at me for a long time before answering.

"I missed you," she says.

"Really?" I say.

"Yes, really. Didn't you miss me?"

"Well, I'm sure I would have if I'd remembered you . . ."

Our fingers brush and then twine together. It feels good to be holding hands.

I gaze at the hills. Three of the sheep with blue slashes on their sides are wandering away from the rest.

"Why are they marked like that?" I ask.

"Luca explained it to us," she says. "It's so the farmers can tell which sheep are theirs when they come to collect them. Anything else you'd like to know?"

"Yeah," I say. "Luca. I can't figure him out."

"What do you mean?"

"Well, it seems like sometimes he takes orders from Uncle, and other times, it looks like he's working for Frank."

"I know," she says. "My take on it is that he works for Uncle only when Uncle is around. But most of the time now, he works for Frank."

"And Uncle is okay with that?"

Abbie shrugs her shoulders. "I don't think he even notices. Uncle has been acting different lately."

"Yeah, I noticed," I say. "Looks like the emperor's got new clothes."

"It's more than that," says Abbie. "It's like he's off in his own little world most of the time. The only thing he talks about is restoring the glory of Scotland of old. He's obsessed with this place and spends most of his time here. I hardly see him at Headquarters or the Compound anymore. He's even cutting back on punishments. Last week, Lydia messed up a snatch—she grabbed a rare jeweled egg from the czar's palace in 1880s Russia but dropped it on the way back. When Uncle noticed a missing gemstone, the only thing he did was tell her to do better next time."

"That's because it was Lydia," I say. "Next to Frank, she's the teacher's pet."

"Maybe. Speaking of Frank, you'd better watch how you talk to him. He's gained a lot of power recently and practically runs the show at Headquarters. He's even got a few of his own goons now. Though he's careful around Uncle. He does just the right amount of groveling and sucking up so that Uncle doesn't get suspicious. And he's been nicer to all of the other time snatchers too. But it's all fake. I'm convinced that Frank's planning something."

"Like what?"

"I don't know. But the way he's acting, it's got to be something big."

"I can't go back to Zach on my own, Abbie," I say after a moment. "They blocked my access."

"I know. Frank was bragging to me about it."

"You've got to take me back."

She lets go of my hand. "I can't."

"Sure you can. Your patch isn't blocked."

"All right. Let's say I take you. Then what? You think you'll live happily ever after? It's not going to happen. Uncle will snatch you right back."

I let her words sink in. She's right. I'm fooling myself to think that I can go back and live a normal life in 1968.

"I've got to know that Zach's going to be okay," I say.

"He will be."

"How do you know?"

"I looked into his situation," she says.

"What do you mean?"

"I went back to check on him."

"You did? Wait. How could you, without it being tracked?"

"While you were in 1968, I was on a mission to 1988. It wasn't Boston, but close enough to take a quick side trip without any time displacement. I didn't speak to him, but I saw him. He was doing fine."

I take a moment to consider what she's saying. She saw Zach when he was twenty-six years old, and he was all right. Relief floods through me.

"Was . . . was I with him?" I ask.

"No. But that doesn't mean anything. It was at a coffee shop, Cale. And only for a minute."

I stare at her. There are so many questions I want to ask her about Zach, but if she only saw him for a minute, I doubt she'll be able to answer any of them.

"We've got to go now," she says.

I nod, but I'm not looking forward to rejoining the others. A feeling of helplessness washes over me. The new life that I thought I had started with Zach and his family wasn't a new life at all. All that time, Uncle still had his hooks in me.

Abbie takes my wrist and taps at her own. The next instant we're back in the small alcove. As soon as our time freeze thaws, we enter the Great Hall and pick up our clothing packets.

"See you soon," she says and goes off to change.

I slip into dark trousers, a white shirt and suspenders. The finishing touch is a straw hat with a flat top and a round brim. Soon after I'm done, everyone else arrives dressed in their 1912 clothes.

"You will all leave now, but your arrivals will be staggered in intervals of two minutes," says Luca. "When you arrive, head right to the seawall, where you will find me with Uncle. Lydia, you are up first."

One at a time, Lydia, Raoul, Abbie and Frank step forward, tap their wrists, fade and then vanish.

"Best for last, right?" I say, stepping up.

Luca doesn't crack a smile or say anything. Only motions for me to get going.

My fingers hover over my bandaged wrist. I've got a bad feeling about this "fun day" that Uncle has planned for us. Maybe I'll sit tight in the castle and wait for everyone to come back.

Luca grabs my wrist and presses so hard I cry out in pain.

"Go now," he says.

Gingerly, I enter the sequence on my patch. As I wait for the timeleap to take hold, all I hear is the distant bleating of the Highland sheep. Even with no fences in sight, they are still prisoners, marked for return by their masters.

Same as me.

# VIII

July 7, 1912, 10:47 A.M.
Pier 6, East River
New York City

I land in a narrow passage between two buildings. A short man wearing suspenders over a stained white apron pushes a hot dog cart past the alley. His sign says ONLY A NICKEL FOR A HOT FRANKFURTER.

Once my time freeze thaws, I head out of the alley and survey my surroundings. A huge crowd is gathered about fifty yards away, and even more people are streaming in that direction. Beyond the crowd, I can see a sliver of the East River and a barge moored at the pier.

A skinny kid wearing a cap that sinks over his ears hands me a flyer.

SPECIAL EVENT

SUNDAY, JULY 7 AT 11 A.M.

Pier 6, East River
One block from South Ferry

HARRY HOUDINI

securely handcuffed and leg ironed, will be placed in a heavy packing case, which will be nailed and roped, then encircled by steel bands, firmly nailed. Two hundred pounds of iron weights will then be lashed to this box containing **HOUDINI**. The box will then be **THROWN INTO THE EAST RIVER**. **HOUDINI** will undertake to release himself whilst submerged under water.

THE MOST DARING FEAT EVER ATTEMPTED IN THIS OR ANY OTHER AGE.

SUNDAY, RAIN OR SHINE

Now, this I've got to see. I'm glad they added the bit about "rain or shine," because thunderclouds are rolling in.

I follow the crowd and soon spot Luca's massive frame near the seawall, opposite the barge. At first I think he's alone, but then I do a double take. Uncle is standing next to him. He's traded in his chain mail for a suit and tie, and his war helmet for a straw boater. He looks like the hundred or so other men jostling for a good viewing spot.

By the time I manage to pick my way through the horde, the other time snatchers have arrived. Frank looks like a mini version of Uncle in a black suit and straw hat, Raoul keeps pulling up his too-large breeches, and Lydia fiddles with the angle of her wide-brimmed hat. Abbie, however, looks like she just stepped out of the Sears catalogue—she's elegant in a maroon dress and matching parasol.

"Welcome, all, to 1912," Uncle says over our mindpatches.

Then he takes a deep breath in, nostrils flaring. "Isn't the air wonderful? It smells of freedom, opportunity and infinite possibilities."

And dead fish. If I'd been thinking ahead, I would have brought one of those pine-scented nose masks that were all the rage during the garbage strike of June 2061. On the other hand, I don't think Uncle would appreciate me bringing attention to our little group by wearing something invented over a hundred years from now.

"I want you all to closely observe the goings-on. In a few moments, I will ask you some questions about what you have seen and heard."

That's fine with me. Close observation is my specialty.

I can't get over how many people have gotten up on a Sunday morning for this. It must be the thrill of possibly seeing somebody die right in front of your nose. It's too bad they can't set up a grandstand underwater. That's where the real action's going to be, I figure.

I spot the hot dog vendor. He's parked his cart at what looks like an ideal location near the seawall. But so far, he doesn't appear to have any takers.

Beyond him there's a guy standing on the seawall surrounded by a small knot of people. He's wearing a black tank top and his dark hair is parted in the middle. Judging from all the attention, he must be Houdini. There's nothing special about him as far as I can see. In fact, he's a lot shorter than I expected.

A gaggle of police officers appear out of nowhere and surround him. I'm too far away to hear all of what's being said, but it's clear they want this party to get started.

After a few minutes, Houdini and his entourage leave the seawall and make their way through the crowd across the pier to a barge. It looks like they're going to do the stunt from there.

Which is bad news for me, because my view of the barge is partly blocked by a line of horse-drawn carriages that are waiting to whisk some of the wealthier gawkers off to brunch as soon as the event is over. The horses seem oblivious to everything, their noses buried in feed bags. Now, there's a great invention: hands-free eating. If I had my own feed bag, I'd fill it with—

"Cale, pay attention!" Abbie's voice comes high and sharp over my mindpatch.

"I am," I say defensively.

"Ladies and gentlemen," says a booming voice. "In a feat never dared before, the amazing Houdini will be handcuffed, shackled, tied up and nailed into this crate. The crate will then be lowered into the East River. Two hundred pounds of iron weights will ensure that the crate does not float to the surface . . ."

Uncle's got a big smile on his face. It always makes me nervous when he's happy. The strange thing is he's not even looking at Houdini or the crate. He's gazing somewhere out over the crowd.

I try to follow where he's looking, but don't see anything out of the ordinary. Just then, there's a commotion from the deck of the barge. I look over to see five burly workmen standing at the rail. They are upending large bags over the side. A flood of squishy pink things pours into the river.

"Jellyfish," whispers Abbie over my patch. "The deadly kind."

A gust of wind comes up, followed by the peal of thunder and the flash of lightning.

This is all great news. Only a minute ago, my count of "Ways in Which Houdini May Die This Morning" was stuck at two: drowning or suffocation. Now I can add death by multiple poisonous jellyfish bites and electrocution by lightning strike to the list. The last one's a little iffy, but I'm still counting it.

Two of the policemen frisk Houdini from head to toe. Next, they fit the manacles onto his ankles, place his wrists in the cuffs and then tie him up with a thick rope. Houdini smiles through it all, which I find amazing.

A slight woman steps forward and kisses him square on the lips.

"The crate in which Houdini will be submerged is not water-proof," continues the announcer. "As soon as it immersed, it will fill with water, and he will have only as long as he can hold his breath to

46

escape from his constraints and break free from his watery prison. Although the Great Houdini has assured us that he can hold his breath in excess of three minutes, he has agreed that if he does not emerge from the crate after two minutes, we may send down the rescue team."

He gestures to three stout men in swim trunks positioned in a rowboat by the barge, axes in hand.

They look pretty sure of themselves, but if it was me in that box, I'd definitely want a backup plan for my backup plan. None of those guys look like they can hold their breath longer than ten seconds.

Houdini waves to the crowd, then folds himself into two and squeezes into the crate. As soon as he's in, the policemen pound nails into the top, sealing it.

"There is nothing quite like the sound of death knocking at your door to bring out one's zest for living, is there?" says Uncle.

His voice in my head startles me. I've been so mesmerized by the show that I almost forgot about Uncle and the others.

Two of the policemen push the crate to the edge of the deck. For a moment, it just teeters there, half on and half off the barge.

My mouth goes dry.

I hastily add death by heart attack to my list.

With a final shove and a gasp from the crowd, the crate splashes into the East River.

The water churns for a moment and then smooths over. The crowd goes deathly quiet. All eyes are riveted on the spot where the crate disappeared.

A minute goes by.

There's no way he's going to escape.

A woman screams. Another faints. The men in the rowboat clutch their axes.

The suspense is killing me. Maybe I should hop forward in time by another minute to see if he makes it.

Then Uncle's singsong voice comes over my mindpatch.

"Ahh, the glory of living in the moment. Raoul, I'd like you to tell us all what is happening this instant."

Lucky for me, but a bad break for Raoul. Going first is never easy.

"Uhh . . . Houdini is inside the crate, trying to escape."

"And?"

"And everyone's watching to see if he can do it," adds Raoul.

"And?"

A bead of sweat is forming on Raoul's forehead. He's done as good a job as anyone could, but Uncle doesn't seem satisfied.

Raoul pauses for a long moment and then says, "That's all, Uncle."

"Are you certain?" says Uncle.

"Yes," says Raoul, but his voice sounds shaky.

"Does anyone else have anything to add?"

Only silence.

"Well, then, let me add my own observations," says Uncle. "There is a woman making her way through the crowd. Do you see her?"

I look to my left. At first I don't see the woman, but then I spot her—middle-aged and wearing an ankle-length forest-green dress and matching hat. She's hurrying along, parasol in one hand and hot dog in the other.

I nod along with the others.

"Good," says Uncle. "Keep watching her."

That's really asking a lot, given that Houdini is about to drown.

The next moment, the woman stumbles and falls forward. Her hot dog goes flying—which is a real shame, because it's a waste of a good dog—and a big dollop of mustard flings through the air, landing on the tan pants of a balding man in shirtsleeves.

The man glances back and swipes a hand on the seat of his pants, which is a big mistake, because now his fingers are smeared with mustard and there's no obvious place to wipe them.

The woman is on the ground, looking dazed and holding her ankle. Mustard Man seems unsure what to do. His gaze ping-pongs from his yellow fingers to the downed woman. A boy shouts "Mother!" and the crowd parts to let him through. He's got blond hair and is as skinny as a wire; I figure him to be a year or two younger than me. He kneels by the fallen woman and helps her to her feet. As soon as she's up, the boy turns toward Mustard Man, pulls out a handkerchief and begins dabbing at the man's stained trousers. Mustard Man attempts a retreat, but is blocked by a wall of people behind him.

Mustard Man shouts at him to stop, but the boy ignores him and keeps swiping at the pants. Finally, the boy stands up, folds his handkerchief neatly, takes the woman's arm and leads her through the crowd.

The duo passes right by the hot dog vendor's cart, and she rests there for a moment, placing a hand on the cart.

"Houdini has been submerged for one minute and thirty-seven seconds." The announcer's voice wavers, and he looks nervously at the guys with the axes.

"Constable, stop that boy. He stole my billfold!"

My eyes flick back. Mustard Man is racing through the crowd, waving his arms.

I turn back toward the water. There are bubbles coming up.

The crowd gasps.

The policeman lunges.

The boy cries out.

The hot dog vendor starts packing up.

And then, most amazing of all, Houdini's head breaks through to the surface.

The crowd erupts into raucous applause. A few of the men throw their hats into the air.

Houdini waves to the crowd before backstroking to the pier. As he hauls himself up onto the dock, my eyes flick back to where the police officer is patting down the protesting boy and coming up empty. The next moment, at the insistence of Mustard Man, the woman offers up her purse for inspection.

"Very well," says Uncle after a moment. "Lydia, how did he manage it?"

"Houdini must have hid a key somewhere on him," Lydia says. "When he was underwater, he managed to pick the locks, untie himself and break out of the crate."

"And the boy?"

"The boy must have lifted the wallet when he was dabbing at the mustard stain on the man's pants."

"Yet Houdini was subject to a full body search before the restraints were placed on him. And similarly, the boy was searched from head to toe. Neither search turned up anything. How could that be . . . Caleb?"

I look up at Uncle, and we lock eyes. My heart is hammering. It isn't lost on me that this is the first time he's spoken directly to me since I escaped with Zach.

"The boy must have slipped the wallet to his mother before he was searched," I say.

"Yet when his mother's handbag was searched, no wallet was found," says Uncle.

He's got me there and he knows it. A smile plays at the corner of his lips.

"And Houdini?" continues Uncle. "How did he manage his escape from the restraints?"

"He had a key hidden on him," I say, repeating what Lydia had said. "It was so well hidden that they didn't find it when they searched him."

Uncle shakes his head.

"The key to Houdini's escape was an event that by its ordinariness went unnoticed by all of you," says Uncle. "Similarly, the snatch of the man's wallet was masked by an event that appeared quite normal."

He pauses for a moment, perhaps waiting to see if anyone will guess. But there are no takers.

We've all failed miserably. Everyone is looking at the ground, except for Frank. He's smirking and looking out over the water as if he doesn't have a care in the world. Well, he's a fool to be so relaxed. Because there's no way Uncle is going to let this one go by. One of the first lessons he taught us when we were small was how important it was to be aware of our surroundings. And not one of us got it right today. In my mind's eye, I see Uncle nodding to Luca, then Luca tying us up, strapping on some of Houdini's iron weights and throwing us into the East River, one by one. He'll probably do it in reverse order of how we came here, which means I'll be the lucky one to go first.

"No one?" says Uncle. "All right, I will tell you. First, the boy. When he was frisked, the wallet could not be found because he had already passed it off to his mother, who had safely disposed of the wallet to the hot dog vendor as she passed by his cart.

"As for Houdini," Uncle continues, "some of you may recall that a woman stepped up and kissed him on the lips moments after he had been searched but before he got into the crate. When they kissed, the woman passed a skeleton key from her mouth to Houdini's. Once

51

out of sight in the crate, he gripped the key in his teeth to undo the locks on his hands and then used his hands to free himself."

I never would have guessed that in a million years.

"You should all have seen these things. There is no excuse. This is not the first time I have spoken of the power of intelligent observation, of not accepting without question what your eyes are telling you has taken place, of seeing with your mind."

My eyes flick to Luca. Any moment now, Uncle is going to give him the signal. I find myself holding my breath, which is a stupid thing to do, because I should save that for when he throws me in the water. Not that it will make much difference, though. Assuming he does a half-decent job tying me up, I'll never be able to hold my breath long enough to break free.

"Soon you will all have new recruits to train," Uncle says. "And I want you to teach them intelligent observation. It will be the key to their future success as time snatchers."

He removes his hat and throws it into the air. Reflexively, my eyes follow the path of the hat. When I look back down, Uncle is gone.

That's it? No punishment? I can't believe it. Abbie is right: Uncle's turning soft. There's no other explanation. Well, maybe one . . . and that is he's gone off the deep end with his obsession about Robert the Bruce and being king and hero to us, his loyal subjects. Whatever the reason, it's too early to celebrate. After all, Frank can do nasty just as well as Uncle, and if Abbie's right about Frank's power increasing, then we're all in big trouble.

Luca hands each of us a satchel. "Here is your clothing for the next stop. Find a place to change. We leave for Paris in ten minutes."

I nod along with the others, but my eyes are scanning the crowd. He's got to be here somewhere. Intelligent observation or not, there's no way even Uncle would have picked up on all of those details unless . . . unless he has been to this time/place before.

Gulls land on the seawall, shrieking. A man, wearing shabby clothes and a fisherman's cap, shuffles toward them, flicking bread crumbs their way. As they dive for the bread, the man removes his cap for a moment to wipe the moisture from his forehead. In that moment, I glimpse Uncle's shiny head. Gotcha!

I smile to myself. Maybe I'm not such a slow learner after all.

IX

I land in an alcove of a building, facing a brick wall. Laughter, shouting and chamber orchestra music waft over to my landing spot. As my time freeze thaws and I'm able to turn, I see maybe two hundred people gathered in a large square. Beyond the crowd and framed in scaffolding is a gigantic sculpture of gleaming copper.

My jaw drops when I recognize what I'm looking at. I've never been this close to it before, and it's not only the size that throws me, it's also the location.

What in the world is the Statue of Liberty doing here in the middle of a city square in Paris, France?

I spot Luca and Uncle at the rendezvous point. As soon as everyone is present, Uncle begins.

"Your eyes are not deceiving you," he says over our mindpatches. "That is the original Statue of Liberty, conceived by Frédéric Bartholdi as a gift from the French people to the American people. We have arrived here in Paris in time for its grand unveiling.

"Impressive, isn't it?" he continues. "After today's festivities, the statue will be disassembled and each piece placed in a separate shipping crate bound for New York Harbor. But the unveiling of the Statue of Liberty is not the reason we are here today."

Why does that not surprise me?

54

"Nor are we here to study the techniques of the Parisian pickpockets, even though they are all around us."

Now he's got my interest. If we didn't come for the pickpockets, then why are we here at all?

"Do you see the red-haired man standing by the scaffolding near the statue's right foot?" Uncle asks.

"Yes, Uncle," Frank says, and I realize for the first time how quiet he has been this whole trip.

"His name is Julien. He is an . . . acquaintance of mine. Lydia, what do you suppose is Julien's *métier*, his profession?"

"Stonemason," she says.

"That is a fair guess," says Uncle, "but incorrect. Look, it appears he is leaving. Let us follow him and see where he goes."

As we follow Julien, I wonder for the umpteenth time what the point of today is. I mean, it's not like we're snatching anything. They say that people mellow when they grow older, and maybe that's what's happening with Uncle—and this trip is his way to show us, his senior time snatchers, how much he really appreciates us.

Nonsense. I think he really believes that today's little excursion will sharpen our skills to deal with the next wave of fresh-faced recruits. Which is more proof that Uncle's losing his edge. Because none of the stuff he's talked about today is new. They're all old lessons he taught us years ago.

Following Julien is easy at first, because there are lots of people milling around to use as cover. But then he turns into a back alley, and not being noticed becomes trickier.

Crumbling buildings line the alley, and there's a strong smell of sewage. This isn't the side of Paris you usually see on postcards. I consider holding my breath until we reach a better part of town, but then our guy stops at a narrow doorway and slips inside.

Uncle signals us to wait.

The alley is deserted, except for a man with an eye patch, who passes with hardly a glance our way.

A few moments later, Uncle beckons us forward and raps on the door.

No answer.

"Our friend is not accustomed to having visitors," Uncle explains.

He knocks again. Still no answer.

"Luca, if you please."

Luca positions himself in front of the door and gives it a solid kick. It splinters open with a loud bang.

Uncle enters first, and we follow. The room is small and plain. Sunlight streams in from a tiny window set high in one wall.

The only piece of furniture in the room is a large wood easel, scuffed and marked with random splotches of paint. Julien stands in front of it, paintbrush in hand.

He turns slowly toward us, and I catch a glimpse of the painting resting on the easel. It's breathtaking: a swirling landscape of ochre and green with a majestic violet mountain in the distance.

"*Qu'est-ce qui se passe?*" says Julien, his eyes wide.

"*Bonjour*, Julien," says Uncle, smiling.

"*Oncle?*" Julien's voice is fearful, shaky.

"I have been looking for you for quite some time, Julien," says Uncle. "You didn't mention to me that you had moved."

"*Mais non* . . . I have not moved," he says, his eyes flicking from Uncle to Luca to the rest of us. "This is my brother's place. I look after it for him while he is in the country."

"I see," Uncle says. "But why did you not tell me, Julien? In fact, it is only by chance that I have found you."

Julien says nothing.

"Julien is a painter," Uncle tells us, although that part I pretty much figured out. "He has all of the skill and talent that it takes to be one of the most important painters of his generation. And he would be, were it not for one small shortcoming."

Uncle paces the small room, stopping to examine the painting on the easel. "You see, my friends, Julien has no imagination. He cannot create original works of his own. He can only copy the great works of others. Isn't that right, Julien?"

Julien stays silent, but his hands are trembling.

"Up until today, we had an arrangement. I own a modest building not far from here. I let Julien stay in one of my rooms, and for that he pays me with his copied paintings. But I have received no payment for going on two months now. Is that what this is about, Julien? Have you been hiding from me to avoid paying rent?"

"*Non, monsieur. Ce n'est pas vrai.* I am an artist. Artists do not hide."

Uncle smiles. "Good. I am glad. Since you are not hiding, you will not object to me taking the rent painting now."

I watch Julien's expression. The line of his lips gets tighter, and his eyes flick to the left, where a canvas, half-covered by a cloth, leans against the wall.

"Frank, why don't you select a painting?" says Uncle, making it sound as if there is a whole roomful of them, when in fact there are only two—the one on the easel and the one by the wall.

Frank takes two steps toward the painting leaning against the wall and uncovers it. My eyes go wide. It's the exact same as the painting resting on the easel.

"*Non!*" exclaims Julien. "It is an original Cézanne! I have only borrowed it from a dealer. Please, *monsieur,* this will be the end of me!"

Uncle smiles a thin smile. "It is not I who chose to break our deal, Julien."

Then Uncle turns to Raoul and says, "Here is your chance to redeem yourself. Do you remember the lesson of earlier this morning?"

Raoul nods.

"Excellent. I'd like you to apply that lesson now. Look with your eyes, but more important, with your mind. Without performing a replica scan, I'd like you to tell me which is the original and which is the copy."

A long moment passes as Raoul studies the two paintings. Then he clears his throat and says, "The one on the easel is the copy, Uncle. He was putting the finishing touches on it when we came in."

"I see," Uncle says. "Does everyone else agree?"

"The other one is the copy," Frank says. "Julien did not immediately react when we burst into the room. That meant he knew we were coming. My guess is that the man with the eye patch tipped him off."

"Go on."

"He had time to switch the paintings so that we would think the one on the easel is the copy . . . when in fact it's the original."

"Excellent observation, Frank. Does anyone else have something to add?"

"Yes, Uncle," says Abbie. "The brush he is holding is dry. He is using it as a prop to make us think that he is completing the painting on the easel."

Uncle gives Abbie a radiant smile. Then he turns back to Julien and shrugs. "I'm afraid my little band of detectives has sniffed out your lie."

Uncle gives a nod to Frank, who grabs the painting off of the easel.

"*Non,*" says Julien, and I can see sweat beading on his forehead. "I beg you, *Oncle.* Do not take that painting. The dealer, Monsieur Letourneau, will be enraged if I do not return it to him. Please, come back *demain.* Or even better, on Thursday next. I will have two new paintings for you then!"

"It is too late for bargaining," says Uncle, drawing a knife from inside his jacket. I recognize it immediately. It's one of the dirks that was hanging in the Great Hall at the castle.

Julien is on his knees, clutching at the fringes of Uncle's coat. "*Non, monsieur.* You do not understand . . . this will crush me!"

"Calm yourself, Julien," Uncle says. "It is not quite that bad. You are an artist, remember? Artists are meant to struggle. So, in a way I am helping you . . . by providing you with a struggle to overcome."

Uncle shakes free of him and takes two quick steps over to where the second painting leans against the wall.

Holding it up for Julien to see, he stabs at the painting with the blade. There's a terrible ripping sound as the knife slices diagonally through layers of pigment and canvas.

Julien is sprawled on the floor, sobbing.

"I'm afraid we must be going now," says Uncle, pocketing his dirk. "*Adieu, monsieur.* Come along, everyone."

Uncle nods to Luca, who hangs back with Julien while the rest of us exit.

"Did anyone notice whether Julien is right-handed or left-handed?" Uncle asks as soon as we are out of the narrow hallway.

"He was holding the brush in his left hand. So I would say that he is left-handed, Uncle," Lydia says.

A terrible scream comes from Julien's studio.

Uncle smiles and says, "That *was* true, Lydia, up until a moment ago. From now on, however, I can assure you that Monsieur Julien will be painting with his right hand. And as adaptable as our friend is, the paintings he will produce with his right hand will never approach the sheer brilliance of his earlier forgeries."

"I . . . I don't understand, Uncle," says Lydia. "If he is not able to paint as well, won't that mean less money for us?"

How caring. A guy has just had his hand chopped off and all Lydia can think about is her allowance going down.

"An excellent question, Lydia. One that I am afraid will take longer to answer than the time allotted to this part of today's outing. Suffice it to say that lately I have done some deep thinking about life's big questions, including the flaws of history and how mankind would be better off if certain historical wrongs were corrected. And I would count as a historical wrong any event that diminishes one of the greatest attributes of civilized humanity—creativity. It is the charlatans and the fraudsters and the second-rate forgers like Julien who by their actions pollute the pristine waters of artistic expression and taint the purity of the world's creativity!"

Lydia nods. No one else says anything, but I'm sure they're asking the same question I am: what the heck is he talking about? Correcting "historical wrongs"? It sounds crazy. And who gets to decide what part of history needs correcting?

The alley is shrouded in fog, and everything seems dreamlike. For a moment, it's as though the haze is penetrating more than just my surroundings . . . it's also inside me. I watch as Uncle turns out of the alley and gets swallowed up by the fog.

Luca's voice cuts through the mist. "Grab your clothes packets and change quickly. Uncle and I will meet you at the next time/place."

Judging from what I've just seen, I take back anything I ever said about Uncle getting soft or losing his edge. And as I change clothes, an even scarier thought occurs to me—Uncle made Julien wait for two months before punishing him. But in the end, Julien's punishment came. In spades.

I wonder how long he's going to make me wait for mine?

May 24, 1978, 6:41 P.M.

Aboard the cruise ship *Bonnie Prince Charlie*

Inner Hebrides, off the coast of Scotland

I'm lying on my back, looking up at the sky, feeling the ship's gentle vibration beneath me.

I know from the quick briefing Luca gave us that we're cruising somewhere off the west coast of Scotland.

As my time freeze thaws, I'm able to move my head. I've landed between two empty deck chairs.

I check the time on my fingernail. 6:41 P.M. I'm surprised there aren't more people out on the deck. Except for a couple playing a game of shuffleboard and two teenagers having an evening swim in the pool, I'm all alone.

"Hey. Are you dead . . . or what?" says a voice.

A skinny boy with straggly black hair is staring down at me. He looks about ten years old and is wearing a bomber jacket that is two sizes too big for him.

"I'm stretching out my back," I say. "The deck chairs aren't any good for that."

"Whatever moves you, Jack."

The boy glances around and then runs off.

Something about him strikes me as odd, but I can't figure out what it is.

I stand up and walk over to the rail. A stiff wind comes up, and I hold on, gazing out at steep cliffs across the gray-blue water.

We've got a break until dinner, and that suits me fine. I need some time to figure things out. Everything has been so confusing. Arriving at Headquarters yesterday, having my brain poked and then going on this whirlwind tour with Uncle.

I wonder what Zach, Jim and Diane are thinking. That I ran away? Or that I was kidnapped? Either way, they'll never believe me when I tell them. And how can I tell them if I never make it back? Or what if I do find a way to time travel there but Uncle yanks me back again?

"Hey, Caleb," says a voice, and I whip my head around to see Raoul standing there.

"Hi," I say.

"Dinner is in twenty minutes . . . in the Clan MacNaughton Room," he says.

"Thanks. What about our cabins?"

"We don't have any," he says. "We're not sleeping here. After dinner, it's the final event and then we go back to the Compound."

"All right, thanks." I turn to look out over the rail again, but Raoul doesn't move.

"The others don't think I should be talking to you," he says, lowering his voice.

"What do you mean?" I say.

"Not Abbie so much. But Frank and Lydia. They say that you're in for it because of trying to escape."

I look at him for a moment and say, "So then why *are* you talking to me?"

"I . . . I don't know. I mean, I do. There's something I need to ask you."

"Okay."

"Do you . . . do you think I'm in trouble with Uncle?" he asks.

That's a tough one. There's no question that Uncle has been picking on Raoul more than anyone else today. But does that mean he's in real trouble?

"Honestly, I don't know," I say. "Sometimes I think this is all a game for Uncle. And part of his game is finding someone he can pick on. He used to pick on me before I . . . went away."

Raoul looks around nervously for a moment, as if to see if there is anyone else within earshot. Then he whispers, "I want to leave Timeless Treasures, Caleb. Can you help me?"

I bite my lip. Does he even really know what he's asking? And why me? I'm the king of failed escapes, not successful ones. Besides, I probably won't be around long enough to help him. Uncle is bound to banish me to the Barrens any day now for my past deeds.

I look out over the water and say, "Are you sure about this? If you get caught—"

"I'm not going to get caught," says Raoul. "There's a place I know where he'll never find me."

I almost feel pity for him. He's naïve if he thinks there's any place or time where Uncle can't reach him. I of all people know how hopeless that is. But I also know that if I had another chance to escape, I'd be gone in a heartbeat.

I glance over at Raoul, nod and say, "Okay."

Immediately his expression changes, and there's a grateful and relieved look in his eyes. As if talking for a minute lifted a huge burden from him.

"Thank you, Caleb, really," he says. "And if you don't mind—"

"Don't worry," I say. "I won't tell anyone. In fact, we never had this conversation."

"Thanks," he says again, and I watch him walk away.

I hang out by the rail for another couple of minutes. I have no idea how I can help Raoul, but I'll try. My thoughts return to Zach. I wonder what he's doing right now. I run a hand lightly over my wrist. Blocked. But what if I go back to 1959 and just wait a few years? Or to 1980. But Zach will be grown up by then and won't remember me.

A bell rings and interrupts my thoughts. "Good evening, everyone," says a man's voice. I look up at the closest screen. He's dressed in a crisp white uniform, and his face is deeply tanned.

"This is your captain speaking. Since our departure from Oban yesterday, the weather has cleared, and the temperature is a pleasant eighteen degrees Celsius. We are cruising at nineteen knots, and in a few minutes, we'll be passing between the isles of Rum and Eigg. If you have a look off the starboard deck, you'll be able to glimpse Askival, the tallest mountain on Rum."

His voice is soothing. It has the same rhythm as the waves. If I wasn't standing up, I could easily fall sleep.

"I'll now turn you over to the cruise director for a few announcements," he says.

There's a brief pause and then another voice, this one high-pitched and squeaky, comes on.

"Helloooo, cruisers. I am Minky MacPherson, your DOFBPC— that's short for Director of Fun on the *Bonnie Prince Charlie*."

It's a woman in a pink shirt, wearing pink eyeglasses and with perfectly coiffed pink hair. Something tells me she likes the color pink.

"I see you, standing there all alone, doing nothing!" says Minky accusingly, and for a panicky moment, I think she's actually talking to me.

"Well, your alone time is over!" She continues, "Time for a wee bit of fun! And there's no better place for fun than the *Bonnie Prince Charlie,* your home away from home. Tonight," says Minky, "there's a Scrabble tournament in the Captain's Lounge and a séance in the Pitlochry Pub. And don't forget to claim your purchased items from this afternoon's art auction of original works by Cézanne."

Maybe if I cover my ears I can block her out.

"Don't forget, cruisers!" Minky enthuses. "In ten minutes in the Loch Linnhe Lounge, I'm giving my popular talk on priceless but affordable Scottish woolens. The first ten people to arrive will receive a complimentary, that means free, ladies, genuine, made in Scotland, cashmere neck warmer, so hurry on down to the Loch Linnhe Lounge!"

It's not working. She's got the type of voice that cuts through skin and bone. The elevator door opens, and I dive for the entrance.

"Well, look what the cat dragged in!" says a voice.

For an awful moment, I worry that Minky's tracked me down, but the image on the television screen is of a large woman in a flowery bathing suit, sprawled on a lounge chair reading a book. The title says *Scotland on Five Turnips a Day.*

"Phoebe?" Wow, Uncle must be getting really paranoid if he's brought Phoebe along. I wonder what he has her doing . . . tinkering with the ship's security system so that no one bothers us? Or, siphoning the take from the ship's casino to Uncle's offshore bank account? Probably both.

"Do you think I'm fat?" she says.

"No," I say. "I think you're normal . . . I mean for a computer."

"Good. Because I've already eaten my five turnips today and guess what?"

"What?" I ask.

"I'M STILL HUNGRY!" she wails.

"Well, then have something else," I say.

"It's not that simple. I need to lose ten pounds. I want to look good for Minky's Scottish woolens talk."

"But . . . her talk's in ten minutes. No one can lose ten pounds in ten minutes," I point out.

"Are you saying that I have no willpower?" Phoebe says.

This feels like old times. If I closed my eyes right now, I could easily be on the elevator at Headquarters. I wonder absently what it would be like having a silent ride in an elevator for a change.

"I think you have great willpower," I say. "Now, can you take me up to five, please? I need to join the others for dinner."

Oops, I shouldn't have said that.

"Dinner? You're having dinner while I stay here alone, suffering? How can you be so insensitive? You're no different than the rest. You don't care about me." Phoebe starts to sob.

"That's not true," I say. "Don't you remember the time I brought you back those earrings from Peru?"

"Y . . . yes," she says in between whimpers.

"Well, doesn't that show I like you?"

She doesn't say anything. Just sniffles quietly.

"And how about that porcelain tortoise I brought back from China? I had to jump into a hot kiln to get that for you."

"I remember," she croaks.

"Good," I say gently. "Now bring me up to five, please, and slide those doors open so that I can step off."

The elevator starts up and then stops suddenly.

What now?

"Let's share secrets!" says Phoebe.

"Let's what?"

"Friends share secrets," she continues. "You're my one true friend, Caleb. Ergo, we should swap secrets."

Ergo? Ergo, I'd like to get off this elevator before she drives me completely nuts. But I've got to humor her to have any chance of getting out of here before next year.

"All right," I say. "Here's mine. When I was in the Barrens, I thought I was going crazy and that I had multiple personalities." It's not much of a secret, but it's the best I can do right now.

"Really?" Phoebe says. "How fascinating. Which was the dominant personality?"

"Someone called Agnes," I say. "She was a bossy type."

"Oooh, delicious," she says. "Now here's mine. The final event Uncle has planned for you guys is a real doozy."

The elevator starts up again and then stops at three. An elderly couple gets on. I look up at the screen. Ancient stones stand alone in a farmer's field, their shadows made long by the setting sun.

The elevator stops at four, and the couple steps off.

"What's the final event?" I ask.

Phoebe's first persona is back. Except this time she has a T-shirt over her bathing suit that has an image of a round of cheese on it with the caption LOCH NESS MUENSTER.

"Please, Phoebe. I've got to know."

She pushes her sunglasses down her nose and whispers, "All I'll say is that it's the kind of napping that you don't do lying down. That's a huge clue. There, I've already said too much."

The doors open on five, and I step out. A nap that you don't lie down for. I wonder what that could mean.

On the way to the dining hall, I take a shortcut through the casino. The place is packed with people feeding tokens into slot machines. I wonder what they would think if they knew there were time-traveling thieves on board? Which leads me to wonder what name Uncle used to check us in under so that he could score the private dining room: Portree Pipes and Drums Band? Lower Manhattan Frisbee Golf Team? Or maybe he didn't check us in at all.

The dining hall is packed and full of the sounds of clattering plates and people talking. There's even live jazz—three performers— a clarinet player, a guy on keyboards and a singer. I wonder how they're going to get to their next gig after they finish their set. Then it dawns on me. In a way, they're prisoners. They can't just pack up and leave. They have to wait until the cruise ends or comes to port to get off the ship like everyone else.

At the far end of the dining hall is a set of double doors labeled CLAN MACNAUGHTON ROOM. As I approach the doors, I take a deep breath before opening them. The room has a giant mural of rolling green hills sprinkled with farmsteads. In the center is a burnished mahogany dining table with seven settings.

But no one is at the table right now. They're all lined up at the buffet next to it.

I join the back of the buffet line behind Raoul. Wow—there's so much food here! All kinds of salads, pasta, seafood, pizza, you name it. There's even a guy in a chef's hat cutting slices off a huge hunk of roast beef.

I heap food on my plate and join the others at the table. No one dares touch the food until Uncle arrives. And for some, including Frank, it's a particularly tough battle. I look at his plate. Lots of eel. You are what you eat, I guess.

"*Feasgar math.* Good evening, people." Uncle sweeps into the room and takes his place at the head of the table. "Did everyone have a great day today?"

We all nod. Uncle is looking sharp in a red and green tartan kilt and argyle jacket.

"Raoul, will you say the blessing?" says Uncle. "In Mandarin, please."

Mandarin? That was yesterday's news. Uncle is already on to his next obsession—all things Scottish. Not that saying the blessing in Scottish Gaelic would be any easier, mind you. That said, Raoul was right. Uncle is definitely after him.

Raoul looks up at the ceiling for a moment.

"I've forgotten," he says, finally.

Uncle's eyes flash.

"Say again?"

"I . . . I have forgotten, Uncle, the words for the blessing."

There is a heavy silence around the table.

Uncle's face is unreadable.

Then he says, "It appears that lately, you have forgotten quite a number of things, Raoul. Perhaps you need to go to a quiet place where you will have time to regain your memory."

Raoul's face drains of all color.

Uncle picks up a saltshaker and drops it to the floor.

"Oh, how clumsy of me. Raoul, will you be so kind as to pick it up?"

Raoul blinks rapidly. The fear on his face is plain.

Slowly, he bends down to pick up the shaker. Before he can reach it, Uncle kicks it under the table.

"Go ahead, fetch it," he says, as if talking to a dog.

As Raoul begins to crawl under the table, Uncle grabs his arm and twists his wrist up. Three quick taps, and Raoul is gone. Just like that.

I'm in shock. I can't believe it. I look around at the others. Except for Frank, they are all staring at their plates. My eyes meet Frank's for a moment, and he smiles. I want to slug him.

Uncle smooths a crease in the tablecloth. "Now, then. Caleb, will you say the blessing, please?"

My hands begin to tremble. I haven't spoken Mandarin in at least five months. But that isn't going to catch me any sympathy from Uncle. All I can see in my head is Raoul's terrified expression. Where did Uncle send him? The Barrens. It had to be. Even if I dared, I wouldn't know where to start looking for him, because when Uncle banishes people to the Barrens it's never the same year that he sends them to. Plus, according to Abbie, ever since my escape from the Barrens, Uncle's tightened up security so that not even Phoebe knows the year. But Raoul still has his wrist patch. He can get himself out of there . . . can't he? And then I remember Frank saying that the new patches can be remotely disabled. I shudder. Raoul's not going to be able to escape.

"Caleb?" Uncle repeats.

My face is getting hot. I can't do this. I'm drawing a blank. I glance quickly at Abbie. There's compassion in her eyes. Why didn't Uncle pick her instead of me? She's much better at Mandarin than I am.

"*Zhù nǐ shēng rì kuài lè,*" I blurt out.

I can almost feel the silence.

After a moment, Uncle smiles. "That was not very good, Caleb. In fact, you just wished me a happy birthday. But I will accept your effort. Very well, everyone, let's eat. I'm famished."

I try to calm my breathing, but this thing with Raoul has got me really rattled. I'm definitely next on Uncle's hit list. I try to count up all the wrong answers I gave him today, but my mind is jumbled. If it wasn't as many as Raoul, it must have been close. Plus, Uncle still has it in for me from before. So why hasn't he punished me?

My hands shake as I lift the fork to my mouth. I eat the tasteless food in silence.

After he's done, Uncle dabs his mouth with his napkin and clears his throat.

"Welcome, everyone, to the year 1978 and to the cruise ship *Bonnie Prince Charlie*. We are presently cruising on the Sound of Sleat in the Inner Hebrides, off the west coast of Scotland."

He pauses, looks out over the room and recites,

"In the highlands, in the country places,
Where the old plain men have rosy faces,
And the young fair maidens
Quiet eyes;
Where essential silence cheers and blesses,
And for ever in the hill-recesses
Her more lovely music
Broods and dies.

"Those, my friends," says Uncle, "are the opening lines to 'In the Highlands,' a poem by the Scottish-born writer Robert Louis Stevenson. Not only was he a poet and writer, but also a playwright, composer of music and inveterate traveler. In July and August 1874, aboard a ship called the *Heron*, he cruised these very waters and passed the same islands that we are presently passing.

"But his travels were not confined to his native Scotland. Stevenson journeyed to many parts of the world. Although for much of his short life he was afflicted by illness, he never stopped writing, traveling and marveling at the world around him.

"In our own life journeys, we must retain the wonder and curiosity of a Robert Louis Stevenson. We must never let our sense of excitement and adventure wane. And we must teach these same qualities to our new recruits."

My eyes wander toward Abbie. She is twirling a loose strand of hair. Her fingers are long and delicate, and I find myself staring at them. She catches me looking and raises her eyebrows slightly. I look away quickly.

"In 1886," Uncle continues, "Stevenson wrote a novel that would later be acclaimed as one of the finest adventure stories ever written. In it, a lad awakens bound hand and foot on board a sailing ship. He is, as the book's title suggests, kidnapped. In today's final event, each of you will snatch a child between the ages of six and eleven years old for training as a new recruit. You will timeleap with him or her from this ship back to the Compound. It is now eight o'clock local time. You have exactly one half hour to complete the snatch."

I can't do it.

I might as well pack my bags for the Barrens right now.

"Before we adjourn, does anyone have any questions?"

No hands go up.

"All right, then, we are adjourned. I will see you all back at the Compound with your guests. Your arrival time at the Compound will be October 5, 2061, at 7:30 P.M."

Everyone gets up and starts filing out of the room.

"I can't do it, Abbie," I say, once we are out of earshot of the others.

"Yes you can," she says. "You don't have a choice."

"I do have a choice. I'll go back to 1950 or 1980 or, even better, 1880."

"Don't you get it?" she says. "If you try to run, he'll track you down again. If you don't do what he wants, he'll send you wherever he sent Raoul. Or worse. Besides, you being a hero isn't going to make one bit of difference. Lydia or Frank will gladly snatch an extra kid to make up for one you don't grab."

"What about you?" I ask. "Don't you have a problem with it?"

"Maybe. But—"

"Maybe? There's no maybe. I will not kidnap a kid to help Uncle grow his business. I'd rather die," I say.

"Well, you just might get your wish," she says before turning and stomping away.

XI

May 24, 1978, 8:07 P.M.
Aboard the cruise ship *Bonnie Prince Charlie*
Inner Hebrides, off the coast of Scotland

I've really done it now. Abbie probably won't speak to me for a thousand years. But does she really expect that I can march into a cabin and snatch someone's kid? There's no way I want anything to do with that.

I head out to the deck and lean over the rail. It's too dark to see the water, but I can hear it lapping against the side of the ship. The wind picks up and blows my hair back from my forehead.

A scuffle behind me catches my attention.

"Leave me alone, you mingin' bampots!" a voice shouts.

Good luck with that. Being left alone only works for people who have communicable diseases or eat stinky cheese. Everyone else is fair game for *not* being left alone.

But the owner of the voice doesn't appear to get that. He's cursing up a storm.

Many of the curses are standard gutter stuff I've heard a million times. But a few of them are colorful ones I've never heard before, and they're drawing me in despite myself.

I look over my shoulder and am surprised to see that the owner of the voice is a stick of a boy. Hey, isn't that the kid I saw on the deck when I first landed?

The two trying to hold on to him are dressed in white crew uniforms.

For a moment, my brain has trouble processing the scene. Have these crew members been hired by Uncle to bring kids to him?

But then one of them says, "Bite me again, girlie, and that's all you're having for breakfast, lunch and supper tomorrow."

Well, that's interesting. The troublemaker is a girl. Or Mr. Bitten thinks he's dealing with a girl.

I follow at a safe distance. They drag her, protesting, to the central stairway. I'm not the only gawker. Five or six cruisers wander over from the casino to see what all the fuss is about. One of the bolder ones asks, "What did she do?"

"Ship's business," is all the white shirt on the left says, which of course isn't an answer at all.

"Get your filthy hands off me, bootlicker!" the girl spits out.

One of the casino crowd, a man with bluish hair and an impressive pinkie ring, takes a half step forward, which looks to me to be more like a stumble than a challenge, but the closest white shirt isn't taking any chances. He glares at the man and says, "I wouldn't interfere, sir. She's a thief. Been stealing from the passengers."

"Liar!" the girl screams, and then proceeds to rake his forearm with her nails. Ouch.

The white shirt grabs the hand that did the damage and twists it until she squeals in pain.

"Your daddy's gonna whip you when he finds out what you've been up to," he says to her through clenched teeth.

"Wrong again, Jack," she says. "The only thing my *policeman* daddy's gonna do is whip your sorry butt so bad that you won't be able to sit on the throne for a week."

Like I said, colorful.

I glance at my fingernail. Thirteen minutes left to complete the snatch.

Hmmm.

They lead her down a long corridor, and I follow at a safe distance. Where are they taking her? To a jail cell? On a luxury ship? Why should I be surprised? Of course they have a jail cell. How else to deal with people who have had too many rum punches?

The small contingent stops at a door about midway down the hall. The beefier white shirt unlocks the door, and they shove her roughly inside. Before they shut the door, the one who got scratched lays in a kick for good measure.

I wait until the men are out of sight, then walk up to the door and place my ear to the wood.

Nothing.

The lock would be a cinch to pick if I had a skeleton key or even a piece of wire. But the only thing I have on me is a slightly bent piece of Juicy Fruit gum that I scored from a candy machine outside the Loch Linnhe Lounge. Not that I'm all that concerned, though. I've got a much easier way to get in.

I walk away and then, a minute later, do another pass-by. This time when I put my ear to the door, I hear breathing. Mentally, I place her at five feet away from the door. That leaves me with a good-sized landing strip. I tap away on my wrist. Delicate now. A tiny leap forward in space with minimal time displacement.

Bingo. Here I am. And there she is. Staring at me from across the room. I can really only see her right eye, on account of her messy hair covering the left. But I can tell from the high blinking rate that my entrance has made an impression.

Still, she doesn't say anything.

"Nice place you have here," I say, going for pleasant.

"Piss off."

"All right. Have a nice day." I touch my wrist, land just outside the door and immediately put my ear to it.

Scuffling sounds and then, "Wait. Come back."

I sigh, count to five, tap my wrist and then reappear inside.

"How did you do that?" she asks.

"Magic," I say.

"Show me," she says, her voice surprisingly husky for someone so scrawny.

"I'll show you . . . after we strike a deal," I say.

She looks at me sideways. I think she's weighing what the odds are of successfully attacking me and forcing me to reveal how I got in and out of the room.

Then she looks at her fingernails and says, "Man, these are getting long. And sharp too. Good thing I don't have an itch that needs scratchin'."

I almost smile. She's tossed out the attack option and is now playing the intimidation card. I have to admire this girl's street smarts. But I'd better not admire her for too long. Time is running short.

"Here's the deal. I can get you out of here," I say.

"So what?" she says. "You get me out, they round me up again. Unless you can get me off this stinkin' tub I ain't interested."

"Off the ship? What about your father?"

She laughs hard. "You bought that story? I ain't got no policeman daddy. But my mom's the queen of England, and if you touch me, she'll send the Mounties after you."

"The Mounties are Canadian," I say.

"What's your point?" she says, looking bored now.

"I can get you off," I say.

She holds a ragged fingernail up to the light, studies it and says, "Where's the catch, Jack?"

"You've got to come with me to where I work. Peacefully. No biting, scratching or fighting. And when we get there, if my boss or anyone asks, tell them I kidnapped you."

She hoots with laughter and then says, "Where's your office?"

"New York City."

Her eyes light up for a second and then she narrows them to slits. "I'll do it for a hundred bucks."

I rapidly calculate how much cash I've got on me. Forty bucks and maybe three dollars in change, tops.

"Never mind," I say, "I'll try the girl in the jail cell down the hall." I begin to make as if I'm leaving.

She shrugs her shoulders, lies down on the floor, sticks a hand inside her shirt and pulls out five rings and a sparkling necklace. "Suit yourself," she says, trying the rings on. "I kind of like it here anyway. Got my own room . . ."

I'm running out of time. I root around in my pocket and pluck out a twenty.

"This is the best I can do. I can give you another twenty when we get where we're going . . . and I'll pay for all transportation," I throw in.

"I dunno," she says, examining the bill. "How do I know you aren't scamming me? That when we get there, you won't take off?"

Heat is rising in my cheeks. Maybe I should forget this whole thing and go snatch some six-year-old from her bed. But I know I could never do that.

"I guess you'll have to trust me on that," I say.

She studies me for a long moment. "All right. Lead on, Jack."

"And since we're going to be traveling together, you can call me by my name. It's Caleb."

"Okay. And you can call me Queen Beatrice the Third. But if that's too long for you, Jack, some people call me Razor."

"Razor?"

"Yeah. It's 'cause I'm a sharp dresser." She sniggers. "By the way, I'll be needing a snack soon."

There's a knock on the door.

"Don't know why they bother knockin'," Razor says. "I mean, there's no way I can open it."

A voice comes over the intercom. "I'm Dr. Posner. Can I speak with you for a few moments?"

She rolls her eyes and mouths the word *shrink*.

"Sorry, Doctor. The place is a mess," Razor says looking at me. "I wasn't expecting company."

"That's quite all right," his voice crackles over the intercom.

"All right, give me a minute to freshen up," she says.

"Okay," he says.

She turns to me. "You're on."

"Fine. Take my hand."

"I don't hold hands on the first date, Jack."

"This isn't a— I need to hold your hand for the magic to work," I say.

"You're not scammin' me, are you?"

"I don't think I could if I tried," I say.

She reaches her hand out, and I grab it.

"So now what?" she says. "You gonna do your vanishing act again?"

I look straight at her. "That's right, Razor. And this time you're coming with me. All you have to do is say the magic word."

"Could it be . . . *scumbag*?" she shouts as she presses the button on the intercom.

"Close enough," I say, touching my wrist.

Scuffling from the other side of the door. A key rattles in the lock. But the good doctor is too late. Razor and I are already halfway to 2061.

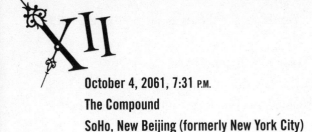

I land on the ground of the alley beside the Compound. When I'm able to turn my head, I see Razor sitting beside me, staring at her hands.

"It's only time freeze. You'll be able to move them in a moment," I say helpfully.

"I'm crippled!" she wails. "I'm suing you for all you got, Jack. These hands are the tools of my trade, man!"

I could mention to her that suing me is a hopeless proposition and that even if she won, my only assets in this world consist of twenty-three dollars and a driftwood carving that I left in 1968. But that would be cruel.

"Try moving them now."

She flexes her fingers and then moves her arms slowly.

"You're lucky," she growls.

I get up and brush myself off. "C'mon. We've got an appointment."

She stands up and looks around. Admittedly there's not much to see: a couple of brick walls and a fire escape. Even so, she looks dazed and confused, which is perfect. If only she can hold that expression until I turn her in to Uncle.

"How did you do that?" she says.

"I didn't do anything," I say. "You're the one who said the magic word."

"Where are we?"

82

"I said I was taking you to New York City. This is it. Except they're calling it New Beijing these days, on account of the Great Friendship. But that's just political stuff. Nothing for you to worry about."

"Where's the ship?"

It's a logical question. Deserving of a logical answer.

"The ship is still at sea," I say.

"So how'd you do it?" asks Razor. "And don't give me that 'it's magic' crap. And where's my other twenty?"

Which question to answer first? "You get your other twenty when we get where we're going," I tell her. "As to how I did it, it has to do with an implant near my right wrist. It can be programmed for any date up to the present. All I have to do is tap my wrist a couple of times and, presto, I'm there."

"Are you sayin' you're a time traveler?"

I smile and nod.

"That's crazy talk. Time travel is strictly science fiction crap."

"I suppose you're right." I switch to a whisper. "If I were you, though, I'd keep that thought to myself. Some of the people you're about to meet really believe in it."

We climb the short flight of steps to the front entrance of the Compound.

"Halt—who goes there?" says a voice as soon as we're inside.

There's a holo-screen above and to our left. Phoebe's persona is wearing a suit of blue armor and carrying a spear.

I sigh. "Hello, Phoebe. It's me, Caleb . . . and a new recruit."

"Some recruit. Looks like she could use a little meat on her."

"Screw off," Razor says.

"Oohh. A feisty one!" Phoebe says.

We don't have time to play, so I begin to walk past the screen. And smack right into a plate glass wall.

"Ouch. When did that get put in?" I ask.

"Yesterday. Do you like it? It's completely retractable . . . only by me, that is. It gives me a chance to spend some quality time with my visitors. Now, what medieval game should we all play?"

"Phoebe, we don't have time for games. Uncle's expecting us."

"Of course he is, and of course you don't. But I'm dying for a game of fox and geese." The screen image changes to a board with thirty-three holes for pegs arranged in a cross. "Who wants to be the fox?" she calls out in a singsong voice.

"Please." I'm trying to keep my tone even. "I've got to report in."

"All right, I'll be the fox. You two are the geese. The geese go first. Your move, girlie."

Razor has a glint in her eye.

Quick as a wink, she reaches into her pocket, withdraws a good-sized stone, cocks her arm back and lets it fly. It bounces off the screen without damaging it and falls to the floor.

"Screw you," Razor says.

A moment of silence follows, which is actually a record for Phoebe. The game board disappears, and Phoebe's knight-in-armor persona comes back on. "Let's see," she says, studying a scroll. "I was right. The rules say that any player who throws a stone at the fox loses a turn. Sorry, girlie. Caleb, your turn."

"Phoebe, how long are you going to keep us here?" I ask.

"That depends," she says. "Usually I'm able to win in about seventeen minutes. But this one could take a bit longer on account of her." She points a gauntlet at Razor.

"Go piss in a junkyard."

"See what I mean?"

"Can't we play something that doesn't take so long?" I ask. "I've really got to get in to see Uncle."

84

A long silence follows. Then Phoebe sighs. "All right. We'll play Name That Dead Rock Band and Album. But just so you know, I'm saving this game for later."

Then she begins to whistle, softly at first but then gaining power. I have no idea what the song is. Still, I've got to try.

"The Rolling Stones, 'Paint It Black,'" I say, taking a flier. Phoebe's a big Stones fan. And they've been dead for a good thirty years, which means they qualify.

"Hah," says Phoebe. "Not even close. Try again."

"I give up," I say.

"You can't give up."

"Yes I can. And I do."

"All right, spoilsport. Do you want to guess, short stuff?"

"Jethro Tull, 'Thick as a Brick,'" Razor says, and a wounded cry comes from the screen.

The glass door slides open, and we step through.

"Impressive," I say.

"Yeah, I know. Like I said, Jack. Razor is sharp."

"Okay," I say, changing my tone to serious. "From here on in, act like I kidnapped you."

"Gimme my twenty bucks first."

Sighing, I fork over my last twenty.

"Good," she says, smiling. "Now, grab my arm."

Luca is waiting at the entrance to the Yard. A line of recruits is being marched out and I don't recognize any of them or their trainers. After they leave, only three dazed kids in pajamas remain in the Yard. These must be fresh off the ship. One, a boy, is crying.

"You're cutting it close," Luca says when we start to go in.

He's right. I didn't plan on it taking so long to get past Phoebe.

"She's like a little tiger, this one," I say, tightening my grip on Razor.

Right on cue, she bares her teeth and swipes at one of my arms with her long nails. She connects, drawing blood. Ouch. Did she really have to go that far?

Luca grabs her and shoves her into the Yard with the others.

"Go to the Viewing Room, Caleb. Everyone else is already there."

I take a last look at Razor. She flashes a smile at me, and I feel a pang of guilt. Sure, she agreed to come, but I didn't exactly tell her the whole truth of what goes on here. Still, I got her off the ship like she wanted. Who knows how long they would have kept her in that cell? Probably until the end of the cruise. And then what?

As far as I know, she's got no family, so they'd probably hand her over to some child welfare department who would stick her in a foster home in Scotland that she'd run away from anyway. Instead, thanks to me, she's in America, the land of opportunity. If she wants to make a break for it now, Uncle might not even bother going after her, not with all the other new recruits he's got. Yeah, looking at it that way, I don't feel so bad.

In the Viewing Room, everyone is seated on chairs, gazing through the two-way mirror at today's catch. The Yard is much as I remember it: a huge room with a rough concrete floor. Except that it looks darker and dirtier than I recall. The new recruits are now all huddled in a corner.

"Caleb," Uncle says, "you are late."

"Sorry, Uncle."

I snatch a glance at Abbie. She's sitting near the back, next to Frank. Our eyes connect. I don't dare mindspeak to her right now. Someone is bound to intercept.

"Frank," Uncle says, "why don't you begin. Tell everyone about your snatch."

Frank stands and struts to the front of the room. He has a variety of different walking styles, none of which I like. This one, which I call his Harvard Strut, is one of my least favorites.

He takes ahold of a pointer and angles it on the two-way mirror. Green light tracers show a path directly to a young boy sitting with his knees to his chest, sobbing.

"That's my catch," Frank says proudly. "Plucked him right out of his parents' bed. They didn't notice a thing."

"Excellent," Uncle says. "Lydia?"

Beaming, Lydia steps forward. For some reason, seeing her happy always depresses me. It's not that she doesn't deserve a little happiness in her life, but when Lydia is happy, it usually means someone else suffered for it.

"Show us your quarry and tell us your story," Uncle says. I can tell he's enjoying every second of this.

"My quarry," Lydia says, taking hold of the pointer, "is that girl, over there." The tracer leads to a short, chubby girl dressed in a two-piece bathing suit that has a green and red anchor design. The girl is wet and shivering.

"She was taking an evening swim with her father. When she did a cannonball into the pool, I quickly dove in after her, grabbed her wrist and timeleaped here, all before she could even come up for air."

There are a couple of admiring oohs and ahhs. I want to ask Lydia how she managed to stay completely dry through all the cannonballs and dives, but I keep the question to myself.

"Nicely done, Lydia." Uncle is beaming now. "Abbie, quarry and story, please."

Abbie steps to the front. Her expression is unreadable. She points to a figure lying curled up on the floor: a boy with curly brown hair and eyeglasses.

Uncle adjusts the audio, and the boy's soft snores can be heard. Frank guffaws.

"I snatched him right from his cabin," Abbie says. "He was sitting up in bed reading a book, and when I grabbed him, he hardly reacted at all. Just kept on reading. I had to be quiet, though, because one of his parents was in the bathroom."

Right from his parents' cabin. I could never do that.

"Well done, Abbie," says Uncle. "And finally, Caleb."

I take the pointer and aim it at Razor. "The only thing I know about her is that right before I snatched her, she was on her way somewhere with a couple of the ship's crew."

"Very well," says Uncle. "It appears that everyone has performed splendidly. And I would go so far as to say that the entire day was a smashing success. Wouldn't you all agree?"

Everyone nods.

I look through the two-way. The kid that was crying before has now settled down and is whimpering softly.

"All right, then. You have all earned a well-deserved rest. Tomorrow morning you will each be assigned two recruits and training will begin in earnest. With that, I bid you good evening. *Oidhche mhath!*" Uncle gives us a little bow.

"*Oidhche mhath,*" we all say, returning the bow.

"Caleb, if I might see you for a moment, please," Uncle says.

"Certainly, Uncle." My palms go all clammy.

Everyone leaves, and I'm alone with Uncle. Only one other person makes me as uncomfortable, and he's just Harvard strutted from the room.

"How are you doing, Caleb?" he says. "We really haven't spoken since your . . . return."

"I'm fine, Uncle," I lie. My stomach is doing somersaults. Here comes the punishment that I've been expecting.

"You and I have a long history together, don't we?" says Uncle.

I nod. I wish he would get on with things and banish me to the Barrens or cut off my big toe or whatever he's going to do, because the waiting is driving me crazy.

"I imagine you have been wondering why I invited you back to Timeless Treasures after your abrupt and, may I say, rather rude, departure."

He calls it being invited back. I call it being tackled by a six-foot-five hulking monster.

"I was kind of wondering, Uncle," I say.

"I invited you to return because, deep down, I know that you and I share similar values, that we both want to do things that are right, moral and true."

My missing little toe is beginning to itch. What is he getting at?

"You may recall me mentioning recently that mankind would be better off if certain historical wrongs were corrected."

"Yes, I remember you saying that, Uncle."

"I now have some ideas on how to bring this to fruition. I am inviting both you and Frank to a private meeting to discuss this further. Are you free at eleven tomorrow morning?"

Am I free? That's a good one. I was free until his goon snatched me and hauled me back here. Now it's fair to say that I'm time trapped. Of course he probably doesn't see it that way, since with my new patch, I can travel to a million different times and places throughout history. It's just that I can't go to the one time and place that matters to me most: 1968 Boston.

"Sure, I'm available," I say.

"Excellent."

"Is that all, Uncle?"

He smiles and says nothing. Goose bumps race up and down my arms. A small wisp of a thought begins to take hold in my mind—that I might actually leave this meeting without being punished. I try to crush the thought before it takes hold because, as unpredictable as Uncle is, he usually inflicts his punishments at the very end of meetings, when you have one foot out the door.

"Yes, Caleb, that is all. Except for one small matter . . ."

I swallow hard.

"As you are freshly back from a rather long absence," Uncle continues, "it would do you good to reacquaint yourself with the Compound. You will see that we have made some changes, including relocating the sleeping quarters for all senior time snatchers to here from Headquarters. Why don't you assist Luca with the tour he will be giving this week's new recruits? It will begin shortly—as soon as they receive their mindpatches and translator implants."

"Certainly, Uncle."

As I walk through the doorway, I don't feel any great rush of relief. He hasn't punished me yet, but it's coming, all right. Sure as the rain comes to Scotland in the spring. I suppose I should be grateful for our little meeting, though. Because, now I have something new to worry about—tomorrow's meeting with him and Frank.

So thank you, Uncle.

October 4, 2061, 8:43 P.M.
The Compound
SoHo, New Beijing (formerly New York City)

Luca is herding eight recruits into a line. A few of them are fingering the backs of their necks where the implants were inserted.

Watching him in action, I'm struck again by how much he looks like Nassim. Which leads me to wonder whatever happened to Nassim. The last time I saw him was when I escaped with him and Zach to 1967.

I continue to watch Luca. Uncle must have given him orders to be gentle with the recruits, judging from the way he's sweet-talking them.

"Make a nice straight line, now," he says. "For anyone who behaves, he'll get a treat at the end of the tour."

The recruits look tired. Razor catches my eye and gives me a devilish smile.

"You mean he or she will get a treat," Razor pipes up.

There are a couple of snickers from the other recruits.

Luca whips his head around. "Who said that?"

Wonderful. That didn't take long.

Razor steps forward. She's not shaking at all, which I find amazing, given that Luca is about three times her size.

"Repeat what you said," he says, smiling.

"I said 'he or she will get a treat,' " Razor says coolly.

"You don't like my English?" Luca says, his eyes gleaming.

"No, I don't like your English," Razor says, and this draws a laugh from the other recruits.

Luca walks around her. The others fall silent.

"You're a very funny girl," he says. "At least I think you're a girl. Does Funny Girl know baseball?"

"Sure," she says. This time, there's a slight crack in her voice.

"Good. Strike one on you, Funny Girl."

"For doing what?" she shoots back.

Luca stares at her. His right hand moves under his shirt where he keeps his E-Prod.

I cringe. This is my fault. I should have warned her that this is no game. That Luca will jolt her if she doesn't fall in line.

"Strike two now. One more, and you're out, Funny Girl."

I hold my breath, praying that she doesn't do anything stupid.

Thankfully, she keeps her mouth shut. I let out a long, slow breath.

Luca resumes walking and leads the group to the north end of the Yard. "This used to be a factory," he says. "You see those machines over there?" He gestures to an iron contraption hiding in the shadows, near the wall. "They had something to do with making shoes. I think one of them was for stretching the leather."

The curly-haired boy with glasses, Abbie's quarry, I think, walks over to one of the machines casual as can be and starts running his fingers over the controls.

"No touching." Luca grabs his arm and pulls him back to the line. "What's your name, recruit?" he says, crouching down to the boy's eye level.

"Dmitri."

"Well, Dmitri," says Luca, leaning closer, "you don't want that nasty machine grabbing your skin and stretching it now, do you?"

"It wouldn't," Dmitri says.

Luca laughs. But no one else joins in.

"How do you know for sure?" he asks.

"That machine isn't for stretching leather," Dmitri says. "It's for perforating fabric."

Luca laughs again. "*Perforating,* you say. Such a big word for a small boy. Would you like to give the tour, Dmitri? Maybe we should switch places. Who votes for Dmitri?"

Not one hand goes up. But as I look around at the recruits, something niggles at me. Something isn't quite right.

"Follow me, everyone," Luca continues. "We're going to the second level."

A parade of feet follows Luca up the stairs. With every step, the sensation of something being wrong is stronger. I can see the heads of seven recruits. One is missing. Razor . . . where is she?

Panic seizes me. I've got to find her, and quickly. I go tearing down the stairs.

"Caleb, where are you going?" Luca shouts from above.

I don't answer. He's obviously not pleased that I've abandoned my post, but he's the least of my worries. If Uncle finds out we've let a recruit escape, I'm the one he's going to blame.

As I take the stairs two at a time, I'm thinking, *That's it, Razor's gone.* She saw an opening and went for it. Who can blame her, really? She must have decided she could do better on the streets than at the Compound.

In that case, I'd better make a good show of looking for her, because things will go worse for me if I don't. I burst into the Yard and shout her name. No answer. I run back out and race to the Viewing Room. She's not there either.

At the top of the stairs leading to the basement, I stop to catch my breath. Should I go down? There's nothing down there except for the boiler room. A noise makes me look up. The front door to the Compound is banging softly against its frame. It's open.

I swing the door open the rest of the way. Razor is lounging on the front steps, staring out into the street.

"What are you doing?" I say. My fantasy of Razor's bold escape from Uncle's clutches evaporates.

"What does it look like I'm doing?"

"Nothing."

"Exactly," she says. "You should try it sometime. Most times, I find doing nothing beats doing something. Especially if it's the kind of something I don't want to do."

I'm torn between screaming at her to run and dragging her back inside. But instead I count to ten and try to calm my breathing.

Better. I walk down the steps and turn to face her.

"You weren't joking, were you?" Razor says.

"About what?"

"About this being the future and all," she says.

"No, I wasn't joking."

"And those kids in there were brought here, like me."

I nod.

"And they're gonna train us to go to the past and steal stuff?"

I nod again.

She stretches her legs out in front of her and yawns. "Well, I guess I'll wait here, then."

"What do you mean?" I ask.

"I already know all about stealing. I don't need more training."

"It doesn't matter if you think you need it or not," I say. "Nothing here is optional. You've got to do what they tell you."

"That wasn't part of our deal," she says.

"We didn't have any deal," I say too loudly. But she's right. I fooled her to get her here. Maybe I didn't lie to her outright, but I left out a few choice parts.

She brings her legs up and rests her elbows on her knees. "Look, I get it, okay? You were just doing your job in grabbing me and taking me to this hole. I'd do the same in your shoes. The thing is, I ain't in your shoes. I'm in mine. And my shoes are telling me to walk."

"So what's stopping you?"

She doesn't say anything for a long time. The only sounds are from the late-night traffic on Lafayette Street.

"I lived in a place like this once," she begins slowly, "all nice solid brick walls on the outside. It makes you wanna believe that the people inside are nice too."

I wait quietly for her to continue.

She rolls up her right sleeve and traces a slim finger along a long scar that goes from the inside of her elbow to her wrist. "This is one of my souvenirs from the brick house. I got others too. But I'm especially proud of this one. 'Cause I didn't scream when he smashed his beer bottle on the wall and then cut me with it. No. Not one peep. I ran away that same night. There's lots of places you can go when you don't have stuff weighing you down."

She rolls her sleeve back down, shifts position on the stoop and looks me in the eyes. "I'm willing to give this whole time snatchers thing a try. But if I don't like it, I'm outta here."

"That's not the way it works," I say, and then add in a quiet voice so that the audio surveillance doesn't pick it up, "This may be your best chance to leave. Right now. Before they start training you."

In the distance, a siren wails. Music spills out of an upper floor window of the brownstone across the street. A woman pushing a stroller pauses under the window to listen before carrying on.

Razor stands up, stretches and says, "What's the food like in this place?"

I breathe a sigh of relief. "Not bad . . . when I'm not cooking."

She looks away. "You'd better be right about the food," she says, and I follow her back inside.

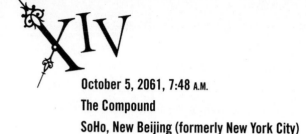

XIV

October 5, 2061, 7:48 A.M.
The Compound
SoHo, New Beijing (formerly New York City)

A noise wakes me. I roll over and open one eye. It's morning. Frank's bunk bed is empty, but Raoul's is occupied.

Raoul! I scramble out of my bunk and rush over to his. I see a shock of blond hair and stop dead in my tracks. Raoul doesn't have blond hair.

So who's sleeping in his bed?

Then I recognize him. It's the boy from 1912—the pickpocket from the Houdini escape at the East River. I can't believe it. Or maybe I can.

"Out with the old. In with the new," Frank says behind me. "You'd better hurry, Caleb. Most everyone else has eaten. You know, for someone freshly back from a long vacation, you don't look relaxed at all. In fact, you look quite stressed."

"Shut up, Frank," I say. "Raoul was one of us."

"He was incompetent, and you know it," Frank says. "And you'd better watch how you speak to me. In case you haven't noticed, Luca has a bit of a violent streak. And, unlike Nassim, he doesn't mind taking orders from me. Especially if they involve inflicting pain on others."

I turn my back to him and get dressed. Frank's right about one thing. The game has changed since I've been gone.

"Cale, are you up yet? We've got to take the recruits to China today," Abbie says over my mindpatch.

"Be right there," I mindpatch her back.

I finish dressing and jog to the dining room. All of the new recruits are already there—none of them is smiling, which I guess is to be expected, since it hasn't even been a day since some were ripped from their families.

Abbie is at a table with four recruits: Razor, Dmitri and two I don't recognize.

"Recruits, this is Caleb, your other trainer along with me," she says. "Caleb, meet our squad. I believe you already know Razor and Dmitri."

Dmitri is staring off into space, oblivious of my presence, but Razor looks me straight in the eye and says, "You've got a real sorry-looking bunch here, Jack. But don't worry. You and me will whip them into shape."

Then she passes a hand right in front of Dmitri's eyes. He doesn't even blink.

"Caleb, this is Judith and Gerhard," says Abbie. "Judith is from 2013 Wales, and Gerhard is from 1987 Munich."

Judith is short and slight with bright eyes. Gerhard looks big and strong. Right now he has his head down and is busy adjusting the distance between his fork and knife. Neither answers when I say hello.

I try to think of a joke to break the ice, but Abbie has given me the two-minute warning, so I decide that the best use of my mouth right now is for eating. There's one more piece of toast left, but as I reach for it, a slender hand darts out and nabs it first.

"Got to be quicker than that!" Razor says, already spreading strawberry jam on it.

I stand up and walk over to the next table. No toast there either. The best I can do is scrounge a bowl of cereal. I eat it standing up.

"I hope everyone had a good breakfast," Abbie says to our little group. "Today we are timeleaping to 1311, Yunnan province, China. Our mission is to snatch leaves from an ancient tree known for producing a type of tea, pu'er tea, that has a strong Qi or life energy. Since this is a training snatch, there will be no official time limit on completing the mission. However, because eventually you will be doing snatches that have thirty-minute time limits, we will stick to that timing. In a minute, I will hand out wristbands. They have been programmed to our current time, date and place.

"When you complete your training," she continues, "you will be fitted for time patches, same as the ones Caleb and I have, but for now, you'll make do with the wristbands. Remember, they're only for emergencies. So long as you are with either me or Caleb, you won't need to use them, since you can hitch rides through time with us. It's only if you get lost or we get separated that you'll need to use your wristband.

"Never take it off. And never touch another person's band. Finally, don't even touch your own band unless it's an emergency or I tell you to. Does anyone have any questions so far?"

Dmitri's hand shoots up.

"Yes?" Abbie says.

"Why do we need to go to 1311 China to purloin pu'er? I expect that pu'er tea is in abundance here now."

I stare at the kid and wonder at his vocabulary. The only time I think I've ever used the word *purloin* was a year ago, and even then, it was only to help Nassim solve a crossword puzzle clue. Or maybe that was *sirloin*.

"Strictly speaking, you are correct, Dmitri," Abbie says. "But the purpose of our field trip today is not primarily the snatch. It's to get you used to time travel and to experience what a mission is like. Now, Razor and Dmitri will go with Caleb. Judith and Gerhard, you two will timeleap with me. We'll be leaping from the courtyard."

Abbie leads everyone down a flight of stairs to the first floor, along the hall and then out the side door.

I've never been in the Compound's courtyard before. It's pretty small, but I can see why Uncle wants all our training leaps to be from here. It's private, and since we can't leap from inside the Compound because of iron in the walls that messes with time travel frequencies, this is the next best thing.

"All right," Abbie says, handing out the wristbands. "Remember, your wristband is only for emergencies. To use it, remove the narrow green strip and press down. You will end up back here. At which point, you will wait until the rest of the group arrives back. Any more questions?"

Judith raises her hand.

"Yes, Judith?"

"This isn't exactly a question. But may I recite a poem?"

Life is full of surprises.

"Well, I suppose," Abbie says, "so long as it's short."

"It is," she says.

Judith clears her throat and starts.

"Angry toenails and the cement juice of exhaustion
forge a blustery end to the feathery rain
pounding the river of my soul."

Wow. Who would have expected that? Not me for one. I particularly liked "cement juice of exhaustion."

"That's very—" Abbie begins.

"Weird," Razor finishes.

"Okay," says Abbie, "everyone make a circle and join hands, please. For this first leap, I suggest that you close your eyes and relax. You may feel a little dizzy, but that's normal."

I take Razor's and Dmitri's hands. Abbie takes Judith's hand, but when she reaches for Gerhard, he stuffs his hands in his pockets and takes one step backward.

"Gerhard," she says with more patience in her voice than I could ever manage. "We have to hold hands in order for the timeleap to work."

"I . . . don't hold hands," he says, with a pained look on his face.

"You don't hold hands?" Abbie repeats.

"That's right," Gerhard says. "But if you like, I can give you my elbow."

Razor narrows her eyes at Gerhard as if she's studying him. "He's a germophobe, Abs. I knew a guy once who was the same way. My advice is take the elbow. It's a good deal."

I begin to wonder if the forest will still be there by the time we finally arrive. Which is a ridiculous thought, since this is time travel we're talking about.

Abbie taps her wrist and puts her hand on Gerhard's elbow. Just before the timeleap takes us away, I sneak a look at the recruits. All of them have their eyes closed except for Razor.

When she sees me looking at her, she cocks her head toward Judith and mouths the words *angry toenails*.

XV

September 3, 1311, 10:22 A.M.
Yunnan province, China
Operation High Tea

We land in a forest. I'm only just out of my time freeze when Abbie walks over with her two recruits lined up neatly behind her.

"Is your group ready, Cale?" she says.

Why does it always seem that I'm playing catch-up? We all arrived at the same time. I guess Abbie's just naturally more organized than I am.

I look around. Dmitri is crouched down, staring at some bug, and Razor is leaning against a tree trunk. I suppose it might be possible for them to form a straight line behind me, but I don't see it happening in my lifetime.

"Ready," I chirp.

"Great. Everyone pay attention. Pu'er tea is a marvel of ancient China," Abbie begins, reciting from the mission data uploaded to our mindpatches. "The leaves come from trees that can tower eighty feet high, and that have trunks three feet wide.

"For a long time, no one knew how they picked the highly-prized leaves from the uppermost branches," she continues. "By one account, the best climbers in all of China were invited by the emperor to come to the Forbidden City. They would train day and night, scaling towers that were built to the same height as the trees. Some of the climbers perished when they fell from the great heights. When

102

picking season came, the emperor entered the great forest and stood and watched as the remaining climbers ascended the huge trees."

It's a good story. I look around and see that Abbie now has Dmitri's attention, as well as Judith's and Gerhard's. Wait. Where's Razor?

A bead of sweat rolls down my back. No need to panic. I'm sure she's close by. After all, where could she possibly go?

I will myself to relax. She's probably just gone to pee. Okay, so I don't really believe that. Still, it's no problem. What we didn't tell the recruits is that there's another reason they've been asked to keep their wristbands on. So that Abbie and I can track them if they get lost.

"Dmitri, where's Razor?" I ask.

"I believe she said that she was going for a stroll," he says.

"A stroll? This is no place for a stroll," I say.

Then I notice something. Dmitri has two wristbands. The first is where it should be—on his wrist. The other he is holding in his left hand. As we talk, he makes a clumsy attempt to hide it.

"What are you doing with two wristbands?" I ask.

"Something," he says mysteriously.

I feel a headache coming on. I'm never going to make it as a camp counselor. "Whose wristband is it?"

"Mine now," he says.

There's a war going on inside my brain. Half of me wants to throttle this kid or at least shake him until the whole truth comes out. The other half is saying forget him and find Razor before she gets into trouble or, worse, gets me into trouble.

"Which way did she go?" I ask.

"Thirty-seven degrees west."

"Show me."

"She went that way," he says, pointing off to the left.

"Wait right here," I say, which sounds ridiculous as soon as it comes out of my mouth. "And don't lose her wristband." I really should just grab it from him. Company property and all that. But I don't think he's going to hand it over easily, and there's no time now to argue with him.

I roll my eyes at Abbie. "Back in a jiffy."

At least I hope so. I start through the trees, calling Razor's name. No answer.

"Razor, we're leaving now!" I shout.

Nothing. Only birds twittering.

I head deeper into the forest. There's a nice breeze blowing, and it carries the scent of pine. If I wasn't preoccupied with finding Razor, I might actually enjoy being here.

"Heading back now," I yell into the forest, "for lunch. There's nothing to eat here. You're going to starve."

"No I'm not, Jack," says a voice behind me. "I scored a bag of peanuts."

I whip my head around. Razor is sitting on the trunk of a fallen tree, munching peanuts.

"What do you think you're doing?"

"Snack break," she says.

I stare at her. I don't like being this angry. "Why did you give Dmitri your wristband?"

"I didn't give it to him."

I frown. "Well, then, how did he get it?"

"Sold it to him." She smiles. "Got a good price for it too. One bag of salted peanuts that he had on him when he was snatched and future consideration."

I skip asking her how she can sell something that doesn't belong to her. "What's he going to do with it?"

"None of my business. But if I were you, he's the one I'd be watching. The kid looks dangerous."

My anger is rising again. "C'mon, let's go."

As we make our way back, a tremendous ripping sound fills the air.

"Abbie, did you hear that?" I say over her mindpatch.

No answer.

"C'mon," I say to Razor and start sprinting through the trees toward the source of the sound.

"Cool," she says. "He did it!"

There's shouting coming from up ahead. We burst into the clearing. Abbie and the recruits are gathered around a large crater that I'm certain wasn't there a few minutes ago.

Dmitri is nowhere in sight. Razor is smiling. My headache is in full bloom.

I gaze into the hole, half expecting to see a meteor or small alien spacecraft. But there is only a tangle of roots. If I didn't know better, I'd say there was a tree there a minute ago and that something huge tore that tree right from its roots. But what could possibly do that? And where did the tree go?

Judith recites,

"Swallowed up whole
by the chicken fingers of desire."

That about sums it up.

"What happened here?" I ask Abbie.

"I was going to ask you the same thing," she says. "It was someone from your group who must have made that hole."

"With what? Her hands?"

Razor is snickering beside me. She knows something.

I glare at her. "Spill it."

"All right. Don't get all hot and bothered," Razor says. "I'm as surprised as you are. I never thought he could pull it off."

"What are you talking about?"

"Dim. I guess I'll have to find a new nickname for him now, since he's not dim at all. In fact, I think he's a genius."

"What did Dmitri do?" I ask.

"Isn't it obvious?" Razor says. "There used to be a big tree in that hole. It's not there anymore. And neither is Dim. Two plus two, Jack. C'mon."

If she's saying what I think she is, that's impossible. No one can move something that big through time.

"Where?" I ask.

"Pay me first," Razor says.

Abbie turns to me and says, "What is she talking about?"

"Have you got ten bucks on you, Abbie? I'll pay you back. Promise."

Abbie glares at me. "You've got some serious explaining to do, mister." But she digs into her pocket and hands me a ten. I fork it over to Razor.

She stares at the watermark on the bill for a moment and then sniffs it. This is maddening.

"Okay. Now where and when did he go with the tree?" I ask her again.

"Times Square, 8:15 A.M., October 5, 2061."

"How? No, forget how. Why?" I ask.

"That was our bet. Frankly, I didn't think he could do it. That tree must weigh a ton."

My cheeks are burning. Even if he could move it, I don't see how the tree could have ended up at Times Square. The default on the wristbands was the Compound courtyard. Unless he did something to the wristband . . .

Abbie turns to me. "You'd better go find him, Cale, and when you do, the snatch will still have to be completed." Her voice is controlled, but I can hear the tension behind her words. This mission is going from bad to worse, and when the punishment comes down, Abbie and I are likely to get the brunt of it.

"Do you mean no one snatched leaves from the tree yet?" I ask.

"Gerhard wouldn't do it," says Abbie. "He's afraid of heights. Judith said she wanted to stretch first. When she was finally ready, that's when the rumbling started."

This is turning into a bad day.

I tap in the sequence for Times Square. Dmitri's got a lot of explaining to do.

Just as I start to fade away, a hand grips my wrist.

"Razor! What are you—"

"I'm coming with you. I got to see the proof before I pay him."

There must be enough of me still visible, because she says, "Turn that frown upside down, Jack. This is gonna be fun!"

I don't say anything. Fun is keeping my remaining fingers and toes. Fun is staying out of Uncle's office. Fun is anything but what I'm about to do.

October 5, 2061, 8:17 A.M.

Times Square

New Beijing (formerly New York City)

Operation High Tea

We land in a doorway on Forty-third Street. Our arrival doesn't draw any attention, because everyone else is looking at the towering tree that seems to have grown right out of the pavement next to the sleek new Mandarin Oriental hotel.

"It looks good there," Razor says as soon as she comes out of her time freeze.

I have to agree with her. I'm no landscape designer. But the tree does improve the look of the place . . . humanizes it somehow.

"Do you see him?" I ask Razor.

"Not yet," she says. "But look, there's a cute little monkey!"

I follow where she's pointing and see it. About a third of the way up the tree. If I read its facial expression correctly, that monkey is terrified.

"We've got to get it back to China," I say.

"Just stick it in the zoo," she says.

"I'm talking about the tree."

The next moment, I see Dmitri. He's standing near the foot of the tree. About twenty feet away from him, a police officer is cordoning off the area with yellow police tape. Other officers are removing people who are inside the cordoned-off area.

"C'mon," I say, ducking under the tape and breaking into a run.

Razor makes it to Dmitri first and claps him on the back. "Nice job, Dim. You win the bet. Here." She forks over the ten that I gave her in China.

"Ha! You did not believe I could extricate and temporarily relocate it."

"That's true," Razor admits. "But I'm a believer now."

"We've got to get that tree out of here," I say, my voice raspy.

"Wait," Razor says. "We gotta do the snatch first."

"I don't think that's a—"

Before I can finish the sentence, Razor begins to moan and swoon.

A policeman rushes over right as she falls to the ground. At the same time, Dmitri slips under the police tape and begins running toward the entrance to the Mandarin Oriental. I start after him but give up when I realize I won't be able to stop him.

By now, a small crowd has gathered around Razor.

"Father, is that you?" Razor says, in a sweet and helpless voice that I can hardly believe is coming from the same person.

"I'm not your father, son," answers the policeman. Then he turns to the crowd. "Is anyone here related to this boy?"

That's my cue to step forward. It's tempting to just hang back for a few seconds and see if anyone else wants her, but I suppose that would be cruel. Cruel or not, she owes me.

Instead I sigh and yell over the crowd, "Hey, Ray! Dad and I have been looking everywhere for you."

There's not a great deal of physical resemblance between us. Razor is black-haired and has gray eyes. I, on the other hand, have mousy brown hair and brown eyes. But this is New York—correction, New Beijing, 2061. Families come in all shapes and sizes.

"Are you his brother?" the officer on the scene shouts back.

No, I want to say. I'm just the guy who kidnapped her to avoid being sent to the Barrens again, which is not such a bad place if you like scorpions, snakes, intense heat and dying of thirst. But having known her for a day, I'm already wondering whether I should have just volunteered straight away to return to the Barrens instead.

"Yeah," I yell.

"Let him through, people," he says, and I smile gratefully.

"Does he have a medical condition?" he asks me, nodding toward Razor, and without skipping a beat, I say, "Paininassosis."

I say it real fast so that it sounds like a true condition. Who knows, maybe in some country of the world it's a real disease.

"Don't worry," I say in a loud voice. "So long as no one breathes his air, they probably won't catch it."

With that, except for a few die-hard gawkers, the rest of the crowd backs up in a hurry. Even the police officer takes two steps back.

Some movement near the top of the tree catches my attention.

There's a person leaning out a window on the eighth floor of the Mandarin Oriental, reaching toward the branches of the tree. Dmitri!

Razor moans again.

"Thank you, Officer, I can take it from here," I say. "He's just having one of his spells. They only last a few minutes and then he's as good as new. But it's important that I get him to a shady spot quickly. Can you let us go under that tree for a few minutes so he can rest?"

He looks around and then back at us. Indecision is written all over his face.

"I'm not supposed to . . . No one's supposed to go near the tree . . ."

Razor writhes in agony.

"Oh, trust me, we won't touch it," I say, reassuring him. "It's only for the shade."

"Well, okay. But only for a couple of minutes."

"Thank you so much, Officer . . . Germanakos," I say, reading the name off his badge.

He helps me get Razor to her feet, then steps away and resumes his position near the police tape.

"Nice work, Jack. Especially that bit about my medical condition." She makes as if she's going to faint again and then laughs.

If I wasn't so worried about the punishment that is bound to come down on us because of this botched mission, I might laugh with Razor. But all I can think about are the bad things that will happen once Uncle finds out how a simple training run turned into major headlines. Maybe we'll get a reprieve because it's the first training mission . . . but I'm not counting on it.

"I have them!" Dmitri shouts, running up to us. Breathless, he loosens the drawstrings of a small pouch and plucks out some green leaves.

"All right," I say. "Now, the next thing is to take the tree back."

Dmitri shrugs. "It is quite possible. But I will first have to reconfigure the wristbands for the return trip. That will take between three and seven minutes."

Reconfigure? Uncle is going to reconfigure his teeth and probably mine too, if he doesn't get this tree back to where it belongs, pronto.

"Look, we can't wait that long. We've got to go right now," I say. "We'll use my patch."

As soon as I say it, though, I realize I have no idea how we're going to do it. It's one thing to timeleap holding someone else's hand

111

or wrist. But it's quite another to bring a whole tree through time. What if it lands on us by accident? Or doesn't come at all?

"No need to," says Dmitri. "I've managed to shorten the prep time considerably, and I'm just . . . about . . . finished."

I take a look around. I wouldn't say the tree looks at home standing in the middle of Times Square, but in the short time it's been here, entire industries have already sprung up around it. One guy is selling T-shirts showing a huge apple falling from the tree with the caption BIG TREE IN THE BIG APPLE. Another guy is selling Big Tree toothpicks, and yet another, maple sugar from the Big Tree, which is quite a trick, since it's not a maple tree at all.

A couple of cops are walking briskly toward us. I guess they didn't speak to Officer Germanakos. Or maybe they did, and they've already had their shots for paininassosis, so they're not afraid of catching it.

"Do it, Dmitri!" I shout.

"I can't," he says. "I need to be touching the tree."

"You there!" shouts one of the officers. "Stand away from that tree."

"Grab the tree, Dmitri!" I shriek.

Dmitri glances from me to the police officers and then makes a beeline for the tree.

Razor and I race after him.

The officers sprint after us.

The last thing I hear before I leave 2061 is Razor's husky voice.

"See you, suckers!"

XVII

September 3, 1311, 11:14 A.M.
Yunnan province, China
Operation High Tea

We land in the forest. The good news is that the tree has arrived with us. The bad news is that it's having trouble staying upright. And the really bad news is that I seem to have landed in its path.

"Timber!" yells Razor.

I roll away just as the ground around me shudders.

There's a thundering sound, followed by the squawking of a hundred angry birds.

Then the forest is quiet. Serene even.

And amazingly, I'm still alive.

I stand up slowly. Then move my arms and my legs. Everything's working.

"Nice scramble, Jack," says Razor. "That was a bet I didn't mind losing."

A moment later, it registers.

"You mean you bet on me dying?"

She looks at me with wide eyes. "What do you take me for? I'd never do that. I only bet how far away you'd be when the big guy fell. Dim said three feet, but I didn't know how quick you really are, so I said two."

I'm totally drained. I've got to get away from Razor and Dmitri. But first I need to get them back to the Compound.

I reach out my hands to them. Razor grabs one hand, but Dmitri waves me off.

"I can navigate fairly well on my own, thank you," he says.

I sigh. I have no energy to fight with him. But if he doesn't turn up at the Compound, I'll be the one who takes the blame.

"Please, Dmitri. I know you don't need my help. But humor me, will you?"

Razor has let go of my wrist and is standing slightly behind and to the left of Dmitri. She's whispering something in his ear.

"I will go with you if I can retain both time bands," says Dmitri.

I have absolutely no authority to bargain with him. The wristbands are Timeless Treasures property, which means they belong to Uncle. And something tells me he wouldn't take kindly to one of his recruits stockpiling them.

On the other hand, I've got to cut some kind of deal with Dmitri—or risk him making a scene when we arrive back. And that's just about the last thing I want.

"I might be able to arrange it, but it's going to take a little time," I say.

Dmitri smiles and extends his wrist. Before he changes his mind, I grab it and then press my own.

Right before we leap, I take a deep breath and look up at the sky. Thunderclouds are moving in. I hope it's not an omen about how the rest of my day is going to go.

XVIII

Get up, Cale. He wants to see you right after you turn in the snatch object." Abbie is standing over me in the alley next to Headquarters with a serious expression on her face.

"I can't move. Still time frozen," I say. "In fact, please send my regrets. It's a bad case of time freeze. I don't see it clearing anytime soon."

"This isn't a joke," she says. "Frank doesn't like it when he has to wait."

Did she say Frank? I begin to breathe a sigh of relief until it hits me that Frank could be worse than Uncle.

"All right. Where does he want us to meet him?"

"Not us. You. In his office," she says. "Right after you hand in the tea leaves to Luca. I can take Razor and Dmitri back with me to the Compound."

I nod and stand up slowly. "Any idea what it's about?"

"No," Abbie says.

I cross over to where Razor and Dmitri sit slouched against the brick wall. I hold out my hand and Dmitri gives me the pouch with the leaves.

"See you at lunch," I say and begin climbing the fire escape stairs.

Luca is sitting behind his desk, eyes fixed on his screen. When I rap on the open door to get his attention, it feels like something is missing. And then I realize what it is. Nassim's surprise attacks. I never thought I'd miss being strangled, but there it is.

The screen above him flashes on, and there's Phoebe's yoga instructor persona dressed in a black leotard, her body folded backward at an impossible angle. It hurts me just to look at her.

"Here they are," I say, handing over the pouch.

He takes it, looks inside and waves me away. Wow, that was easy. I turn to go.

"Not so fast," says the voice from the screen.

Darn.

"You've got to make sure they are the real thing, Lucas," says Phoebe.

Luca glares at the screen, which tells me he doesn't appreciate Phoebe bossing him around, let alone getting his name wrong. Then he dips two fingers into the pouch and withdraws a single leaf. He's about to touch it with the tip of his tongue when Phoebe squawks.

"Don't you dare! What if he's trying to poison you? Make him try it first."

I sigh. I always wondered what Phoebe does in her spare time, and now I know. She watches bad murder mysteries.

I grab the leaf from Luca and lick it. It tastes bitter. I try not to make a face.

"See? Still alive," I say.

Phoebe frowns, but only for a moment. Then her yoga instructor face morphs into a sea of tranquility. "Get him to spill 'em all out," she tells Luca.

Luca shrugs and I pour the contents of the bag onto his desk. Phoebe makes as if she's studying them and then finishes off by scratching her head with her big toe. "They're all wrinkled," she says finally.

"They're supposed to be wrinkled," I say. I try to keep my voice from rising, but it's impossible. Phoebe is being difficult.

"Tell him to go back and get fresh ones," she instructs Luca, finally unfolding and assuming the Cherokee warrior pose.

"That's ridicu— I can't go back," I say. "Frank wants to see me right away."

Luca looks undecided. Well, I'll decide for him. I get up to go.

"I'll have to tell Uncle about the wrinkles," he says.

"Fine," I say over my shoulder. I half expect him to jump up and block me from leaving, but he doesn't.

"Tuck your shirt in," yells Phoebe, mistress of the last word.

I walk down the hall to Frank's office. The door is open, and Frank is seated behind a large desk with a glass tabletop, gazing at his screen. The walls are bare except for a photograph of Frank presenting the first flag of the Great Friendship to a smiling Uncle. It irks me every time I see that, because Frank poached my snatch to get that flag.

I stand at the entrance, waiting for him to notice me. After what seems like forever, he looks up and says, "The morning news. Have you seen it?"

"No," I say. "I never read the news. Too depressing."

"You may want to have a look."

He turns his screen and I see an image of the giant tree, framed by the large Toshiba sign. The caption under the image reads "Church Group, Bowling Alley Operator and Mothers Against Logging all claim responsibility for the Miracle at Times Square."

I'm rooting for the bowling alley operator. It's tough to keep a small business going these days.

"Interesting," I say. "What does this have to do with me?"

"Don't play coy, Caleb. I know that one of your recruits did this."

"Are you serious? No one can move something that size."

Frank circles the desk and comes up behind me, which is really annoying. The back of my neck prickles, but I resist the urge to whip my head around.

"You've caught a break this time," he says. "Normally, this kind of attention would make Uncle very angry."

Did he say "normally"? A small ray of light pierces the gloom of my thoughts.

"But you're lucky. He's not angry at all. In fact, he didn't mention any punishment for you. What intrigued him was how the tree got there."

My mind is racing. There's good and bad in what Frank's saying. The good part, of course, is that I get to keep my remaining toes for at least another day. The downside is that Uncle probably wants the intel on how the tree was moved.

"He wants to speak to the recruit who did it," Frank says, confirming my fears.

My stomach clenches. If I say no, that will be seen as directly challenging Frank. But if I say yes, who knows what will happen to Dmitri once Uncle gets his mitts on him.

"I don't know who did it," I lie.

"How could you not know?" Frank asks. "You were there, weren't you?"

"Yes and no. I was in the forest, but I was chasing down a recruit who had wandered away from the snatch zone. When I returned, the tree was already gone."

At least that part is true.

"I see," says Frank. "Which recruit had wandered away?"

I was afraid he would ask that.

"I forget," I lie.

Frank smiles and says, "Play it that way if you want to. But I'll find out anyway."

He looks down at his handheld. "Judith, Gerhard, Razor and Dmitri . . . I will meet with them one by one. Oh, and tell Abbie I'd like to see her also."

"I can't," I say. "I mean they can't. At least not right now. They're busy. Abbie's briefing them on the next mission."

I've got to buy some time so I can prepare Dmitri.

Frank studies me for a moment. I can tell he's weighing the pros and cons of delaying the meetings.

Ten seconds of awkward silence follow. A single droplet of sweat forms on my forehead and threatens to make a break for it down my cheek, but I resist the urge to wipe it away.

I'm counting on him not wanting to make Uncle angry, which could be the result if we weren't on schedule for our afternoon snatch.

"All right, Caleb. I won't insist on seeing them right now," he says finally. "But as soon as your team's next snatch is completed, send all of your recruits to my office."

"Sure," I say.

"And to put your mind at ease, you don't need to worry about the recruit responsible for moving the tree being punished. In fact, he or she will be rewarded. You see, Uncle has a great interest in what could be a new technology."

As he says this, he brushes the hair away from his right ear. Or what's left of it after Uncle lopped off the top part of it last summer as punishment for turning in a replica of the Xuande vase.

There's something about this meeting that bothers me. Frank just doesn't seem that interested, period. It's almost as if the entire screw-up with the tree is a minor annoyance to him and no more than that. The old Frank would have been all over me for it.

But this Frank is eerily calm. There's only one possible explanation. It's what Abbie told me at the castle—he must be planning something big. But what could that be?

"Are we done?" I say, looking him square in the eyes.

"Yes, of course. Go ahead and join your little group."

I wait until I'm out of view before running the back of my hand across my forehead to wipe away another bead of sweat.

How did it go?" Abbie asks. We're standing across the street from the Compound, which is as close as you can get without having your mindpatch monitored.

"As well as I could expect."

"Meaning?"

"Meaning, Frank knows that one of the recruits moved the tree," I say. "But he doesn't know who it was . . . yet. He wants to see all of them individually. And he wants to speak to you too."

"Right now?"

"I managed to stall him until we get back from our next snatch. By the way, what is our next snatch?"

"Didn't you scan the mission schedule?" she says. "This afternoon, we're off to 1886 Atlanta, Georgia, to snatch the first-ever glass of Coca-Cola. I'm calling it Operation Fizz."

"That sounds okay," I say. In fact, if it was just Abbie and me doing the snatch two years ago, I might have said "that sounds fun," but lately I've learned to keep my expectations low.

"I'll prep Judith and Gerhard about the meeting with Frank," Abbie says. "You do Razor and Dmitri."

"What's our story?"

Abbie scrunches her eyebrows. "That it was a freak accident. A one-in-a-million shot. Some kind of malfunction with Dmitri's wristband. That he did it but doesn't know how. Besides, Frank can ask the others all he wants. I'm positive they didn't see him do it."

"But if it was a freak accident," I say, "how could it happen twice? You know, the tree returning to the past after its little trip to Times Square."

"I don't know," Abbie says. "Maybe it was part of the same freak accident."

"I don't think Frank will believe that," I say.

She runs her fingers through her hair. "You're right. But it might buy us some more time to figure something else out."

"All right," I say. "I'll talk to Dmitri and Razor. Right after my meeting with Uncle."

"Uncle wants to meet with you?" she asks.

"Yeah, with me and Frank. Eleven o'clock at the castle."

"What about?"

"He didn't get into details," I say, "but it has to do with his idea about fixing history."

"Okay, good luck."

"Thanks," I say grimly and begin to enter the sequence for the castle.

"Wait," she says, putting a hand on my arm. Then she leans in and kisses me.

"Th . . . thanks," I say. "What was that for?"

"For more good luck."

There are no bad seats in the tower room at Doune Castle. In all directions, there's a commanding view of the rolling countryside.

After ten minutes, Luca pokes his head into the room and says, "Uncle said to tell you he's running a little late. He will be here momentarily."

I nod. I don't like waiting. It gives my brain time to think of unpleasant things. I take some deep breaths to calm myself. About a minute later, the patch of air two feet away begins to shimmer.

Even before he goes solid, I can tell from the swirl of colors that it's Uncle. Frank is never that bold a dresser. Uncle slowly materializes in a tartan kilt in the colors of the Clan of Bruce, a Prince Charlie jacket and a wing-collar shirt with bow tie. He's not carrying a sword or an ax or any other weapon, as far as I can see. But then again, a person could store all sorts of knives and daggers under that kilt.

Still, I can feel my hopes creeping up ever so slightly.

When he emerges from his time freeze, Uncle tips his head toward me in greeting and takes his seat at the head of the table.

We sit there silently, waiting for Frank to appear. About thirty seconds later, there's a shimmering in the air halfway between us. As Frank's form materializes, I can't wait to hear his explanation as to why he's late.

It looks like he's been out shopping. He's wearing a silver and black skin suit and has on black leather boots that look buttery soft. There's a gold chain around his neck and he's also sporting a flashy pinkie ring. I've never seen Frank dress this sharp before. Where is he getting the money for his new wardrobe?

"Sorry I'm late," he says once he's thawed. "I had a disciplinary matter to deal with."

That's it? A disciplinary matter? I don't buy it. I think what he's really doing is testing the boundaries with Uncle . . . seeing what he can get away with.

I brace myself for the inevitable barrage of abuse that Uncle is about to unleash on Frank.

But amazingly, it doesn't come. All Uncle does is smile and say,

"Very well. Now that you are both here, we can begin. The reason I have called this meeting with you, my most senior and trusted time snatchers, is to discuss a matter that is near and dear to my heart."

Did he just say he trusted me? Of course he said it in the same breath as saying he trusts Frank, which tells you something about Uncle's sense of judgment these days. Still, I haven't heard the word *punishment* yet.

"When I have spoken of this matter before, it was only an idea, a wisp of a thought. Of course, action does not occur in isolation; it always originates with an idea, a concept, a notion. Without the notion, the action is meaningless. The same can be said of an idea not tethered to execution—it is but a pie in the sky, a flight of fancy."

I have no idea what he's talking about. But if there's a choice between execution and pie, I choose pie.

"*Mo charaidean*—my friends—the time is ripe to take Timeless Treasures in a new direction . . ."

I glance at Frank. Outwardly, he looks calm, but my guess is he's sweating big-time under that expensive skin suit.

"And that direction is the pursuit of what I call 'historical correctness,'" Uncle continues. "History is fraught with events that have tainted its true and correct course. There are many examples of historical events that, had they not occurred, the world would be a much better place. And I am not talking only of wars and plagues that have decimated humanity, although those too are worthy of reexamination and in certain cases, correction."

Reexamination? Correction? I think Uncle's finally jumped off the deep end. Stealing small stuff from the past and bringing it back to 2061 is one thing. But deliberately going back in time to try to alter, or as he calls it, to "correct," history is a whole other can of beans.

"Starting tomorrow, there will be a new division in Timeless Treasures called the Historical Correction Division. Caleb, I would like you to head up this new division. Together, we will right the wrongs of history!"

Did he just say Caleb? Is he sure he didn't mean to say Frank and my name slipped off his tongue by mistake? No, he's looking straight at me, so he must mean me.

"I . . . certainly, Uncle," I stammer. Here I was expecting punishment, and he offers me a promotion.

"I see that you are surprised," he says.

"A little," I admit. "I mean, when I left, things were a bit tense between us."

The understatement of the year.

"Here is how I see it," he says. "You are the first one I brought on board. My first orphan, my first trainee and my first time snatcher. That is why I brought you back from 1968."

Frank has been awfully quiet so far. His face is expressionless. What I wouldn't give right now to know what he's really thinking.

"But that is not why I am giving you this opportunity," Uncle continues. "The reason I have selected you to lead the Historical Correction Division, Caleb, is because you are most like me. We both share strong convictions. We both have a keen sense of what is right and what is wrong. We are both guided by a strong moral compass.

"Inadvertently changing history is one thing," says Uncle. "But molding it, shaping it and correcting its many flaws is another thing altogether. It requires a deft touch, an artistic flair and, above all, an unshakeable determination to do what is right. Of all my time snatchers, there is only one who possesses all of these qualities . . . and that is you, Caleb."

He shifts to look at Frank, and I let out a long, slow breath.

"I am sure you are wondering, Frank, what this new direction will mean for our mainstream operations that you have been so capably running from New Beijing. The answer is that there will be no effect whatsoever. The growth of the time snatching side of the business will still be a priority for many years to come. Rest assured that the changes begun last year with Project Metamorphosis will continue.

"In fact, the core time snatching operation will be more important than ever. The righting of historical wrongs could be an expensive proposition. We will need the revenue from our mainstream operations to fund the activities of the new division."

I can't imagine that Frank is happy about any of this. Especially the part about his division bankrolling mine.

"That all sounds excellent," says Frank. Then he turns to me. "I look forward to working with you, Caleb, in your new role."

Frank's face breaks into a smile. Uncle smiles at him, then both of them smile at me, and I smile back. All of this fake smiling is making me nauseous. I still have no idea what he means by historical correctness. If it's about going back in time to stop the Braves from beating the Yankees in game seven of the 2058 World Series, then I'm all for it, but something tells me that's not what he has in mind.

"Before you both go, I'd like to tell you a story. A true story of Robert the Bruce."

Okay, here we go. I knew he couldn't get through a whole meeting without mentioning his new hero's name.

"It was a dark period in Robert the Bruce's life; a time when he was experiencing defeat after crushing defeat at the hands of the English. Feeling desolate, he was close to giving up his lifelong dream of freedom for the Scottish people. One cold and stormy night, as he lay alone in a cave, hiding from the English, he looked up and saw a spider. The spider was trying to weave a web from one part of the ceiling to another. Six times the spider tried to sling its web from one part of the ceiling to the next, and six times it failed. But on the seventh try, a thin tendril of web clung and held. The spider had persevered and won. At that moment, inspired by the never-say-die spirit of the spider, Robert the Bruce decided that he would never give up fighting for the things he believed in.

"And so it must be with us. We must stride forward with renewed hope and confidence. We must be like Robert the Bruce's spider: tenacious and determined to accomplish all that we set out to do."

Uncle's eyes are shining. The last time I saw him this excited was when he announced Project Metamorphosis. Still, this whole thing is giving me a stomachache, and I can't wait to get out of here.

Uncle gets up first and then Frank and I stand.

"*Chi mi a-rithist thu,*" says Uncle, dismissing us. "And remember, I'm counting on you two for great things."

"Yes, Uncle," we both say at once. No sooner are the words out of his mouth than Frank vanishes.

I'm about to tap away at my own wrist when Uncle signals me to wait.

Rats.

He smiles and points at something on the floor. I look but all I can see is a small, dark speck. The next moment, the speck begins to move. It's a spider.

The spider is gaining speed now, skittering across the tower room floor.

Uncle takes two quick steps toward it and crouches down. His hand lashes out quick as a viper and snatches the spider. Then he walks back to me and opens his hand. The spider hops off his fingers onto the floor and again tries to skitter away.

This time, Uncle raises his leg and stomps down hard, crushing it. Then he removes his boot, examines the underside and shows it to me.

"As with people, Caleb, no two spiders are exactly alike. That little fellow did not appear to like it here. He tried to run away. The first time I brought him back and gave him a chance. But as you saw, he squandered it and tried to escape again. I'm afraid twice is unforgivable."

I shudder. "Can I go now, Uncle?"

"Yes, of course," he says, smiling.

My fingers reach for my wrist, but they're trembling so badly that I have trouble keying in the sequence. I'm feeling many things right now, and not all of them are fear of Uncle, although there's that too. When he said that stuff about me being his first time snatcher and how I want to do what's right, I felt a warm tingle and had a flash of an earlier time—when I was a small boy on his lap, telling him about my day, feeling safe and secure.

But that was a long time ago. I'm not that little boy anymore, and Uncle certainly isn't the same either.

Finally, I succeed in keying in the sequence and am relieved to feel the familiar sensation of the timeleap taking hold.

The last image I have before I leave the castle is of the tiny spider ground into the heel of Uncle's boot.

"Where are we goin'?" asks Razor as soon as lunch is over.

"You'll see," I say. "Please change into your mission clothes and make your way to the courtyard. We're leaping from there in five minutes."

"Why are you acting so serious?" she asks.

"I'm not," I say. In fact I am. I'm still trying to make sense of the meeting with Uncle and Frank. Uncle also hasn't told me what all I'm supposed to do in my new role. One thing is crystal clear, though. If I try to run, he'll find me and crush me, like he did that spider.

"Suit yourself," she says. "But Dim already told me where we're going."

"So then why are you asking me?" I say. There's a hard edge to my voice, but I can't help it. I have no patience for Razor right now.

"I'm just fact checking. You can't really put your money on anything coming from Dim's mouth. He operates in some kind of bizarro world of his own. He's not ordinary like you and me."

Did I really hear her refer to herself as ordinary?

"So what are we gonna steal?" Razor asks, fingering her new wristband.

"You'll find out soon enough."

"I hope it's something big," she says, "like that tree."

"We weren't supposed to snatch the tree," I remind her, "just the leaves."

"You don't know anything about horticulture, Jack. If you want the leaves to stay fresh, you gotta keep them on the tree as long as possible."

I could stand here and argue the finer points of horticulture with her. Or I could get on with my life. "Get ready to go," I say, checking my fingernail. "We're leaving in . . . three minutes."

Before she has a chance to answer, I'm already halfway down the hall.

Abbie and the rest of the recruits are already in the courtyard when I arrive. As I approach, Abbie and I make eye contact. I want to tell her about my meeting with Frank and Uncle, but there's no time right now. It will have to wait until after the mission.

"Staggered landing," Abbie says when Razor arrives. "Judith,

Gerhard and I will land first. Dmitri, Razor and Caleb a couple of minutes later. Once you're thawed, look for Jacobs' Pharmacy at the corner of Peachtree and Marietta. There's an alley right next to the pharmacy. We'll meet up there."

"What are we snatching?" Razor asks.

"Didn't you brief her?" Abbie says over my mindpatch.

"Not fully . . ."

Abbie looks from me to Razor. "You'll find out when we get there."

Razor kicks at a stone and then whispers something into Dmitri's ear.

A shocked look comes over his face.

"Ignore them," Abbie says over my mindpatch.

"Gladly," I answer as Abbie and the others begin to fade away.

I stand alone for a moment, wondering about my life. In some ways I think everything was simpler when I had no memories. Because all I could do was look forward. And there was a lot to look forward to . . . growing up in Boston with Zach and Jim and Diane. My new family. Yeah, my future was in the past, if that makes any sense. But now my future is one big question mark. And even worse, when I think about trying to do something about my situation, all I feel is helpless.

I close my eyes and listen to the traffic sounds. I read somewhere that every five seconds a horn is honked out of anger in Manhattan. Which means that every five seconds, twelve times a minute or over seven hundred times a hour, someone in New Beijing is angry at someone else. And that's only the people who drive. There must be thousands of other angry people walking around New Beijing right now.

"C'mon," Razor says, tugging at my arm. "We got to catch up to them."

"It's not a race," I say. "Besides, it doesn't matter when we leave. This is time travel, remember?"

"Whatever. Let's just go, okay?"

"Sure."

I grab Dmitri's and Razor's hands. Razor's fingers are surprisingly slim and delicate.

Whoever thought up the phrase "appearances can be deceiving" must have had Razor in mind.

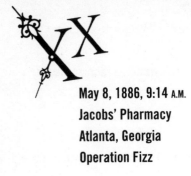

May 8, 1886, 9:14 A.M.
Jacobs' Pharmacy
Atlanta, Georgia
Operation Fizz

The first thing I notice when I land is the tickle in my nose. A moment later, I let go with three sneezes in quick succession.

As soon as my time freeze thaws, I'm up and looking around. We've landed behind a shed in someone's backyard, right next to a planter filled with daffodils. That accounts for my sneezing. I gather up the others, and we make our way past a well-tended hedge to the front. The first sign I see says PEACHTREE STREET, and a minute later I spot the sign for Jacobs' Pharmacy.

I sneeze twice more and head for our rendezvous spot. It's a good thing this is going to be a quick snatch. I don't want to spend a minute more in this city than I need to.

Abbie smiles when she sees me. I blow my nose in greeting.

"All right, listen up," she says, once we're all assembled.

Dmitri's hand shoots into the air.

"How can you have a question, Dmitri? I haven't even said anything yet."

"Yes you have. You said, 'listen up.' I would prefer you not use that phrase. Sound waves travel through the air in a spherical motion, and therefore it is a misnomer to say listen *up*. Listen *around* would be more accurate."

Abbie rolls her eyes at me. I shrug and wipe my nose.

"Fine," she says. "Here's what's going down. Three minutes from now, a woman named Clara Rowbottom will walk into the Venables Fountain in Jacobs' Pharmacy, seat herself on the third stool from the end of the counter and order a glass of cola syrup from Sam Jacobs, the owner's son. Sam will fill Clara's glass with one-third cola syrup and, at her request, instead of filling it the rest of the way with spring water, he will add soda water. By making it this way, Sam will have poured the first-ever glass of Coca-Cola."

"So where do we come in?" asks Razor.

"Our mission is to snatch the first-ever glass of Coke before Clara drinks it," Abbie answers. "One of Uncle's clients is paying big bucks for it."

"How much?" Razor says.

"I don't know," Abbie says. "I just know it's a lot. But you don't need to think about that. Just think about performing the snatch smoothly. No mistakes. Dmitri, you will seat yourself across from Sam. You'll be able to identify him by his distinctive handlebar mustache. Your job is to strike up a conversation. Sam's interests are golf and guns. Do you think you can do that?"

"Unquestionably," answers Dmitri. "I am skilled at pleasantries, small banter and other pointless forms of communication."

"Good," Abbie says. "As soon as Sam finishes pouring the glass of Coke for Clara, you're to let out a groan, crash to the floor and act like you are ill. At that moment, Sam will put the glass down on the counter and hurry over to see if you are all right."

Dmitri raises his hand.

"Yes?"

"How do you know that he will place the glass on the counter?" Dmitri asks. "Why would he not first give it to the customer before he attends to me?"

133

"Human nature, Dmitri," answers Abbie. "If someone is in trouble, the normal reaction is to put aside what one is doing and to see if one can help."

"If it were me, I'd keep on serving," Razor says.

Abbie ignores her and continues. "When he sets the glass down, Judith, your job is to snatch it and bring it back here, without spilling a drop."

"Why does she get to snatch it? I wanna do that part," Razor complains. "Besides, Judith is a klutz. She's gonna spill it all over the place."

"I will not," Judith says.

"You will so!"

"Enough," says Abbie. "Razor, it's Judith's turn. You had your chance in China."

"No I didn't," says Razor. "Dim stole the tree before I had a chance to climb it."

"This isn't up for discussion. Caleb and I already decided who is going to do what."

"Well, you haven't said what I do yet," Razor says.

"You and Gerhard are to stay outside with Caleb and me. We're all going to watch the snatch through the window."

"That sucks," Razor says. "Can't I at least be inside, closer to the action? How am I gonna learn anything if I'm out here?"

Abbie and I exchange looks.

"If she goes in, you should too, Cale, to keep an eye on her," she says over my mindpatch.

"Okay," I say to Razor. "You can come. But we're staying near the door."

"How about my buddy Gerry over here?" says Razor.

I glance across at Abbie.

"All right," she says. "We all go. But like Caleb says, everybody except for Judith and Dmitri stands by the door."

Razor smiles and claps Gerhard on the back. "We're in, Ger!"

"Don't do that!" Gerhard yells. "I told you I don't like to be touched! And I don't like to be called Ger or Gerry."

"Sorry," Razor says. "I forgot how sensitive you are." Then she turns to me and says, "I swear we won't mess things up. On Gerhard's grandpa's grave."

"Hey, why my grandpa?" Gerhard says.

"Enough!" Abbie says. "We're going in."

A bell tinkles as we enter the pharmacy. There's a long bar of dark polished wood. Four customers are seated at the counter, nursing their drinks. Two men and a woman are behind the bar mixing drinks. Luckily only one of them has a handlebar mustache.

I nudge Dmitri, and he steps forward, positioning himself at the far end of the bar opposite Sam.

"I find that the firing mechanism on the new 1886 Colt functions optimally when lubricated with seal fat," Dmitri says in a loud voice.

I groan under my breath. Sam looks up from what he's doing, squints at Dmitri and then goes back to pouring drinks.

Gerhard takes a step toward the stools. As I grab his arm to bring him back, Razor skips past me toward the back of the store. I'm about to go after her when I see that she's not causing any trouble; just standing by a rack of small blue bottles. With any luck, she'll stay there—out of the way.

"I like nothing more than measuring the trajectory of a little white sphere on days such as today, when the wind patterns are agreeable," says Dmitri.

Sam looks up again. "What did you say, son?"

"Your choice of appellation is interesting. I am fairly certain that I am not your son, although there is a one-in-three-hundred-million chance that I may be your great-grandson. That aside, I was remarking on the pleasures of partaking in a game of golf."

"Hey, Judith, get over here. You gotta see this!" shouts Razor.

Judith looks over her shoulder for a moment but refuses to take the bait.

"Suit yourself," says Razor. "But there are some cool ingredients in these little jars. This one says it's got sassafras in it."

The bell to the front door tinkles, and a woman enters. She's petite and carrying a paisley umbrella. She plunks herself down on one of the stools between Dmitri and Judith.

"Hello, Clara," Sam says, moving over to wipe the spot of counter in front of her. "How are you today?"

"I've had the most dreadful morning, Sam," Clara says. "My cousin Rita has decided to stay in Atlanta for another fortnight. That woman is eating us out of house and home!"

"Sorry to hear that," Sam says.

"And she simply will not stop following me. I had to take a circuitous route here, and even then, I'm not entirely certain she didn't see me slip in." She eyes the door.

"Well, perhaps a refreshment to calm your nerves?" offers Sam.

"Yes, Sam, that would be just the ticket. How about one of your new syrups?"

"Of course. Which would you like? The cola or the root beer?"

"Hmmm." Clara strokes her chin. "It is so difficult to decide. I believe I will take the cola."

"Smart choice, lady."

I cringe when I see Razor making her way to the bar.

She plunks herself down next to Clara, smiles up at Sam and says coolly, "I'll have what she's having."

"This isn't your snatch, Razor," I say over her mindpatch, trying to put as much menace into my voice as possible.

"Relax, Jack," she mindpatches me back. "I'm not gonna do anything. I just want a front seat for the main action, that's all."

"I don't believe your parents would approve, young man," says Clara. "Cola is a digestive remedy."

"Perfect," Razor says, "because this whole scene is giving me heartburn." Then she looks up at Sam and says, "Hey, if you don't mind, Sam old buddy, why don't you pour some fizzy water in mine. They say bubbles are good for settling the old tum tum."

"That is exactly what I was thinking, young man!" says Clara. "Sam, I'll have the same, if you please."

"Two fizzy water colas coming up," Sam says.

He pours the drinks, sets the first one down in front of Clara and is about to set the other one down when Dmitri falls off his stool. On his way down, one of Dmitri's flailing arms rakes Gerhard's sleeve.

"Don't touch me!" yells Gerhard.

"He didn't mean it, Ger," says Razor.

"Thin slices of rubbery solitude amid a wasteland of wine gums," recites Judith.

"Judith, what are you doing?" Abbie shouts over Judith's mindpatch and mine. "Grab the glass of Coke!"

"But Dmitri is hurt," she says.

"He's not hurt!" Abbie answers. "It's part of the act."

Judith doesn't seem to hear her. Along with everyone else, she just stares at Dmitri, who is alternating between lying completely still, jerking various parts of his body and shouting out names of Kentucky Derby winners from the 1920s and '30s.

"What do you make of that, Clara?" Sam says, coming from behind the bar and gazing at Dmitri's intermittently jerking body.

"TWENTY GRAND!" screams Dmitri.

"He could be having a fit," Clara says, knitting her eyebrows. "Of course, it's the strangest looking fit I've ever seen—"

"BUBBLING OVER!"

"Or heard," finishes Sam.

Sam brings two fingers to his mouth and whistles. A big, hulking boy wearing suspenders emerges from the back of the shop.

"Help him up, Jimmy, and bring him outside," says Sam.

"BEHAVE YOURSELF!" shouts Dmitri.

Jimmy lifts Dmitri up with ease, slings him over his shoulder and carries him, sack of potatoes style, to the door.

"Judith, finish the snatch!" shouts Abbie.

Judith reaches for Clara's glass of coke, but Clara grabs it first and raises it to her lips.

Before she can take a sip, Razor clutches her middle and falls to the floor, moaning.

Not again.

"Young man, what is the matter?" exclaims Clara.

"Oh . . . oh, my stomach!"

"You poor dear little man. Here, have this." Clara kneels down next to Razor and brings her glass of fizzy cola halfway toward Razor's lips.

Just then, the front door swings open and a woman comes rushing in. She's built like an icebox—short and square.

When Clara sees who it is, her face turns white and her hand slips off the glass.

But Razor has a firm grip on it and as Clara's hand slides away, Razor lifts the glass the rest of the way to her mouth.

138

"Razor, don't!" I scream over her mindpatch.

"Found you, cousin!" shouts Rita.

"Strawberry sentries scatter like toast crumbs in the night," recites Judith.

Razor ignores me and tips the glass toward her lips.

Abbie and I lunge for it at the same time.

But Razor's too quick. In one fell swoop, she drains the contents.

"Ahh," she says.

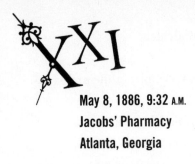

I stare dumbly at the empty glass.

Razor jumps to her feet and brushes herself off. "That was swell. What's the matter, Jack? You look like you've seen a ghost. Come on. Pull yourself together. I can't wait for our next adventure."

I'd rather be sent to the Barrens than go on another "adventure" with Razor. In fact, Uncle might just grant me that wish. I should have grabbed that glass of Coke when I saw that Judith wasn't going for it. But then I'd probably get punished for not allowing a recruit to finish a snatch.

I watch as she steps lightly to the door.

Something is tugging at my arm. But I can't be bothered to look. All I can think about is the torture ahead when Uncle finds out about the failed snatch.

"Excuse me," says a voice that a distant part of my brain acknowledges as Judith's.

"Let's go, Judith," I say, looking at her. "We're done here."

"I thought so. But I was just wondering if . . ."

"Sorry, Judith. But there's no time for any more poems."

"No, it's not that," she says. "I was wondering if you thought it would be useful if I took this with us."

In her hand she holds a glass filled with an amber-colored liquid.

Razor made me so angry, I'd completely forgotten about the second glass of Coke!

"Yes," I say. "Let's take it with us."

"But there's only one thing," Judith says.

Why is there always one thing? Why can't there be *no* things for once?

"What is it, Judith?"

"We haven't paid for it yet," she says.

"Judith," I say, trying hard to keep my voice even, "we are thieves. Thieves steal stuff. Go ahead. Just take it, and let's get out of here."

The only movement she makes is to hold out her hand in front of me, palm up.

I sigh, scrounge around in my pocket and hand her a nickel.

"Thanks!" she says and scoots back into the store.

Razor is whispering something in Dmitri's ear. Gerhard is tying and retying his shoelace.

"All right, everyone," Abbie says as soon as Judith is back. "We're going to Headquarters now. As soon as your time freeze thaws, Frank wants to meet with each of you in his office."

"Why?" Judith asks.

"He wants to talk to all of you about the tree incident," I say.

Judith looks up and says, "I didn't see anything."

"Well, then tell him that," I say. "Dmitri and Razor, stay here with me for a moment, please."

I watch the others fade and vanish.

"Dmitri, you first," I say. "Razor, please wait over there, across the street."

She looks where I'm pointing and then says, "I wanna be here when you talk with him."

"No. I just want to talk to Dmitri in private for a moment, okay? Your turn will be next."

She doesn't budge.

"Razor, this doesn't concern you," I say, my voice rising.

"Sure it does. I'm Dim's lawyer. Anything you say to him you gotta say in front of me," she says.

"But you're not a lawyer. In fact, you are the furthest thing from a lawyer I've ever seen."

"Wrong again," she says. "I'm a criminal attorney. I specialize in defending scoundrels, like Dim over here."

"I am not a scoundrel," Dmitri says.

"You are so," Razor says. "Look at your shifty eyes. But don't you worry. I'll have you off death row in no time. I got the perfect defense. You were insane at the time you committed the crime. In fact, I think you're still insane now!"

"Razor, enough!" I snap. "Dmitri, Frank is going to ask you if it was you who moved the tree from China to Times Square. And if you tell him it was you, he's going to want to know how you did it."

"Very well," Dmitri says. "That does not pose any problems."

"And," I add, "he'll want to keep you cooped up until you can show him exactly how you did it."

"Yeah," Razor agrees. "It'll be like being in the slammer, Dim. Lunch will be thin soup and one slice of stale bread. Ask for whole wheat, if they have any."

I give her the look of death.

"I have no problem with sharing my technical knowledge of large object time transport with the senior management," Dmitri says.

I try to think of things from his perspective. The problem is that he doesn't know what Uncle and Frank are really like. He's never seen them hurt a fly. No wonder he's not afraid of them.

"All right, Dmitri. I'm not going to tell you to lie. I suspect they know that you did it by now anyway. But if you pretend that you don't know how you did it, it might go easier for you."

"Yeah, you might get a bit of mystery meat in your soup, Dim," Razor says, making a slurping sound.

October 5, 2061, 2:43 P.M.
Timeless Treasures Headquarters
Tribeca, New Beijing (formerly New York City)

All's quiet when I land under the fire escape in the alley next to Headquarters. The usual city noises are subdued. Maybe it's a long weekend and everyone's gone to Jersey. Whatever the reason, I like it this way.

I watch as Razor and Dmitri clamber up the fire escape and enter Headquarters. I could follow them but that would spoil my sense of peace and quiet. So instead, I linger another minute and then take the long way around to the front entrance.

As soon as I'm inside the elevator, the doors close and a booming voice shouts out, "Hit the floor and hold your breath!"

I drop to the floor and cover my head with my hands.

"It's okay, you're safe now," Phoebe says from the screen above me. She is dressed in one of those protective suits scientists wear when they are dealing with a deadly, contagious virus.

"What just happened?" I ask.

"Nothing you need to worry about anymore. But if you like, you can thank me for saving your life."

I am having a very confusing day. "How did you save my life?" As soon as I ask, I immediately regret it.

Phoebe chuckles her know-it-all chuckle. Or is it her you-know-nothing chuckle? I have trouble telling those two apart.

"I wish I could say. But that's Top Secret." She switches to a whisper. "Don't worry, though; it's been contained. It will never hurt you unless I let it out. And I would never let it out around someone I like."

I'd better not go there.

"All right," I say. "Thank you for saving my life, Phoebe. Can you take me up to four, please?"

"As soon as you say the magic word," she says.

"I already said please," I say, starting to get annoyed.

There's that chuckle again. "So you did. But that's not the magic word."

I take a deep breath. Maybe it's not too late to get my room back at the castle. I'd rather deal with a million winding stone steps right now than an elevator ride with Phoebe.

"C'mon. Take a guess. Give it your best shot. Be bold!" she says.

I don't want to be bold. But I don't want to stay here forever either. "Haggis," I say, taking a flier.

Phoebe's screen persona removes her mask, and I can see the astonished look on her face.

"How did you know? I just changed to that password an hour ago. And I didn't tell anyone."

"Just lucky, I guess," I say. "Can you take me up now?"

The elevator starts to move.

"Congratulations!" says Phoebe as we go up.

"For what?" I ask.

"For training a winner. Frankly, I didn't think you had it in you."

"What are you talking about?"

"Frank gets on my elevator and starts jabbering about one of your recruits—you know, the spaced-out one. Then he tells me to get a new office ready. The nerve. Do I look like a furniture mover to you?"

The elevator door opens, and I stand there for a moment. I can't

145

believe it. Frank is actually rewarding Dmitri. Still, I've got a bad feeling about this.

"Ahem," Phoebe says.

"Yes?" I say.

"In case you haven't noticed, this is four. GET OUT!"

I stumble from the elevator and hit the button on the couch. As I walk down the hall, something Phoebe said niggles at me. There's a connection that I haven't made yet. But it feels tantalizingly close.

"We caught a break," says Abbie when I enter the lounge.

"Really? How?" I look around the room. She's the only senior time snatcher here, along with a couple of newbie trainers.

"Luca took the glass of Coke, no questions asked," she says.

"Well, then, something is up," I say, lowering my voice.

"Why do you say that?" Abbie says.

"Think about it. Two botched snatches. No punishment. That's not . . . natural."

"Yeah, but these days anything is possible," says Abbie. "It's like I told you before. Uncle is obsessed with his castle and Scotland. Punishment isn't top of his list anymore."

"Neither is time snatching," I blurt out.

"What do you mean?" Abbie says.

"I mean you are looking at Timeless Treasures' new head of the Historical Correction Division."

"Historical Correction?"

I nod.

"What part of history does he want you to correct?" she asks.

I shrug. "I don't know yet."

"How did Frank react to all of this?"

"He said he would be happy to work alongside me, blah, blah, blah. But I know he was just saying that because Uncle was there."

We both stay quiet for a moment.

"Did you hear about Dmitri?" I say.

She shakes her head.

"He's getting a cushy new office."

"Hmmm. I hope he can deliver what they want," Abbie says.

"Me too." Things are happening too quickly. If I was ever in control of my life, I'm sure not now. All of the stuff that's happening around me, with Frank, Uncle, and now Dmitri, is making me really nervous.

"Uncle sends his regrets," Luca says. "He had been hoping to but now it appears he will not be able to join us for dinner this evening."

No surprise there. He's probably busy crushing spiders. But more likely, the castle renovations are keeping him away. Maybe he's putting in a new moat or something. Not that I'm complaining. I find it more relaxing to eat when Uncle's not around.

"But even though he can't join us," continues Luca, "he gave me an agenda of items he wants covered."

So much for a relaxing meal.

I stare longingly at the buffet table. It's all-you-can-eat Thai food, which is quite an improvement from the old days when we had to cook for each other. I wish Luca would get on with things so we can go ahead and eat.

"First, Uncle had a question for you, Caleb," he says.

Sighs of relief come from the other time snatchers.

"Shoot," I say, which is probably a poor word choice.

Luca reads off his handheld, "What is the most valuable lesson you learned from your recruits during today's snatches?"

Why is he asking that?

"Do you have any multiple-choice questions instead?" I say. "I do much better on multiple choice." As soon as I say that, I regret it. Luca isn't fond of jokes, and I doubt he'll appreciate my feeble attempt at humor. Still, I need to stall as long as I can, because I can't think of anything to say.

"Just answer," he says predictably.

"All right," I say. "The most valuable lesson I learned from my recruits during one of the snatches performed today, the first snatch being Operation High Tea, where we snatched leaves to make pu'er tea and second, Operation Fizz, where—"

"We know what your assigned snatches were. Hurry and answer, or I'll write 'no answer given.'"

I wonder if "no answer given" is better than "wrong answer given."

"Okay," I say. I'm drawing a blank. The only thing that stands out in my mind is my feeling of absolute terror when the tree almost landed on me. If I hadn't rolled left, I would have been smushed like a bug.

"The lesson I learned from my recruits was . . . when it feels like the world is crashing down around you, it important to know which direction to take."

Luca looks at me through slitted eyes. I think he's trying to figure out whether I'm joking or not. Thankfully, after a moment, he turns away and enters something on his handheld.

"Frank." Luca looks up. "Uncle also asked if you might say a few words about some of the exciting work you are doing at Head-quarters."

"Gladly," says Frank. He stands up and smiles.

What's that on his wrist? It looks like a real Rolex. Those don't come cheap. Why does he even need one? He can read the time off his fingernail like the rest of us.

"As all of you know," Frank says, "Uncle is extremely busy. Between dealing with client relations and plotting the strategic direction of Timeless Treasures, he is always on the go. He's often expressed to me at our weekly breakfast meetings how thankful he is that he has me, his trusted lieutenant, to guide the ship at Headquarters and the Compound while he's away."

So now they're eating breakfast together.

"While there are a couple of projects that are too confidential for me to share with you just yet, I can report that Uncle and I are also working on some new technology that you will all soon have access to. For instance, we recently developed an ear patch that will enable the user to hear conversations happening up to a mile away."

Wow. A mile away. I wonder if it comes with an app that filters out coughs and sneezes.

"Another thing that Uncle and I have been discussing is a built-in GPS enhancement to your ocular implants so that by blinking, you will be able to switch modes from night vision to a map of your physical location."

Now there's something I could use. Still, if he says "Uncle and I" one more time, I think I'm going to puke.

"And those are only a couple of the projects we're working on. I'm also looking at ways to streamline our main time-snatching operations to make Timeless Treasures a leaner and meaner organization."

Hold on. Uncle has just taken in a new bunch of recruits. Is Frank saying that we don't need them all?

He sits down and as he does, he gives me a look that says, "I don't care that Uncle appointed you as new division head. I'm still much more important than you'll ever be."

"Thank you, Frank," says Luca. "Everyone can eat now."

I jump from my seat, happy to be out of there. I pile my plate up with pad Thai noodles, ginger fried chicken and papaya salad and am on my way back to the table when I see Luca give his handheld to Frank. Frank gazes at the screen for a moment, presses some keys and hands it right back. What was that all about?

I manage to get my first few bites in before Luca says, "Since you are all here, I may as well brief you on tomorrow's missions. All teams will have a morning snatch. There will be no afternoon mission. Instead you are to continue with training sessions in the Yard. Caleb and Abbie, your team's mission will to be to snatch an object that led to one of the greatest discoveries of all time."

Let me guess. He's sending us to steal the thing that puts the cream filling in Oreo cookies.

"You are to go to 1666 England and the home of Sir Isaac Newton's mother," says Luca, reading from his handheld. "On April 17 of that year, Sir Isaac was out in the garden when he saw an apple falling from a tree, which led him to discover gravity. Your mission is to snatch that apple."

I thought the whole apple-falling-from-the-tree thing was just a made-up story. I guess I was wrong.

"Uncle has asked that you use the opportunity of this mission to impress upon the recruits some of the principles he taught during your recent outing with him. Specifically, he mentioned 'seeing with your mind' and 'intelligent observation.'"

It's a nice thought, but I've got a hard enough time trying to keep Razor and Dmitri in line, let alone trying to teach them Uncle's principles.

I think back over the day. Two far from perfect snatches and no punishment. I don't need intelligent observation to tell me that sooner or later, no matter how sweet, every lucky streak comes to a sour end.

April 17, 1666, 2:31 P.M.
Woolsthorpe Manor
Lincolnshire, England
Operation Gravity

Ouch! A million tiny needles pierce my body. All right, maybe just five or six. But it feels like a million. I had programmed my patch to land *behind* some bushes . . . not *inside* them.

When I'm finally able to move, I pluck the thorns from my shirt-sleeves and pants. About a hundred yards away is the snatch zone, Woolsthorpe Manor.

"What are your new digs like, Dim?" I hear Razor say. "Did they give you CoffeeValet?"

I snort. Even Uncle doesn't have CoffeeValet, the latest in premium intravenous coffee drips.

"I am not supposed to talk about my appointment," Dmitri says. There's a certain smugness in his tone that I've never heard before.

"Well, excuse me for living," Razor says. "Just remember, Dim. None of that would be yours without me."

"What do you mean?" he says.

"Do the math, Dim. Whose idea was it to move the tree? And who got you the supplies you needed to do it?"

Dmitri sets his lips in a thin line and says nothing.

"We're about to move to the snatch zone, guys," I say. "Do you all remember your roles?"

"Yes," Judith says. "I will stay with you in the garden and compose sonnets."

"Gnome," Razor says under her breath.

"What was that, Razor?" I say.

"I was thinking about Alaska. I always wanted to go to Nome. D'ya think if we ace this snatch, Uncle will let us go there, you know, as a kind of reward?" She gives me her best fake sweet smile.

"Gerhard?" I ask.

"I will be standing near apple tree number one, ready to grab any apple that falls."

"Good," I say. "Dmitri?"

No answer. He has a faraway look in his eyes.

"Earth to Dmitri," I say.

"Y . . . yes?"

"Your station, Dmitri. Where will you be?"

"In the garden, in the vicinity of apple tree number two," he says.

"Correct," I say. "And your job?"

"To wait," he says.

"For?"

"For the apple to fall."

"Razor?"

"Here I am," she chirps.

"You will stay with me," I say, and before she can object, I add, "Abbie will be stationed inside the house, in case Sir Isaac takes the apple inside. Let's go, everyone."

I'm feeling pretty good about things. Abbie's right. The only way to deal with Razor is to take a firm line. Maybe she's finally starting to respect me. I take a deep breath and let my shoulders relax.

The afternoon is glorious. There's a light breeze blowing in the garden when we arrive. The air carries a slight scent of lilac. Under the shade of a big oak is a wagon whose doors have been painted in reds and greens. "MayFair Puppet Company" is painted in gilded letters on its side. That's strange; the briefing materials didn't say anything about a puppet play.

About two dozen chairs face the puppet theater in rows. Guests stroll about the garden, admiring the different varieties of flowering plants. A man dressed in a black waistcoat wanders among them, offering glasses of fresh julep.

"This is delightful," says Abbie, smoothing her hair. She's looking very stylish in a silk and lace gown trimmed with silver thread. Come to think of it, I can't remember a mission where Abbie didn't look stylish. I watch her head for the house and when she's out of sight, I shift my eyes to the puppet stage. A man is standing in front of it, twirling the ends of his mustache. His long dark hair falls in loose curls almost to his shoulders.

For a split second, I glimpse another person, a tall man, who emerges from behind the puppet stage to adjust the curtain in the front. He quickly retreats behind the stage before I can see his face.

But neither man is the one we've come here to see. According to the mission data, Sir Isaac has a full head of shaggy blond hair and is of average height, which for 1666 translates to approximately five feet six inches tall.

A trio begins to play soft music. Razor, Judith and I take seats near the back. The doors of the puppet theater swing slowly open. The crowd hushes, and everyone leans forward.

The play is about to begin. So where is Sir Isaac? I crane my neck in each direction but don't see him. It looks like they are going to start without him.

"Good afternoon, ladies and gentlemen," says Mr. Mustache Twirler. "My name is Henry Pendergast. It is with extreme pleasure that I present to you a play by Sir Andrew Mulcair, entitled *Mother Shipton and the Devil's Remorse.*"

Polite applause all around. A chilly wind comes up, and I can feel goose pimples on my arms. Storm clouds are rolling in. I wonder what they'll do if it begins to rain. The puppet theater is definitely too big to move inside.

The curtains of the puppet theater part. At first I see nothing but a dark shape. After staring at it for a moment, I make out jagged edges. It's a cave.

And inside the cave, something begins to stir.

This isn't starting out like any puppet show I've ever been to. In fact, now that I'm thinking about it, apart from the ones I brought with me, there isn't a single kid in the audience.

A figure emerges from the cave; it's a woman puppet. She's dressed all in black and has a long crooked nose and wild hair. That must be Mother Shipton. I can see part of a hairy wrist with a thin scar guiding the puppet, which kind of ruins the moment for me.

But the others all seem to be sitting on the edge of their chairs.

"Begone, Devile, I will have no truck with the likes of ye," says the Mother Shipton puppet, her voice deep and husky.

Another puppet, this one red-faced with big, curved horns for ears, prances right over to Mother Shipton and looms over her.

"Was it not ye who summoned me presently? I will gladly take my leave as soon as our business is done." The Devil puppet half turns toward the audience, and I can see a sly smile painted on his wooden face.

Mother Shipton cocks her head to one side as if considering the Devil's answer.

"I have no business with the Prince of Lies." She practically spits the words.

The Devil laughs. "That is most amusing coming from one who

only last evening uttered the words, and I quote, 'To have the gift of far sight, I would trade my very soul to the Devile.'"

Mother Shipton stays still for a moment, apparently trying to decide whether or not to accept the Devil's offer.

"Very well," she says finally. "Give me the gift."

"And?" says the Devil.

"And my soul is yours, Son of Hades," she answers.

"This is boring. I'm going to take a break," Razor says.

She gets up to leave, but I yank her back into her chair. "Stay here until it's over."

"How much longer?" she asks.

"Not long," I say, although I really have no idea.

The Devil turns to Mother Shipton and smiles.

A commotion erupts at the back of the crowd.

"Stop," shouts a voice. "Begin again!"

There's a groan from the audience. A man with frazzled hair strides up to the stage. It's him! Sir Isaac!

"Begin again, I say!"

A woman appears at his side and says, "There is no need for Master Pendergast to begin all over again, brother. You have seen this play many times before, remember?"

Sir Isaac turns to her, and his look softens. "All right, then. But, Mary, please tell him to jump ahead to the choice bits near the end."

"I'm with him," mumbles Razor. "Go right to the end. This play sucks."

"No," Mary says firmly. "The others have not seen the play. They must see it in its entirety in order to enjoy the finale."

From the resigned look on his face, it appears that Mary has won this battle. Sir Isaac slumps into a seat in the front row.

The Devil has left the stage now, and Mother Shipton stands

alone at the mouth of her cave. It must be a trick of the light, but her eyes seem different somehow, more . . . knowing.

She begins to recite:

"Carriages without horses shall go,
And accidents fill the world with woe.
Primrose Hill in London shall be
And in its centre a Bishop's See.

"Around the world thoughts shall fly,
In the twinkling of an eye.

"Water shall yet more wonders do,
Now strange, yet shall be true."

I gasp. This is remarkable. The puppet has just predicted cars, e-mail . . . and maybe even hydroelectric power!

"Boring," mumbles Razor beside me.

I stare at the puppet, forgetting for a moment all about Sir Isaac and the snatch.

"Iron in the water shall float,
As easy as a wooden boat.
Gold shall be found, and found,
In land that's not now known."

Razor nudges me. "Look, he's getting up!"

But I hardly hear her. I'm totally mesmerized by the Mother Shipton puppet, who has opened her mouth to speak again.

Razor is tugging at my arm, but I ignore her.

"For travelers through both time and space,
In dress familiar to this place,
Their master's kindnesses of late,
Will turn to unrepenting hate.

"A lifelong quest, an ancient stone—
The wrongful heir upon the throne.
Death and suffering line the path.
None will be spared the master's wrath."

My mouth has gone completely dry. She's talking about Uncle!

The Mother Shipton puppet retreats deep into the cave and then the music starts up. The curtains of the small puppet stage close to a smattering of applause.

No, that's crazy. I'm just imagining that she's talking about Uncle. It can't be. Besides, there's no connection as far as I can tell between Uncle and an ancient stone or a throne.

I must talk to the puppeteer. Something very strange is going on here. But as I get up, Razor pulls hard on my arm.

"C'mon, get with the program, Jack. We've got a snatch to do."

I try to shake her off, but she's relentless. I sigh and let myself be pulled along. Soon I see Sir Isaac. He's sitting under apple tree number two, looking up at the sky.

And there's Dmitri, sitting on the other side of the tree, doing the same thing. They don't seem to be taking any notice of each other.

I glance at my fingernail and gasp. Only three minutes left to complete the snatch. Where did the time go? Still, we can't snatch what we don't know. There must be a dozen apples on that tree. There's no choice but to wait for one to fall.

"Pssst."

I look up. Razor is sitting in the branches of the apple tree.

"What are you doing up there?" I say.

"Just helping things along," she says. "Bombs away!"

"No, don't!" I shout.

But I'm too late. Apples rain from the sky, thudding on the ground. A couple hit Dmitri and Sir Isaac, but they don't react.

This is not how it's supposed to happen. I count the apples on the ground. Nine. One for every year I'll spend in the Barrens when Uncle finds out.

Razor leaps from the tree and lands beside Sir Isaac. "Here you go, Izzie," she says, picking up a random apple and handing it to him. "Hurry up and discover gravity, so we can get out of here."

Sir Isaac stares at Razor openmouthed. She stares back at him, hands on her hips, foot tapping the ground.

I shake my head and look for the puppeteer. There's an open space by the oak tree. The puppet theater is gone. And so is my chance to speak to the puppeteer.

"Time's up," says Razor, snatching the apple back from Sir Isaac and handing it to Dmitri. "Here, Dim," she says, "we'll call this your snatch."

"Who . . . who are you?" asks Sir Isaac.

Just then Abbie arrives with Gerhard and Judith in tow.

The gang's all here, so I turn to Sir Isaac and say, "Would you please close your eyes for a moment, Master Newton?"

"Why?" he asks.

"Because we are about to travel through time, and he doesn't want you to see the part where we go poof and disappear," Razor pipes up.

I glare at Razor, but Sir Isaac just laughs and says, "Very well. I will close my eyes for a count of three."

Then, amazingly, he shuts his eyes,

Abbie takes Judith's hand, and Gerhard offers up his elbow. They are gone even before Sir Isaac gets to "two."

I grab Razor's and Dmitri's hands. Right before we fade away entirely, Sir Isaac says, "Three," and opens his eyes wide.

The last thing I see before we leave 1666 is those same eyes growing even wider.

XXIV

We land in the alley across the street from Headquarters.

"Razor, come with me for the check-in with Luca," I say as soon as my time freeze thaws.

"Sorry, but I've got other plans," she says.

"No you don't," I say. I must have added a special ingredient to my voice, because she actually stays quiet for a moment.

"Dmitri, as soon as we get to the fourth floor, find Abbie and ask her to meet me at my thinking place after check-in," I say, taking the apple from him. "She'll know where I mean."

"Wait, I want that job," says Razor. "Dim, I'll switch with you. You go with Caleb to see Luca the Spooka."

"No switching, no betting and no complaining. I've had enough!" I yell.

Razor looks at me with narrowed eyes. "Listen," she says, "I'll make you a deal. I'll be good . . . so long as I get to do the next snatch."

"No more DEALS!"

"Fine. See what happens if I don't help. It's your funeral, Jack."

She sure has that right. It's my funeral.

We cross the street and enter Headquarters. As soon as we're inside the elevator, the doors close and it starts to go up.

"Who are you, the Glum Sisters?" cackles Phoebe. Her persona is a ticket seller in a little booth.

I don't say anything, and thankfully, neither do Razor or Dmitri.

"That apple looks a little wormy," says Phoebe, handing a ticket to a tall woman whose hair is on fire. "I don't think he'll take it."

I stay quiet. Anything I say will be twisted or used against me, so what's the point of talking? And so long as the elevator keeps moving, we're okay.

"Don't you want my advice?" she adds, stopping the elevator.

I sigh. "I'm in a bad mood, Phoebe. Can't we just make a deal— you bring us up to four and let us out, and next ride, I'll listen to all your advice."

"Why will you make deals with her and not with me?" says Razor.

"Because you're an ungrateful, untrustworthy little runt," cuts in Phoebe.

"Gimme me that apple, Jack!" says Razor. "I'm gonna break that screen."

Phoebe's ticket taker persona takes a half step from her collector booth, sticks her tongue out and then runs back in.

"Enough," I say. "Phoebe, I will take an extra ride with you once we've reported in and listen to any advice you'd like to give."

"Make it two rides and we're there," says Phoebe, and the elevator starts up again.

"Done," I say. "Two rides."

We arrive on four, and the doors open. The elevator screen changes to a close-up of the ticket collector booth sign that now says WELCOME TO HELL. SENIOR TIME SNATCHERS HALF PRICE.

Dmitri goes off in search of Abbie, and Razor and I head to Luca's office.

He frowns when he sees us. "What have you got for me, Caleb?"

"The snatch object from the Sir Isaac Newton mission," I say, handing him the apple.

161

Luca holds it up to the light, turning it this way and that. "Not in great shape, is it?" he says at last.

"What do you mean?" I say. "It's a perfect apple. Not a mark on it. It came straight from the tree in Sir Isaac Newton's mother's garden."

"Are you certain there are no marks?" he says. "What about that one?"

"What are you talking about? There are no—"

And then Luca does an amazing thing. He takes a bite of the apple.

All I can do is stare. Even Razor is speechless.

Finally, I find my voice. "Why did you . . . ?" I begin to ask.

Luca looks across at me and takes a moment to swallow, before answering.

"I believe you are mistaken, Caleb. It must have been your recruit here who took a bite of the snatch object." He nods at Razor. "That wasn't very wise."

Razor growls, and it looks like she's ready to launch herself at Luca. I place a restraining hand on her shoulder.

I can't believe it. Uncle would never order Luca to ruin a perfectly good snatch, even a training snatch. What's going on?

"You're right," I say, looking him right in the eye. "I'm mistaken. Someone did take a bite of that apple. But it wasn't her. It was me."

I can feel Razor's eyes on me. Luca studies me for a moment and then grins.

"If you insist," he says.

As I turn to leave, Luca says, "Uncle wants to see you and Abbie after supper."

"He's here at Headquarters?" I ask.

"No," says Luca. "He's at his castle. He'll be on holo-feed in his office at the Compound."

"What about?" I ask.

"Your next mission."

It must be an important one if Uncle wants to brief us himself. Usually he leaves that kind of stuff to Luca.

I nod, and as Razor and I leave Luca's office, the crunch of him biting into the apple follows us out.

"How did it go with Luca?" Abbie asks as soon as we meet up at my thinking place in Central Park.

"It was going fine until he got hungry and took a bite of the snatch object," I say.

"He what?" says Abbie.

"Right there in front of me, too. Took a big slobbering bite."

"Why would he do that?" she asks.

"I don't know," I say. "Maybe he needed some extra fiber. Abbie, he looked at me with a big smirk on his face and said that it was Razor who took the bite."

Abbie pushes back a stray lock of hair and says, "I was afraid of this happening."

"What do you mean?" I say.

"Luca's not doing this on his own," she says.

"He's got to be," I say. "Uncle would never allow him to ruin a perfectly good snatch object."

"No. But Frank would," she says quietly.

"What do you mean?"

"Haven't you noticed? Luca's taking his orders from Frank now, not Uncle. And Frank doesn't want the recruits to succeed. He isn't punishing mistakes so that they'll keep making them."

"But if they fail," I say, "how does that benefit Frank?"

"It's part of his master plan, Cale," she says. "He wants to show Uncle that he can take care of operations even when things go wrong. That he's the only one who can run the business right. And once he has fooled Uncle to the point where Uncle has handed over all power to him, then it's good-bye, Uncle."

"That's crazy," I say. "It'll never work."

"No? Think about it. Frank already has Uncle's trust to the point where he's running the operations. Plus he's controlling the money coming in from snatches . . . so that means his plan is working."

It takes a few seconds for me to process what Abbie is saying. It makes sense. All the signs are there, including the expensive clothes and jewelry. Frank is planning a coup. And if he succeeds, things are bound to get a lot worse for the recruits . . . and for me and Abbie too.

"Abbie, there's something else."

"What?" she says.

"Do you remember at the snatch this morning there was a puppet show on the back lawn?"

"Sure," she says. "Except I missed it, since I was inside. Was it any good?"

"Well, it wasn't like any puppet show I'd ever seen before. One of the puppets, an old witch type, was making predictions . . . about the future."

Abbie beings to laugh. "A puppet prophet? Cool. What kind of predictions?"

"'Carriages without horses shall go,'" I recite. "And, 'Around the world thoughts shall fly, In the twinkling of an eye.'"

"Interesting," says Abbie. "But you know, those kinds of things can be interpreted in a million different ways. It doesn't really mean the puppet was telling the future."

"No?" I say. "Well, what do you make of this one?" I scan my brain for the exact words and recite: "'For travelers through both time and space, In dress familiar to this place, Their master's kindnesses of late, Will turn to unrepenting hate.'"

"Wow," Abbie says. "That one sure hits close to home. Did you see who the puppeteer was?"

"I only got a glimpse. He was really tall. I was going to find him and talk to him after, but I had my hands full with Razor and Dmitri. When I looked for him later, he was gone. Abbie, I think someone is trying to send us a warning."

"Who?" she asks. "And if they were, why didn't they just meet us somewhere and tell us straight out, instead of speaking through a puppet?"

"I don't know. The whole thing's really weird. But I tell you, it felt like that puppet was actually looking at me and talking right to me."

A rustling sound interrupts my thoughts.

I look toward the bushes. Nothing.

"We'd better go," says Abbie, switching to mindpatch.

I nod and stand up. I can't shake the image of the Mother Shipton puppet staring at me. Her words run through my head over and over again. I also have a strong feeling that things are going to go very wrong very soon unless Abbie and I do something about it. But what can we do against Frank and Uncle? They hold all the cards. Well, maybe not *all* of the cards. Maybe there is still something we can do. The first inklings of a plan begin to take shape in my mind.

October 6, 2061, 7:33 P.M.
The Compound
SoHo, New Beijing (formerly New York City)

Right after supper, Abbie and I head for Uncle's office. There's no aquarium in this one, which means no snapping turtles. That's a good thing because those turtles of his are downright nasty. Shu Fang in particular dined on my wrist once.

Luca is already here. He closes the door and leans against a wall. There are no chairs, so we sit cross-legged on the floor.

No sooner are we seated than the office darkens until it is pitch-black. A pinpoint of light appears. It grows bigger and bigger until it takes Uncle's shape. If I squint, it seems like he is actually in the room with us—that's how lifelike the holo image is.

"*Feasgar math,* Abbie and Caleb," he says. He is dressed in a simple leather jerkin and carrying a two-handed broadsword.

"*Feasgar math,* Uncle," we chime.

"It is a very special day today. Do either of you know what day it is?"

He'd better not call on me.

"Caleb?"

"I believe it is Tuesday, Uncle." That's actually a guess on my part. It could easily be Wednesday. When you don't get weekends off, it's kind of hard to keep track of the days of the week.

Uncle chuckles and says, "Actually, it's Thursday. But, Caleb, I meant what is special about today?"

He's got me there.

"I don't know, Uncle."

He doesn't seem put out by my answer. In fact, he smiles even more broadly. "On this day in 1296, Robert the Bruce became Constable of Carlisle Castle. On that same day, he also swore allegiance to Edward the First, King of England and Overlord of Scotland, who figures prominently in the matter we must discuss."

A good thing I didn't guess. I never would have gotten that one.

"Excuse me for a moment," Uncle says. His image blinks out, and we're left sitting in the dark.

The pinprick of light reappears, and a moment later, so does Uncle's form. "Thank you for your patience. I had to explain to one of the workers that the original stonework of the outer castle is not to be compromised in the renovations.

"Now, I'd like to turn to the matter that I brought you here for. I have a mission for you and your recruits. One that is dear to my heart. It is a mission that I have been dreaming of for a long time. It is also the inaugural mission of our new Historical Correction Division, of which Caleb is the head. But until today, until your success in the forests of China, this mission would have been doubly difficult, if not impossible."

My left leg is falling asleep, so I uncross it and give it a good shake. If I heard Uncle correctly, he wants to send our team on a mission. He doesn't want to punish us. That's definitely good news.

"Gaze upon this, my friends," he says, and a holographic image appears two feet from our noses.

The image is of a big rock, roughly two feet long and a foot and a half high.

"The object you see before you is the Stone of Destiny," Uncle says.

Now, there's a catchy name. I can easily picture it as the title of a made-for-holo miniseries.

"The Stone of Destiny has been used in the coronation of every King of Scotland for the last eight hundred years," Uncle continues. "And even before then, to crown the kings of ancient lands. In very early days, it was known as Jacob's Pillow and was rumored to be the very stone upon which Jacob of biblical fame laid his head to rest as he dreamt of a ladder reaching all the way up to heaven. The prophet Jeremiah is said to have brought the stone from ancient Israel to Ireland, and from there, it found its way to Scotland. If this stone could talk, my friends, think of the stories that it could tell."

None of my business, but I don't think a conversation with a rock would be that interesting.

"In 1296," he continues, "the stone was snatched from the Scottish by Edward the First. His successor, Edward the Third, promised to return it to Scotland, but alas, the promise was broken, and the stone was not returned. So on Christmas Eve in 1950, a group of Scottish students hatched a daring plan to right a wrong, to make good the unfulfilled promise of Edward the Third.

"Their mission was to snatch the stone from Westminster Abbey in London, England, and to return it to Scotland, its rightful ancestral home, so that all the people of Scotland could gaze upon it."

I still don't see where we come in.

"The students indeed snatched the stone from Westminster Abbey and returned it to Scotland. Eventually the stone was deposited on the altar at Arbroath Abbey. When the British discovered it there, they took it back to Westminster. There it stayed until 1996, when it was finally returned once again to Scotland and to Edinburgh Castle for display, along with the crown jewels of Scotland.

"However," Uncle continues, "there is some uncertainty surrounding the provenance of the stone that is now kept at Edinburgh Castle. Some believe that shortly after it was stolen from Westminster Abbey, the original stone was hidden and that the stone on display in Edinburgh is a copy."

Uncle raises the broadsword high over his head and then makes a downward slashing motion. Through some trick, the blade shimmers a brilliant blue as it cuts through the air.

"Tomorrow you will have only one mission to carry out: it is a mission to correct history. You must snatch the original stone from the student thieves immediately after they steal it and bring it to me here in Scotland, where it belongs.

"Now, there are two more pieces of information that you should know," he continues. "First, the stone weighs in excess of three hundred pounds. It is not easily moved through time. But with the new, cutting-edge, technology that one of your group has pioneered"— Uncle smiles—"transporting the stone—and the replica stone of the same weight that you will replace it with—should not pose a problem."

Really? Tell that to Dmitri. It may be true that he's our go-to guy for moving heavy stuff through time, but can I count on him in the crunch? The jury is still out on that one.

"And second," Uncle continues, "I realize that the training of new recruits has not yet been completed. However, this will be considered a regular mission, not a training mission."

My hands go cold. A regular mission means no margin for error. And it also means punishment for failure.

"I'm counting on you to make this snatch a success," he says.

Well, at least he didn't single me out.

"And, Caleb, this will be your chance to redeem yourself for your escape from the Compound. Perform well, and everything between us is erased."

There it is. A single chance to wipe the slate clean.

"That is all," says Uncle. "In the morning, Luca will provide you with more specific information concerning the mission. Ask him any questions you may have. Sleep well, and good luck."

Uncle's image starts to fade away. When the pinpoint of light disappears, I let out a long breath that I didn't realize I had been holding.

"Dmitri will go with you," says Luca when Abbie and I meet up with him at breakfast. "The replica stone, made to the exact specifications of the original, will remain in the courtyard of the Compound until right before the snatch. At that time, using the new technology Uncle mentioned last night, Dmitri will remotely retrieve the replica and arrange for its instantaneous transport to the snatch zone."

Wow. Remote accessing a replica from another century. Who would have thought that was possible?

"You and Abbie will take anti-time-fog pills for this mission," Luca continues. "They're good for three hours, which is the same as the mission length. If you stay in the past longer than that, you'll be susceptible to time fog."

I nod. I wonder why Uncle's giving us so long? Regardless, I'll be thankful for the pills. Time fog is definitely no fun. Lucky for the recruits, since they don't have wrist implants, they don't have to worry about getting it.

"The mission data is being uploaded to your . . . Hold on one second," says Luca. He looks away for a moment and then turns to face us. Uncle must be talking to him over his mindpatch.

"There will be a small change in the mission," he says. "You will take all of your recruits with you."

What? Uncle said this was going to be a regular mission. Obviously we need Dmitri, but Razor is bound to cause trouble, and Judith and Gerhard will just be two more recruits to worry about. Then it occurs to me. It wasn't Uncle who mindpatched Luca. It was Frank! He wants us to fail. And what better way is there to do that than to make us take all of the recruits along?

"Finally," continues Luca, "on this mission, you will be snatching from three other thieves. They may be armed."

May be armed? What kind of intel is that? In any case, three armed thieves against two veteran time snatchers shouldn't pose a problem . . .

Until you factor in Razor and Dmitri, that is.

XXVI

Christmas Day, 1950, 1:59 A.M.
Westminster Abbey
London, England
Operation Coronation

We land a minute apart in an alley two blocks from Westminster Abbey. I check my fingernail. One minute to two o'clock in the morning, London time. Just about any second now . . . and there it is. The most famous clock tower bell in the world, Big Ben, begins to chime.

I go over the mission data in my head. The three thieves are college students—two guys and a girl. They will already be inside Westminster when we arrive there in five minutes. At precisely 2:10 A.M. local time, or ten minutes from now, they will lift the stone from its place in the Coronation Chair inside Edward the Confessor's Chapel and proceed toward the southeast door at Poets' Corner. However, at 2:20 A.M., a night watchman on his rounds will come too close for comfort and the thieves will abandon the stone on the floor of Poets' Corner, only ten feet from the exit door. At precisely 2:45 A.M., they will reenter Westminster and complete the snatch.

So our window to complete the snatch will be twenty-five minutes—from 2:20 A.M., when they leave the stone, to 2:45 A.M., when they return to retrieve it.

I feel a rush of adrenaline and look over at the others. Abbie is stretching and Razor looks to be still time frozen, but Dmitri is already up and about, fiddling with something he has pulled from his pocket. Judith is watching Gerhard collect small stones and place them in perfectly straight lines. Each of us is wearing a heavy coat and winter boots for this mission, which is a good thing, because there is a definite nip in the air.

"What is that you're holding, Dmitri?" I ask.

"You will soon see," he answers evasively.

"Ready to rock," announces Razor. "Get it, Dim? 'Rock,' as in 'Stone' of Destiny."

Dmitri doesn't appear to hear. He just keeps playing with his contraption.

"Okay," I say. "Here's what's going to happen. We walk two blocks to Westminster Abbey. When we arrive, we split up—Judith and Gerhard, you'll go with Abbie to a position near the night watchman's station by the west door. Razor and Dmitri will come with me to the door at Poets' Corner. When we get there, we sit tight until after the night watchman has made his rounds and the thieves have left.

"The first part of this mission is surveillance only. And you must observe not only with your eyes but also with your brain," I say, throwing in an Uncle-ism.

"The brain does not have the capacity for observation," says Dmitri. "It is inaccurate to speak of it in such a context."

"All right, then forget that part," I say. "Just watch what's going on, okay?" I refuse to get into an argument with Dmitri over words.

"There's something else you should all know," I say. "This isn't a training mission. Uncle is treating this as a regular mission. Which means that each of you will get credit if the mission succeeds . . . but if it fails, there will be punishment."

"What kind of punishment?" says Razor.

"I don't know. That's up to Uncle . . . and Frank," I say. "But trust me, it won't be pretty."

The recruits are silent for a moment and then Judith's hand goes up.

"Why do they call it Poets' Corner?" she asks.

"Lemme handle that one," Razor says, turning to Judith. "It's simple, Judy. It's called that because that's where they bury the really bad poets. They bury them alive, right under the floor. So, if I were you, I'd be keeping a low profile on this mission."

Judith hisses at Razor, who ignores her.

"No more discussion," I say. "Let's go."

We walk in silence, keeping to the shadows. After a few minutes, we round a corner and the two enormous towers of the west front of Westminster loom in front of us.

"Stay cool, Cale," mindspeaks Abbie as we split up. She goes off with her recruits to find a hiding place with a view of the night watchman's station. Razor, Dmitri and I continue along toward Poets' Corner.

We pass a white car parked in the lane. I feel its hood as we walk by. Still warm.

Poets' Corner comes into view. My heart skips a beat when I see a broken padlock lying on the ground next to the door. There's no question: the thieves are inside.

I lead the recruits to a line of low sheds right across from the door and sit down to wait.

"Got any munchies?" Razor asks.

"No," I say.

"This is boring," she says.

I try to ignore her.

"I can't take this anymore," Razor says after about five seconds. "Why do we have to wait out here?"

"Because that's the way we planned it," I say.

A car engine starts up. That can't be! The car parked in the lane was empty when we passed it. Also, no one has come out of the Poets'

Corner door, and the only other way for someone to approach the car is from the other side of Westminster, which wouldn't have happened without Abbie noticing and mindpatching me.

Dmitri is chuckling softly.

"What did you do?" I ask, already guessing the answer.

"Drive it around, Dim!" Razor whispers.

"That is possible," he says. "But to do so, I will need to be inside or in closer proximity to the vehicle."

"How about the horn, then?" Razor says. "Give us a toot!"

"Don't!" I mindshout. "Close it off, Dmitri. That's their getaway car!"

"Exactly!" says Razor. "We don't want them getting away, now do we? Trust me on this one, Dim's got the right idea."

I glare at her. Doesn't she get it that the stakes are a lot higher for this mission than all the others we've been on?

"No more car starting," I say, grabbing the device from Dmitri. "Both of you, just watch the door."

The next moment, I hear, "Hey, look at that!" and before I know it, I'm falling for the oldest trick in the book. By the time I look back at Razor, she's already across the lane and halfway through the door.

"Come back!" I shout over her mindpatch, trying to inject as much threat as I can. She looks back once and smiles before disappearing inside.

I want to cry. My life is over. Maybe I can cut a deal with the thieves. I'll trade them Razor and Dmitri for the Stone of Destiny. Better yet—I'll *give* them Razor and Dmitri and they can also keep the stone.

Enough self-pity. I've got a decision to make. Go after Razor or stay put? And if I go after her, what do I do with Dmitri?

Just then I hear another noise. A creaking sound.

"Don't turn anything on, and don't move anything," I whisper to Dmitri.

"Indubitably, I—"

"And don't speak!"

Seconds later, the door to Poets' Corner opens from the inside. A girl who looks about eighteen or twenty years old stands in the doorway. My first impression is that she doesn't look at all like a thief. For one thing, she's wearing high heels that must make a terrible racket when she walks. And second, a bright yellow scarf is wrapped around her neck—certainly not standard issue for thieves who work at night. She steps out of the shadow of the doorway, struggling to carry something bundled up in a sweater.

It can't be! It's too small to be the Stone of Destiny.

"Do you see her?" Razor says over my mindpatch.

"Yes," I say. "Stay out of sight!"

"Don't worry about me," says Razor. "I've got a great hiding spot. Right next to the tomb of some dead guy. Looks like they must have dropped it."

"What do you mean?" I say.

"She's only got a piece of it."

"Where's the rest? Can you see?"

"Nope. Want me to look around?"

"NO! Stay put," I say.

Something is wrong. This was not supposed to have happened. The mission data said nothing about the stone being in two pieces.

I watch the girl carry her bundle past our position toward the lane.

"Abbie, one of the birds has flown the coop," I mindspeak. "She only has part of the stone."

"That's not possible," Abbie says. "The briefing data didn't—"

"I know," I cut her off. "What do you think we should do?"

My patch is silent for a moment. Then she says, "We can't let her take off without knowing where she goes. I know. Take Razor's wristband and somehow get it inside that car. The band has a tracking function."

"Uhhh . . . Razor is unavailable right now," I say meekly.

"What?" Abbie says. "Okay, forget her wristband. Grab Dmitri's, then."

"Will do."

"Dmitri, give me your wrist," I say.

Amazingly, without a word, he extends his hand to me, palm out.

"I'm borrowing this," I say, as I undo the clasp of his band.

He smiles, looks past me and says, "This is turning into a most excellent adventure. It appears that we have more company."

I look up. A flashlight beam is bouncing off the sheds up the line from us. The night watchman! He's not supposed to be doing his rounds yet! Sweat breaks out on my forehead. I can't worry about him now. I've got to get the wristband in the car before she drives away.

"By my estimate," Dmitri says, "in seven point five seconds, unless we relocate, the flashlight beam will shine on my left shoulder and your right elbow."

I grab Dmitri's arm, and we scramble to the back of the shed. We won't be able to see the door anymore, but at least we won't be seen either.

A motor starts up. No!

"Dmitri, here," I say, shoving his gizmo back in his hands. "You know the car you started up before? I want you to shut off the engine."

He squints at me. "I do not understand. Only moments ago, you were quite adamant that I was not to use my device. Are you having a change of heart?"

"Yes!" I mindshout. "I'm having a change of heart. Just do it!"

"Very well."

He pushes some buttons. The roar of the engine fades and then stops altogether.

Two seconds later, it starts up again.

"What happened?"

"I turned it off. She turned it back on," he says.

"Keep turning it off," I say. "I'll be right back."

I hurry up the lane, hugging the walls of the abbey to stay out of sight.

As soon as I see the back of the car, I crouch down. If she looks in her rearview mirror, she will probably still see me, but I'm counting on her being distracted by trying to get the car going.

"Ahem," says a voice over my mindpatch. It's Razor.

"What now?" I mindshout.

"The other two are heading your way . . . with the rest of the stone."

No. This is not happening. They aren't supposed to have the stone with them! At least not the first time.

"Got it," I say. "Abbie, the other two birds are flying the coop. They've got the stone." I switch to Dmitri. "Stay out of sight!"

"Affirmative," he answers.

"Have you got the wristband in place yet?" says Abbie.

"Almost."

"Do it! I'm on my way. The mission intel was all wrong."

You're telling me.

Staying low, I crabwalk the rest of the way to the car. I'm close enough to hear her pounding on the steering wheel and cursing.

I fish Dmitri's wristband from my pocket. The car starts up again. I've got to do this quickly and get back.

But where can I put the wristband? The obvious place would be inside the trunk or inside the car—neither of which is an available option right now. I glance quickly at the rear bumper—there's no place to hang it.

My hands are clammy, and I wipe them against my pants. Come on. Where?

The engine is still going. Why hasn't Dmitri shut it down yet?

There! Right beneath the rear window—the gas tank door. But she'll see me.

No time to think about that.

Then the sound of a gear shift sliding into place.

I sprint to the car and in a single motion, open the small flap and stick the wristband in.

A second later, the engine roars and the car drives away.

XXVII

Christmas Day, 1950, 2:27 A.M.
Westminster Abbey
London, England
Operation Coronation

The band's in place. I'm coming back!" I yell over Abbie's and Dmitri's mindpatches.

"No!" shouts Abbie. "Stay there and get out of sight! The thieves have got the rest of the stone and they're heading your way."

Out of sight where? I glance left and right. Solid stone walls on either side of the lane. No doorways, no alcoves, not a single place to . . . Wait. There! Twenty feet away. A narrow break in the wall. I race to it and press my back against the shallow recess. In broad daylight, this would be a laughable hiding place. But I'm counting on the night shadows to hide me.

The sound of footsteps and grunting kick-starts my senses into high alert.

I can do this. I am a tree. Solid and unmoving. Wrong image. Now all I can think of is Razor yelling "timber" and that giant tree coming down and missing me by inches.

"Damn thing weighs a ton, Angus," says the voice of one of the thieves. I don't dare look, but by the sound of his voice I'm guessing he's not more than five feet away.

"It's a wee bit heavy, I'll grant you that, Colin," says the other thief. "But it's a good weight, if you get my meaning."

I get his meaning. I know all about good weights and bad weights.

A good weight is a mile-high stack of blueberry pancakes with maple syrup. A bad weight is the feathery touch of Uncle's blade on your little toe.

"Put her down a minute, mate, so I can catch my breath," says the one called Colin, in between huffs and puffs.

They set the stone down right there in the lane. Just as they do, I hear footsteps approaching.

They must hear them too because Colin whispers, "It's the night watchman. He's not supposed to be on his rounds."

Good. Their intel is as bad as mine.

"Don't panic," Angus says.

"I ain't," Colin says. "But we don't want to get caught here with our trousers down."

Trousers down. I'm beginning to like these guys. Or at least Colin. He knows how to be miserable just like me.

"Right," Angus says. The next second they've abandoned the stone and are hightailing it down the lane.

The footsteps stop for a moment. I watch the beam of the watchman's flashlight as it shines first on the wall opposite my hiding place and then onto the lane.

My left leg is cramping. I badly need to massage it. But there's no moving from here yet.

"Anyone there?" yells a gravelly voice. All the while the flashlight beam bounces here and there but amazingly doesn't land on the stone.

I am a statue. Strong, silent, unyielding, motionless—

The night watchman's footsteps start up again. This time they are receding—he's walking away!

I peek out from my hiding place. There's no one in sight.

Taking a deep breath, I step out and massage my leg.

"What's happening Cale?" Abbie asks over my mindpatch.

"They just took off . . . without the stone," I tell her.

"Good," she says. "We have to split up. Gerhard, Judith and I will track down the first thief and her piece of the stone. You, Razor and Dmitri snatch the piece we've got. I'm sending Dmitri over to you now."

"All right," I say, peering down at the stone. Draped in shadow and sitting on the cobbles as it is, it doesn't look too impressive. Still, I'm tempted to sit down on it myself and see if it makes me feel kingly.

"Cale, change of plans. Hide!" Abbie's voice sounds frantic.

"What's happening?" I mindshout.

"Thief number four just left Poets' Corner. He's coming your way."

Did she say thief number four? That's impossible. Because there's only supposed to be three. But then again, nothing surprises me at this point.

I slip back into my hiding spot and wait. Seconds later, I hear footsteps followed by heavy breathing. Right after this snatch, I'm putting them all, except maybe thief number one, on an exercise program.

I sneak a peek and see Number Four taking off his overcoat and sliding it under the stone.

Next he's dragging the stone along the lane.

"Where's Dmitri?" I mindshout. "I can't snatch it without him!"

My patch is silent for a moment and then Abbie's voice comes on. "Sorry, we're having a little trouble here. Dmitri says that there is something important he has to do first."

"What could be more important than snatching the stone?" I say.

Down the lane, Number Four is making good progress. In another few seconds, he and the stone will be out of sight. But how is he going to . . . ? A car. He must have his own car parked nearby.

"Razor," I mindpatch, "get over here, and bring Dmitri. I don't care how you get him to come. Just do it. And tell him to bring his gadget."

"That's a big ten-four, boss man," answers Razor.

I take off my shoes to muffle my footsteps and race to the end of the lane. Peering around the corner, I see Number Four open the passenger door of a black car. Then he heaves the stone up so that it is standing on end and pushes it through the door.

Footsteps come clattering behind me. It's Razor and Dmitri.

Just then the car's engine starts up.

"Dmitri," I yell, "do your thing. Stop that car!"

Mid-stride, Dmitri pulls out his gizmo and starts pressing buttons.

But nothing happens. No, that's not true. Something does happen—the car starts driving away.

"I'm afraid my device is not calibrated for a V-12," says Dmitri.

"What are you talking about?" I yell.

"That car is a 1938 Allard," says Dmitri. "It uses a Lincoln-Zephyr V-12 engine, which is basically a flathead V-8 that has been updated to narrow the angle between cylinder banks and add four more cylinders. Now, if it had been a later model Allard, it would likely have the much more common but less powerful V-8 engine, in which case my device would function admirably but—"

"Okay," I say, cutting him off. "Then we have to find a way to follow him. You and Razor stay—"

Razor! Where is she?

A horn blasts and I look up. Twenty feet away there's a rusted red van, engine idling.

Razor's head pokes out the driver's side window. "Hop in, everyone!"

"Where did you—"

"Learn to break into and start a van?" she finishes for me. "At art school. Where else? I majored in the Art of Stealing Motor Vehicles. I got lucky, though . . . he left the keys for us."

"Dmitri," I say as we squeeze into the front seat beside Razor, "can you make your device drive this van?"

"Yes," says Dmitri. "Reconfiguring for an autopilot feature is certainly—"

"Forget that," Razor says. "There's no time. Besides, I want to drive."

"And I want to retire and live by the lake," I say. "We can't always get what we—"

Razor ignores me and steps on the gas. The van lurches forward and glances off the side of the building. She promptly reverses, and we smack into a trash bin, sending the contents flying.

"I am experiencing heart palpitations," says Dmitri. "It may be the result of stressors such as a perceived loss of control."

"Razor! You are *not* driving," I shout. "Move over."

"Sorry, but there's no time to switch," she says, throwing the van into first gear. "The bad guy is getting away."

Wrong. The bad guy is sitting next to me.

XXVIII

Christmas Day, 1950, 3:02 A.M.
Westminster Abbey
London, England
Operation Coronation

You and Dim should relax and close your eyes," Razor says, turning onto Northumberland Avenue. "I'm an expert driver."

Relaxing is the last thing on my mind. "Dmitri, get this thing on autopilot ASAP," I say.

Unbelievably, I can still see the Allard's taillights. It's stopped up ahead.

"I'm gonna ram him," says Razor.

"No! Don't!" I yell.

"Just testing to see if you're still awake," says Razor, laughing. "I'd never ram someone . . . unless he deserved it."

Dmitri nods to me and says, "It's ready."

Finally, something is going my way. "You can let go of the steering wheel now, Razor. Dmitri has set up the autopilot."

"No way," says Razor. "I'm not putting my life in his hands. Did you see what he did to that poor tree?"

"You are the one who wagered that I could not move the tree both temporally and geographically, which I succeeded in doing," Dmitri says.

"Hands off, Razor," I say, trying to sound firm.

A car swerves in front of us. Razor jerks the wheel to the right and slams on the brakes.

"Whew. That was a close call. Good thing I didn't listen to you, isn't it?"

"Cale, what's happening?" says Abbie over my mindpatch.

"We're gaining on 'em, Abs! Got the pedal to the floor, hear this baby roar!"

"Razor, I want to speak with Caleb. Kindly get off this frequency."

"Hi," I say meekly.

"Hi? What's going on?"

"Everything's under con— WATCH OUT!" I yell.

Razor zigs right and brakes to an abrupt halt, barely avoiding a street lamp. And it starts to snow.

"That's it, I've had enough," I say, jumping out and running around to the driver's side. "Move over."

I grab the keys from the ignition and wait. I can barely make out the taillights of the Allard.

"Aww, c'mon," says Razor. "You're no fun."

I say nothing.

She opens her mouth again but then closes it. She moves over.

"Okay, Dmitri, take over," I say, starting the ignition.

"With pleasure," he says, sitting up to get a clear view of the road.

The steering wheel starts to move by itself, and the car lurches forward.

As it does, a wave of dizziness comes over me. That's strange. I don't usually get dizzy . . . unless I'm time fogged. But it can't be time fog. I took an anti-time-fog pill, and Luca said they're good for three hours.

Yeah, but he also said there would be only three thieves.

"You drive like a granny, Dim!" Razor yells. "Step on it, or we're going to lose him!"

"Very well," he says. He presses a button on his gizmo, and the van begins to go faster. In moments, we're zipping along.

For the next hour, Dmitri somehow manages to keep the van on the road with Number Four's car in sight. I'm not doing as well, though. I go in and out of feeling dizzy, whether my eyes are open or closed.

When I can finally focus, I see Number Four's car just ahead of us. It has its brake lights on.

"Looks like he's stopping," Razor says.

The thief's car turns onto a small dirt track off the main road.

As we reach the place where he turned off, I signal Dmitri to stop the van.

"Don't stop! We're gonna lose him again," Razor says.

"We wait here for a minute," I say. "If we turn too soon, he'll know we're following."

The getaway car climbs a slope.

As we watch, a siren wails behind us. Wow. That was quick. The stone was stolen only about an hour ago, and the police have already tracked down the getaway car. The Allard is about three-quarters of the way up the hill now.

"Move us over a little so the police car can get by," I instruct Dmitri.

He edges the van over, but instead of passing us, the police car slows and then rolls to a stop. A burly-looking police officer steps from the vehicle and heads toward us. My stomach does a quick flip.

I adjust my night vision to full zoom. The Allard is stopped at the top. The door on the passenger side is open, and the thief already has the stone halfway out.

"Quick, grab my hands," I say to Razor and Dmitri. "We're time-leaping the rest of the way."

Neither of them makes a move, so I grab Razor by the wrist and reach around her to nab Dmitri.

"Your hand, Dmitri!" I shout.

But by the time he looks up, the officer is already tapping at my window, motioning for me to roll it down. Rats.

"Good morning, Officer," I say, letting go of Razor.

The policeman shines his flashlight full in my eyes and then does the same with Razor and Dmitri.

"Driver's license, please," he says to me.

I make a show of patting my pockets and then say, "Uhh. I must have forgotten it at home. Look, I live just over that hill . . . if you wait here, I can drive over to my house and get it."

"Kindly turn the engine off and step out from the vehicle," he says to me. "And your friends, too."

I'm focused on the scene unfolding at the top of the hill. The thief has the stone out of the car now and is duck-walking it to a spot on the hillside near some snow-covered shrubs.

He struggles with the stone for a few more feet before laying it down and kicking snow on top of it. I can't believe it. He's just going to leave it there—in the middle of nowhere!

"Step out from the vehicle, now," repeats the officer, this time with an edge to his voice.

I turn the engine off, and we all clamber out of the van. As we stand by the side of the dirt track, he pulls a notepad out of his pocket and shines his light on it. Then he aims the beam at the van's license plate.

After a moment, he looks at me and says, "How old are you?"

My mind races. For the life of me, I don't know what the legal driving age was in England in 1950 but I'm guessing it was either sixteen, seventeen or eighteen.

"Nineteen," I say, just in case. "I've got a rare skin disease. Makes me look younger than I really am."

Razor guffaws.

"These are my . . . brothers," I continue. "We're on our way home from visiting our grandmother."

Razor smiles up at the officer. Dmitri, as usual, doesn't appear to be paying any attention to the goings-on around him. He runs his fingers over the buttons on his black box.

"I'm not buying your story, son," says the officer to me. "For starters, if you're a day over fourteen my nan's a pilot with the RAF. I'm afraid I'm going to have to take all of you back to the station," he says. "This vehicle is reported as stolen."

"You ride with me in the front," he says to Razor. "You two go in the back."

As Dmitri and I slide into the backseat, the officer talks into a radio receiver.

"Central Dispatch, this is car forty-seven. I'm just south of Cat-claw Hill and have located the stolen vehicle. The three occupants are children, approximate ages, thirteen, ten and ten. No adult in sight. I'm bringing them in to sort this out. Over."

"Car forty-seven, this is Central Dispatch. Copy that. Carry on. Over."

I look up the hill. The getaway car is nowhere in sight. The stone sits on the hillside half covered in snow.

Why did the thief just leave it there? Then it occurs to me. Half of England is soon going to be on the lookout for a black Allard carrying the Stone of Destiny. He must be hiding it until the heat is off and then he'll come back in a different car and drive it the rest of the way to Scotland.

"Any update, Cale?" says Abbie over my mindpatch.

No sooner does she say this than another wave of dizziness hits me, this one stronger than the first.

"Abbie, are you . . . have you experienced any symptoms of time fog?" I ask.

"No," she says. "Why? Have you?"

"Yup."

"Well, there's nothing we can do about it," she says. "Try to hang in. What's going on right now?"

"Not much," I say. "I've just been arrested for vehicle theft and underage driving, and we're all about to head to the police station."

"What about the stone?" she asks.

"I can see it from here," I say. "Number Four dumped it and drove off. My guess is he's going to come back for it later."

"There's no time for you to go to the police station," says Abbie. "We're already running behind on the snatch."

She's right. What seemed like oodles of time has now dwindled down to a measly forty-seven minutes. And it's bound to get even tighter, since now I've got to budget some time for busting out of prison.

"Don't worry, Abs, they'll never take us alive," says Razor, cutting in.

"Razor, get off this frequency!" I mindshout.

"Can you get any decent rock stations on your radio?" Razor asks the police officer.

"What?" he says.

"Rock and roll," repeats Razor. "You know . . . some Stones, or even Moody Blues? Oh cripes, I forgot. What about Elvis? He was big in the fifties, wasn't he?"

The officer gives her a strange look. "No more talking, son."

The car starts up, reverses and then turns onto the main road.

As we bump along, I can see the back of Razor's head through a small mesh window, but I can't reach out and grab her. Which is what I'll need to do in order for the three of us to timeleap out of here.

I'll just have to be patient and wait for my chance.

I turn to look at Dmitri. He's completely occupied with what looks like a plastic mouthpiece, alternately putting it in and taking it out of his mouth. It amazes me how he can tune everything out. Maybe if I lived in my own little world like he does, I'd be a lot happier.

He curls his lips around the mouthpiece and glances my way. His eyes are full of mischief.

"Car forty-seven. Car forty-seven, this is Central Dispatch, come in. Over," says a voice.

I do a double take. I swear that Dmitri is saying the words, but they sound exactly like the voice of the police dispatcher. And not only that. It sounds like his voice is coming from the police radio in the front seat.

"This is car forty-seven. Over," says the policeman from the front.

"Update on the stolen vehicle report," Dmitri says in the dispatcher's voice. "The vehicle reported stolen has been recovered and returned to its owner. I repeat, the vehicle has been recovered and returned. Over."

"Copy that, Central Dispatch. Over," says the policeman.

"Car forty-seven," Dmitri continues, "the three you have picked up check out. They live on the north side of Catclaw Hill. You had best return them to their vehicle. Over."

"Are you certain?" says the police officer. "The driver looks awfully young. Over."

"Car forty-seven. We located the father of the driver, and he confirmed that the boy suffers from a rare skin condition that makes him look much younger than his years. He has a valid driver's license. Over."

"Copy that," says the policeman. "Will bring them back now. Over."

The police car turns around and starts heading back.

Dmitri removes the mouthpiece and smiles at me.

Ten minutes later we arrive, but something about the scene is different.

There are ten or fifteen vehicles parked at the top of the hill, including a mixture of cars and horse-drawn wagons. About thirty men and women are milling around, a few of them putting up tents. They must have just arrived, because only twenty minutes ago, the place was deserted.

The officer opens the back door for Dmitri and me. "Out you go," he says. "It seems there's been a bit of a mix-up. You're free to carry on."

"Thank you, Officer," I say. "Come along . . . children."

He tips his cap at us, gets back into his car and drives away.

I scoot in behind the steering wheel. Razor and Dmitri scrunch in beside me.

I'm surprised that Razor hasn't said anything to me about wanting to drive, but I'm not about to bring up the subject.

"Hurry up and start this thing," says Razor, rubbing her hands. "It's freezin' in here."

I fumble around in my pocket for the keys but can't find them.

"Dmitri, did you—"

"Looking for these?" Razor asks, dangling a ring of keys from her fingers.

"How did you get those?" I say, grabbing them from her.

"I learned from the best!" she says, leaning across to toot the horn. "Now, step on it, Jack. Next stop, the Stone of Destiny!"

XXIX

Christmas Day, 1950, 4:22 A.M.
North of London, England
Operation Coronation

I throw the van into gear and it skids for a moment before the tires grip the snow. We're halfway up the hill when Abbie's voice comes over my mindpatch.

"Cale, we snatched our part of the stone."

"Good work," I say. "We're still working on ours."

We reach the top of the hill, and I park near a beat-up gray sedan. As I step from the van, I'm hit with another wave of dizziness so bad that I have to grip the door to keep from falling.

"What's the matter, Jack?" Razor asks.

"Nothing. Just a little dizzy, that's all."

A boy appears out of nowhere. He's as tall as I am but looks younger, maybe Razor's age. His hair and eyes are dark. Although he's dressed in only a thin shirt, the cold doesn't seem to bother him.

"Lemme handle this," Razor says. "Hey, kid, what's up?"

The boy doesn't answer. He only looks at us and then trails behind as we continue making our way across the top of the hill. Other boys join him, and soon we have our own small contingent following us along.

We walk through an area where men are busy putting up tents and then past a campfire where about a dozen people are gathered around, sitting shoulder to shoulder. One of the men is playing a lively tune on a violin, and a few of the women are clicking their tongues in time to the music.

A dark-bearded man in a faded green parka approaches us.

"Nice setup you've got here," Razor says to him. "Real cozy."

He stares at her.

Razor has started prattling on about something else when he raises his hand. It's got a lot of miles on it; it's all wrinkled, and the fingers are gnarled. But it does the trick—she stops talking in mid-sentence.

For a moment, I think he's going to speak. But instead, he beckons for us to follow, leading us along a path in the snow that has already been pounded down by boots. We pass within two feet of the stone, and I frown when I see two men seated on it, chatting.

Our silent companion leads us to the flap of the only tent that's fully up. As soon as we enter, I pause and look around. The inside of the tent is filled with a hodgepodge of mismatched and worn-looking pieces of furniture.

There's a small fire going, and we're instructed to sit on the layers of blankets covering the ground near the fire. This place reminds me a little of Temüjin's hangout in the Barrens, minus the smell of camel dung.

The man gestures for us to sit and then escorts two others into the tent. I recognize them immediately: Colin and Angus from Westminster Abbey! They sit down on the ground next to us, confused looks on their faces.

Razor's eyes are wide, and her jaw hangs open. I have to admit that I prefer her this way. Dmitri has his usual distracted look.

"I know why you are here," says a new voice. It's deep and husky; a woman's voice.

Through the swirling smoke, I see the outline of a figure sitting on a cushion behind the fire. Her head is covered by a dark blue kerchief, and she's wearing multiple layers of faded patterned clothing.

"I have been expecting you," she continues, and her words chill me. It feels like she is speaking to me and me alone.

The smoke clears, and I can see the woman more clearly. She has a strong face with large eyes and a generous mouth. I can tell that she must have been beautiful when she was younger.

"You each believe that you have a claim on it," she says. "But you are all mistaken. For it cannot be claimed. It is the stone that decides."

I gulp. How can she know that we've come for the stone? This must be some trick. No, not a trick. Simple observation, seeing with the mind, like Uncle says. Before they set up camp, they must have seen Number Four unload the stone. And they must also have seen us getting into the police car. There, I solved it. No mystery here at all.

The tent flap opens again, and Abbie, Gerhard and Judith are standing there. Gerhard's foot is furiously tapping.

"Ahh, the other travelers," she says. "It appears that all are here. We can now begin."

This lady is seriously spooking me. How does she know we are time travelers? No, she didn't say that. She said "travelers." That could mean almost anyone.

She gestures over the fire, silver bracelets gleaming on her wrist and a ring on each of her fingers.

The flames suddenly leap up a good foot, and I feel a rush of heat on my face.

Tricks. These are all parlor tricks. Just like Houdini. I force myself to relax.

The woman has cards in her hands now, and as she shuffles them, she looks at each of us in turn, eyes gleaming and lips curled up ever so slightly. When her eyes meet mine, the intensity of her gaze makes me look away.

"Five times lost and four times found," she says. "Three times captured and two times freed. The heads of kings and the heads of state. All have vied for the stone. And all have failed to hold her. A journey of a thousand years, a thousand wars and a thousand tears."

That all sounds pretty and poetic, but if she's making a point, it's completely lost on me.

"Among you are those whom I shall call the 'patriots'—ones who would have the stone to wake a nation from its slumber and stoke the flame of independence."

I look across at Colin and Angus. Even in the firelight I can see that the blood has drained from their faces.

"And there are also those among you who are the travelers—who seek the stone for reasons less noble."

That would be us.

"But it is not for you to decide what shall be the fate of the stone. The stone does the choosing."

I'm feeling lightheaded again. Sweat starts pouring down my forehead. A chill comes over me, and I bring my knees to my chest and wrap my arms around them. This must be time fog. What else can it be?

I glance at my fingernail. I can't believe it. Only thirteen minutes left to complete the snatch!

With knobby fingers, the woman smooths the patch of blanket in front of her and lays down the deck of cards. Next she cuts the deck three times, all the while staring straight ahead.

"I will need two now. One patriot and one traveler. You decide who."

"You go, Cale," Abbie says.

197

"Yeah, Jack," echoes Razor. "You're the man!"

"I don't want my fortune read," I say.

Abbie gives me the look of death, so I look up at the woman and say, "Count me in for the travelers."

She nods and caresses the cards.

"And me for the . . . patriots," says Colin.

She nods at him. "We shall begin with you, then."

I breathe a sigh of relief. For once I don't have to go first.

She draws a card from the top of the deck and places it facing Colin.

The image on the card is of a man seated at a table. In his right hand he holds a wand, and resting on the surface of the table are a knife, a cup and some coins.

"The Magician," says the woman. "Very good."

Then she draws another card and places it next to the first. The card shows a woman seated on a throne. In one hand she holds a sword, and in the other, a pair of scales.

"Justice," she says.

Her fingers move to the deck for a third time. The card she chooses depicts a woman riding on a chariot pulled by two winged horses, one black and one white.

"And finally, the Chariot."

She pauses for a moment, studying the cards. Then she taps the Magician card and says, "Past," taps the Justice card, "Present," and the Chariot card, "Future."

This is all very confusing, but at the same time, I can't tear my eyes away.

"Patriot," she begins, "the Magician, which is your past, symbolizes creative energy and action. This card speaks of infinite possibilities for expressing yourself.

"The Justice card," she continues, "is your present. It is a card that is concerned with fairness and doing what is right. That is your present predicament, is it not? You are here to do what you see as honorable and just.

"And finally, the Chariot card. This is your future. This card speaks of travel—of a journey you are about to take or have already embarked on. When combined with the Justice card, it tells me that your journey is . . . how shall I say it . . . 'morally justified.'"

I gulp. There's no mistaking what Colin's "journey" is; it's the same as mine. To steal the Stone of Destiny. But she's saying that he's doing the right thing.

She collects the cards, replaces them in the deck and shuffles. My palms are sweating. Is it too late to back out? Maybe Dmitri wants his future read. Or maybe I can bribe Razor to go in my place.

Only seven minutes left to complete the snatch.

"You are next, Caleb," she says. The woman knows my name. That's an easy one. She heard Abbie say it. No, that couldn't be. We've been mindpatching each other, not speaking out loud.

She cuts the deck three times and lays three cards in front of me.

The first card shows a man holding an hourglass hunched over a walking stick.

"The Hermit," the woman announces, "your past."

The second card is of a man hanging upside down, with one foot tethered to a tree.

"The Hanged Man," she says, "your present."

The final card gets me shaking. The image is a horned and winged beast with the face of a man. In his mouth, he holds two naked figures, one male and one female.

"The Devil. Your future," she says.

Well, I'll be going now. And not at a leisurely pace either. I want to run screaming from this tent and never look back. Because no one wants the Devil card, do they? And that Hanged Man doesn't look like a winner either. The problem is my legs feel like jelly and the only things on me that move right now are my eyes.

"This is very interesting," the woman says, which doesn't help my blood pressure.

"Hang in there, Jack," Razor mindspeaks. "Oops, sorry . . . bad word choice."

"The Hermit," says the woman, "is a solitary figure whose path through life is guided by his own inner strength. This is your past."

That doesn't sound too bad. Can we turn the cards around and make this one my future?

"Your present is dictated by the Hanged Man. The Hanged Man symbolizes that your life's path is not yet decided, but that in order to realize your full potential, you must be open to seeing things from a different perspective, to changing your way of viewing the world."

"I think she means letting me drive," Razor whispers.

But I hardly hear her. I am completely focused on the woman's hand as it passes over the third card.

"It is rare for this card, the Devil card, to appear on a first reading," she says. "It denotes that an important choice, a life-changing choice, needs to be made. Although you may feel that there is nothing you can do, that you are enslaved to your present situation, that is not true. You are not powerless in this decision, Caleb. You can make a choice that will change the course of your life and perhaps others' as well . . . for the better or for the worse. One six eight nine trusts that you will make the right choice. But it is your decision and yours alone. Choose wisely."

I'm about to ask what one six eight nine is when something

bumps my shoulder. I whip my head around and see Abbie sprawled on the ground.

"Abbie!"

"I . . . I don't know what happened, Cale," she says, eyelids fluttering. "I got really dizzy all of a sudden."

No! Now Abbie's got it too.

"It's time fog," I say. "I'm taking you back right now," I say, gesturing to Gerhard to help.

"No," she says. "I'll be okay. I just need some air."

Gerhard helps me get Abbie to her feet. The woman is already standing and beckons us to follow.

She leads us outside and past a line of tents that weren't there before. They must have been put up while we were inside during the reading. A blue car is parked next to our van. I'm guessing it belongs to Colin and Angus.

Finally, the woman stops and gestures for us to gather around.

"This is what you seek," she says, pointing to the stone.

I crouch down next to the stone and place my trembling fingers on it. It would be a shame to come all this way for a replica. The next moment, the scan comes back positive. This is it, all right. The real Stone of Destiny!

She clears her throat, and I'm certain she's going to tell us who the stone has chosen. But she says nothing. Only turns and walks back toward the line of tents.

All of us, including Colin and Angus, are left standing there.

It's come down to this. I check my fingernail and gulp. Only three minutes left to complete the snatch.

"Mumbo jumbo, that's all it is," says Razor. "Let's snatch it now before this wind turns us into Popsicles!"

Razor's words spur me to action. "Dmitri, the duplicate," I mind-patch him. "Transport it, please, to the spot right next to the stone."

Dmitri nods and pulls out a device I haven't seen before, and the next moment, it feels as though I'm seeing double. Or almost double. A second stone has materialized on the crest of the hill now, right next to the real Stone of Destiny. The only difference is this new stone doesn't appear to have a chunk missing from it.

Colin gives a shout of surprise.

A gust of wind blows snow in my face. Abbie is gathering the recruits around her, getting ready to timeleap. All that's left is for me to do the same with my recruits and to give Dmitri the word to transport the Stone of Destiny when we leave.

Uncle's words flash through my brain. "Together we will right the wrongs of history." Well, bringing the Stone of Destiny to him so that he could keep it all to himself, locked up in his castle, would be a massive historical wrong.

"No!" I say, mindpatching Abbie and the recruits at the same time. "This isn't right."

"What are you talking about?" says Abbie. "Uncle is going to go ballistic!"

"Yeah, listen to her," says Razor. "If we come back empty-handed, your ass is grass."

"We're not going to come back empty-handed. Dmitri, scan the original, please."

"What's the point?" Abbie says. "You already did that, didn't you?"

"Bear with me for a moment, okay?" I say.

Dmitri touches the stone. "Scan completed."

"All right. Now transpose the scan results onto the duplicate."

Dmitri gazes at me with knitted eyebrows for a moment. "The

scan cannot be transposed. The only thing I can do, perhaps, is to superimpose the scan of the original onto the scan of the duplicate. But anyone checking closely will notice the difference."

A wave of sickness washes over me, and I clench my teeth. I have to fight it.

Barely over a minute left.

"What if they only do a quick scan?" I say.

He's quiet for a moment. "In that case, a scan of the duplicate may exhibit features that would lead one to believe that it is in fact the original."

It's far from perfect.

I look across at Abbie. We have to agree on this. Because if Uncle finds out we're pawning a replica off on him, then we're both going to be facing some heavy-duty punishment. To say nothing of what will happen to the recruits.

She has a fierce look in her eyes. "Do it, Dmitri."

Next, she nods to Gerhard, who disappears and then returns a moment later, carrying a large object wrapped in an overcoat: the broken off piece of the Stone of Destiny that Abbie, Gerhard and Judith had snatched from the girl thief.

Thirty seconds to go.

"Give it to them," Abbie says to Gerhard.

He hands the bundle to Angus.

I shake hands with each of them and say, "Good luck."

Just before the timeleap takes us away, I see them clearing the snow away from the real stone.

I close my eyes with the satisfaction of knowing what will happen next. They will heave the stone up and onto the backseat of their car. And then they will drive north and bring the stone back home to its rightful owners, the people of Scotland.

October 7, 2061, 12:09 P.M.
Doune Castle, Scotland

We land in a field. A stiff wind blows, rippling the grass around us. The walls of Doune Castle are solid and imposing. I imagine archers lining the parapets, ready to fire flaming arrows down at the enemy. I wouldn't want to be on the receiving end of that. According to Uncle, though, the castle has been taken many times over the years, once by siege, and three times by armies who pounded the walls with catapults and burst through the gate with battering rams.

The others are all in various stages of thawing from time freeze. The duplicate Stone of Destiny lies in the grass about ten feet away.

I stand up and then immediately fall back down. It's the lingering effects of the time fog. Even though I'm back, I'll have to take it easy for a while until it clears. I glance across at Abbie. She's looking a little pale, but judging from the fact that she's actually standing, she seems to be doing better than me.

"Hey, Caleb, have you got a minute?" Razor asks. Something about her voice is different. It's softer somehow. Also, it's the first time I can ever remember her using my real name.

"Sure," I say.

She leads me a little away from the others, then turns and says, "I had you pegged all wrong."

"What do you mean?" I ask.

"What you did back there with that rock . . . I mean that you let those other guys have it . . . I wasn't expectin' that. That took guts."

A warm shiver goes through me.

"Thanks," I say. "But I don't think it was really guts. I was just doing what I thought was right."

"Trust me on this, Jack. That was gutsy," says Razor. "And now that I know you got guts, I wanna see you using them every day."

"Every day?"

"Of course," she says. "Having guts is like owning a dog. If you don't walk it every day, then it gets fat and lazy. You don't want that happening to you, do you?"

"No, I suppose not," I say.

"Good," she says, clapping me on the back, "that's the right attitude."

The castle's massive front doors are opening. The next moment, Luca appears, pulling a wagon.

As soon as he reaches our position he motions to Gerhard to help him. The two of them heave the duplicate stone up and onto the wagon, turn and start heading toward the castle. The rest of us follow behind.

A strong feeling of dread comes over me. I don't want to go in. I can't face Uncle. I have to get out of here. And I can . . . it's so easy. All I have to do is tap on my wrist, and I can go anywhere. Well, almost anywhere. But I know I'm fooling myself. Wherever I go, he'll find me and bring me back.

Our small procession enters the castle and continues on to the Great Hall. When we arrive at the far end of the hall, Luca signals a stop.

"Come with me," he says to Gerhard, and they disappear from

the room. A moment later they return, carrying a huge chair between them.

It's the fanciest chair I've ever seen. Each arm and leg is beautifully carved and there are intricate designs on its high back and sides. Four gilded lions serve as its feet.

They set the chair down and lift the stone into a compartment under the seat.

A moment later, familiar footsteps approach. I take a deep breath as Uncle strides into the hall wearing a shirt of mail over a tunic with the colors of the House of Bruce.

Smiling broadly, he walks quickly past us, eyes fixed on the chair.

Except that now it's not only a chair. It's a throne. Uncle's throne.

I expect him to sit, but instead he crouches in front and reaches a hand out until it touches the stone.

Don't scan it! Please don't scan it.

He runs his fingers lightly over the stone, almost in a caress. I can't tear my eyes away. At this moment, it feels like my entire existence hinges on what those fingers will do.

They stop about halfway along the stone.

And linger there.

I'm toast. He's running a scan. I'm sure of it.

Finally, after what seems like forever, Uncle removes his hand, straightens up and turns to face me.

His expression is unreadable.

My life flashes before my eyes. I've had a good run. Expert time snatcher and mediocre driftwood carver, beloved adopted brother to Zach and cherished adopted son to Jim and Diane. HE LEFT THE WORLD WAY TOO SOON, my tombstone will say.

"Exquisite," says Uncle, smiling, and at first I don't believe my ears. He's only saying that to lull me into a state of calm before he unsheathes his sword and proceeds to show the others what happens to someone who dares to try to fool him with a replica.

Instead, he turns to Luca and says, "Do up invitations. Here is what they should say: All trainers and recruits are cordially invited to attend my coronation as King of Timeless Treasures, to take place here in the Great Hall of Doune Castle."

"Yes, Uncle," says Luca. "Is there anything else you want me to put in the invitation?"

"Hmmm," says Uncle, considering. "Yes. Why don't you say no gifts. Or even better, in lieu of gifts, a donation to the Doune Castle Restoration Fund will be gratefully accepted."

"Very well," says Luca. "And the date and time?"

"October 14, 2061, at midnight," says Uncle.

"Okay," says Luca. "Anything else?"

"Yes," says Uncle. "You must stay here and assist me in the preparations for the fulfillment of a lifelong quest: my ascension to the throne. Everyone else may return to their normal duties."

A lifelong quest. The words trigger something in the back of my mind; a wisp of a thought or maybe a memory—but I can't reach it. I sense it's important, but that doesn't help me remember.

"Oh, and, Caleb," says Uncle, "may I have a word with you before you go?"

"Certainly, Uncle."

I feel a pain shoot through the place where my little toe used to be. The game is over. Uncle knows the stone is a fake and he's waiting for everyone else to go before he hands out my punishment. There can be no other explanation.

I fidget nervously, watching as Abbie and the recruits fade and then vanish.

Now it's just me, Uncle and Luca.

"Luca, will you leave us alone for a moment please?" says Uncle. "Caleb and I have some business to discuss."

Yeah—the business of deciding whether to send me to the Barrens straight away or to torture me first. But even as I think it, a slim ray of hope penetrates my gloom. Why send Luca away if I'm about to be punished? Wouldn't Uncle prefer to keep him around to do the dirty work while he watches?

"Caleb, you have done admirably well in your first Historical Correction mission," he says, pacing the floor of the Great Hall.

"Thank you, Uncle."

"Do you know the finest quality a leader can have?"

"No, Uncle," I say.

"It is the ability to recognize his own faults. I will confess to you one of my faults. Once I am convinced of something, I cannot be easily swayed from that notion."

"I see," I say, although I don't really. How is that a fault? But I don't give it much thought. I'm feeling slightly dizzy trying to follow him with my eyes. He's stopped pacing back and forth and is now doing laps around his new throne.

"Lately," Uncle continues, "I have been gathering evidence. At first I was able to shrug it off as anecdotal. But the more I probed and examined, the clearer it became."

He stops in front of the throne, bends down and strokes the stone, which sends a cold chill up my spine.

"I have come to the realization that I acted too hastily in sending my time snatchers out on certain missions. History is not as immutable as I once thought. What I had perceived as pebbles sinking harmlessly to the bottom of a river, causing nary a ripple, have on occasion turned out to be boulders that have set the waters around them churning."

I shift my weight to the back of my heels. I wish he would cut to the chase and tell me what this is all about.

"I have spent some time in my personal library researching historical accounts dating from the very beginnings of Timeless Treasures and found a few anomalies. Do you recall your snatch of the Frederick Blackman umbrella from the Brolly Shoppe in 2006 London?"

"Yes." Operation Bumbershoot—I remember it quite well. I pretended to be the brother of the king of Lower Slobovia, and Abbie was my loyal aide-de-camp.

"Well, when you and Abbie snatched that umbrella, you unwittingly initiated a series of events that culminated in an unfavorable historical result."

"We did?" That surprises me. As far as I could remember, it was a clean snatch.

Uncle nods. "After you completed the snatch and walked off, the shopkeeper left his shop unattended for approximately ninety seconds while he caught up to speak with you."

I think back to the snatch. I can't remember whether the shop owner came after us or not, but I'm willing to go with Uncle on that point.

"During that brief interlude, a man entered the shop and stole an umbrella. One wouldn't think that such an ordinary theft would cause a ripple in the fabric of history. But it did.

"You see, two weeks after your snatch, a prominent British physicist named Damien Toulson was finishing his cup of coffee at the same Kensington coffee shop that he had frequented each Saturday morning for the previous twenty-three years. As he exited the shop, he felt a prickling sensation in his calf. When he looked up, he saw a heavyset gentleman drop his umbrella.

"Upon returning home that evening, Toulson began to feel unwell. Three days later, he died. Although it was never definitively proven, it was suspected that Toulson was assassinated. Can you guess how he died?"

I shake my head. I've got plenty of theories about how I might die, but happily that subject's not on the table right now.

"He died," says Uncle, the corners of his mouth lifting, "from being struck by a poisonous pellet fired from a specially rigged umbrella at close range. The umbrella that fired the deadly shot was the umbrella stolen from the Brolly Shoppe."

I take a moment to digest all of this.

"Caleb, had Toulson survived, he would have invented a device that would have provided the West with a competitive edge in the nuclear rearming race of the 2020s. That is what the historical accounts in my personal library described. Instead, much of the world's attention during that time was spent appeasing rogue nations who threatened this or that with their primitive nuclear capabilities."

"Uncle, are you saying that all of this happened because the shopkeeper left his shop for a couple of minutes to talk to me and Abbie?"

He nods and smiles.

I try hard not to stare at him, but it's not working. If I needed proof that Uncle's gone around the bend, I've certainly got it. Anybody could have stolen that umbrella at any time. If he hadn't done it when Abbie and I were talking to the shopkeeper, the thief would have found another way. Besides, what was so special about that particular umbrella? The thief could have gone to any of a dozen other umbrella shops and stolen another umbrella that he could have rigged just as well. Or he could have used a half dozen other weapons. And apart from all of that, there must have been a million other reasons why the West didn't have the jump on other countries in the race to rearm with nukes. To imply that all of this happened because Abbie and I completed a routine mission is . . . well, it's beyond ridiculous.

"I am considering sending you and Abbie back to 2006. To undo the snatch."

Undo the snatch? Is he nuts? Scratch that last question. I already answered it.

"And there are a couple of other snatches as well, including your mission to 1871 Bridgeport, Connecticut, that may need rectification as well."

Does he mean Operation Fling? The snatch of the world's first Frisbee? I gulp. This is sheer madness. Besides, I've already got my hands full with snatches that need doing, without having to add ones that need undoing.

"That is all for now, Caleb. You may go. I would, however, like to meet with you again this evening to discuss this matter further."

"Yes, Uncle."

I can't wait to get out of here. As I key in the sequence for the Compound, I play the conversation with Uncle over in my mind. The more I think about it, the crazier it all seems. But crazy is the flavor of the week, isn't it? I wonder what Frank thinks of all of this. Does he even know?

I close my eyes and try to quiet my thoughts. Blessedly, the timeleap takes me away.

I arrive back at the Compound to a buzz of activity.

Rows of folding chairs have been set up in the Yard facing a makeshift stage.

Trainers and recruits stream in, quickly filling the seats.

I spot Abbie and our recruits near the back. "What's going on?" I ask, walking up to them. Abbie shrugs and shakes her head.

The fact that Abbie doesn't know makes me especially nervous. She's usually on top of everything happening around here.

We take seats with our recruits between us.

It's amazingly quiet in the Yard. But it's not a comfortable kind of silence. You can cut the tension with a broadsword. Everyone is waiting to see what will happen.

Suddenly the overhead lights flick off and the Yard is plunged into darkness. I sit up straight and force myself to breathe normally.

A moment later, a single beam of light illuminates the stage. It's soon joined by another and another. Someone steps from the shadows and into the spotlights. At first all I see are his shoes; soft and gold in the tradition of the great emperors of China. Then the rest of him comes into view: a dazzling orange and blue *hanfu* decorated with leaping dragons down the front and a jeweled sword tucked beneath his sash.

My eyebrows shoot up when I realize the person standing there is not Uncle.

It's Frank.

Does he know what he has just done? Doesn't he get that Uncle is the king of the hill around here and the only guy who's allowed to dress like an emperor?

As I listen to the applause greeting Frank's arrival onstage, I feel a swirl of emotions. By his actions, he is openly challenging Uncle's authority. But Frank is shrewd. He planned all of this for when he knew Uncle would be away at his castle in Scotland.

He simply stands there, basking in his own magnificence. I sink deeper into my chair.

"Thank you, everyone, for coming to this Gathering of recruits and trainers," says Frank. "Unfortunately, Uncle can't join us this afternoon. There are pressing matters that he must take care of. He has asked me to fill in for him."

Fill in, my foot. Uncle probably has no idea that this is even taking place.

"As you all know," Frank continues, "Uncle's goal in this past year has been to grow Timeless Treasures. That is why there are many more of you here—both recruits and trainers—than ever before. Of course, merely being here does not guarantee your future success. Only the best will make it to the next level."

What's he talking about? What next level? And what happens to the ones he doesn't think are the "best"?

Frank jumps around and paces the small stage as he speaks. Whoever is manning the spotlights is doing an amazing job of following him.

"We will face challenges," Frank says. "But in order to be the best, as Uncle always says, we must meet all challenges head-on. And we will make mistakes along the way, but in order to be great, we must learn from our mistakes and carry on."

The spotlights blink off. Something big is about to happen. I can feel it in my bones.

A moment later, the lights come on again. A young girl has joined Frank on the stage. She looks eight or nine years old.

"This is Priscilla," says Frank. "Priscilla is the Recruit of the Day."

There's a murmur among the audience. She looks so slight and fragile.

"Now, Priscilla," begins Frank gently, and I swear he looks and sounds like a young Uncle, "let's talk a bit about how you came to be selected as Recruit of the Day. First, who's your team leader?"

"You are," she says.

My only surprise is that Frank is still training recruits. I would have thought that was beneath him.

Frank smiles. "And what was your team's assigned snatch today?"

She shifts from foot to foot. "Our mission was to snatch a hat."

"Yes," Frank says. "But it wasn't just any hat, was it?"

She shakes her head.

"Priscilla's team's mission," Frank says, "was to snatch the two-cornered—bicorne—hat famously worn by the great emperor of France, Napoléon Bonaparte, during the battle of Waterloo. A wartime snatch is difficult under any circumstances, but to steal something as personal as a hat from the world's most powerful man is near impossible.

"Why do you think I chose you to perform the actual snatch and not one of the other team members?" Frank asks.

Priscilla shrugs.

"She's so modest." Frank smiles. "I'll tell you why. I picked Priscilla because she's cool under pressure. Did anyone try to stop you from completing the snatch, Priscilla?"

She nods.

"Tell us what happened, please."

"Well," she says, "right after I snatched the hat from Napoléon's desk and substituted a replica, his bodyguard grabbed me, and said '*Je t'ai attrapé!*'—I caught you."

"Really. How rude! And what did you do then?" Frank asks.

"I tried to wriggle free, but I couldn't," Priscilla says.

"Yes. And then?"

"Then he lifted me by my ear and turned me around to face Emperor Napoléon."

"And?"

"The emperor frowned and called me *une petite voleuse*—a little thief. I cried and begged him not to tell my parents. Then I reached under my cloak and handed him the hat."

Frank smiles. "Forgive me, Priscilla, but how is it that the snatch was successful if you had to give back the snatch object?"

"I didn't give him back the snatched hat," she says. "I gave him back a replica."

"A replica? I don't understand," Frank says. "Didn't you already place a replica on the desk when you snatched the original?"

"Yes, I did. But I had two replicas with me."

"Two replicas." Frank nods approvingly. "And whose idea was that?"

"Mine," Priscilla says, smiling.

"Yours," repeats Frank, patting her on the head as if she was a good dog.

Then he turns to the audience and says, "Didn't Priscilla do well?"

There's a smattering of applause.

"Good work, Priscilla," he says. "Congratulations."

"Thank you." Priscilla smiles brightly, turns and begins to head off the stage. But Frank reaches out a hand and places it firmly on her slim shoulder. I shudder, imagining that hand landing on my own shoulder.

"Not yet," he says. "You have one more task to perform. Please wait."

She dutifully stands next to Frank as he turns to a burly trainer I don't recognize and says, in a voice loud enough for us all to hear, "Bring him in."

The trainer disappears behind the curtain, and a moment later he is back, leading a short, pudgy boy recruit onto the stage.

There is a gasp from the crowd. The boy's hands have been tied behind his back.

I switch my ocular implant to full zoom.

"What's your name, recruit?" All of the sunshine is gone from Frank's voice.

"J . . . Jaimini," the boy says.

"Jaimini," Frank repeats, his hand stroking his chin.

"Whose snatch team are you on, Jaimini?"

"I'm on Lydia's team," he answers.

"And what was your snatch?"

"We went to 1789 Virginia to snatch President Thomas Jefferson's waffle iron."

A few people snicker, and if the tension in the room weren't so high, I'd be laughing along with them. But instead, I'm at the edge of my seat waiting to see what will happen next.

"And was the mission successful?" Frank asks.

Jaimini mumbles something under his breath.

"Speak up please, Jaimini. I want everyone to hear your answer. I will ask again: was the mission to snatch the waffle iron a success?"

"No."

The boy's legs are shaking badly, which is no surprise. In fact, I'm amazed that he's still able to stand.

"And why not?" Frank asks.

"I . . . I forgot to snatch it."

Frank turns and paces the length of the stage. The lighting guy is a little slow this time to follow, and for half a second, Frank disappears into shadow before the spotlight finds him again. He lingers near the edge of the stage for a moment before returning to stand beside Jaimini.

The audience has fallen completely silent. I bet they can hear my rapid breathing.

"You forgot," Frank repeats, slowly. Although his voice is soft, each syllable, each word, sounds as if he's whispering in my ear. There is a great weariness in Frank's voice. It's clear he wants us to know that Jaimini has disappointed him.

"Could it be that the reason you forgot was that you were distracted?" asks Frank.

Jaimini nods and says, "Yes."

It's clearly the wrong answer, but what else could he say?

"And what do you suppose you were doing, Jaimini, that made you distracted?"

"I was . . . eating waffles," the boy says in a small voice.

"Louder!" commands Frank.

"I WAS EATING WAFFLES!" screams the boy, and then he collapses on the floor of the stage, a whimpering heap.

"There, there," Frank says, bending down to help him up.

But even as he does this, he nods to the trainer, who disappears again behind the curtain.

My stomach twists in a knot.

The trainer reappears on the stage. He's wheeling a basket the size of a bathtub. It's filled to the brim with something. He angles the basket toward the audience, and I catch a glimpse of its contents.

Waffles. The tub is filled with waffles.

"It must be a bit nerve-racking to be up here in front of everyone," Frank says.

Jaimini says nothing, but his wide eyes tell the story. He is terrified.

"Would you like a waffle to calm your nerves, Jaimini?" Frank asks in a sickly sweet voice.

The boy nods, and the corners of Frank's lips curl upward in a sympathetic smile.

He gestures to Priscilla and she steps forward. "Priscilla, would you be so kind as to give Jaimini a waffle? But I'm afraid you'll have to feed it to him . . . he doesn't have use of his hands right now."

She plucks a waffle from the basket, walks over to Jaimini and feeds it to him, a bit at a time. As soon as he is done, Frank asks, "Would you like another?"

Jaimini shakes his head, but Frank ignores him and instructs Priscilla to bring another waffle.

She hesitates, looking from Frank to Jaimini and then back again to Frank.

"Go ahead. It's okay," Frank says, smiling.

A shudder goes through my body.

As before, Priscilla places the waffle close to Jaimini's mouth, feeding him pieces.

But no sooner does she finish feeding him than Frank points to the basket of waffles and instructs, "Give him another."

Priscilla's hand shakes as she takes another waffle, tears it into pieces and begins feeding them to Jaimini.

"Not like that," Frank says. "Here, let me show you." He reaches into the basket, grabs a waffle and stuffs the whole thing into Jaimini's mouth. The boy makes a motion to spit it out, but Frank is quicker. He clamps Jaimini's mouth closed.

"EAT IT!" he roars.

Jaimini's jaws are working furiously, chewing the waffle. Tears are streaming down his cheeks, and his face is turning red. But even before he is able to finish the waffle in his mouth, Frank is shoving another in, commanding Jaimini to chew.

I can't watch anymore. But try as I might, I can't tear my eyes away either.

Frank releases his hand just long enough for Jaimini to spit out a mess of half-chewed waffle. The boy is making great rasping sounds.

"Still hungry?" Frank asks.

The boy shakes his head furiously.

"No, I suppose you're not," Frank says. "Take him away . . . and then send him away."

Two trainers appear on the stage and drag Jaimini away. Priscilla follows, and Frank is left alone on the stage.

"This is training camp, not summer camp," Frank says to the audience. "And, like I said, only the best are going to make it. My advice to you is—be the best."

The curtains close.

I sit there stunned, unable to move. I have a vague awareness of people around me starting to get up and head for the exit.

Get up and leave with everyone else, a voice in my brain urges.

But I'm not listening. Only feeling. And the overwhelming feeling I have right now is anger, anger at Frank for thinking he can do anything to anyone he wants, including new recruits whose only "faults" are acting like the children they are. If I ever said that Frank is just a younger version of Uncle, I take it back. Uncle would never be this cruel to young kids.

The rage boiling inside me is transforming, morphing into something cold and hard. When I finally do stand, the only thing I feel is numbness. Numbness and a strong resolve to do one thing.

I have to save the recruits.

October 7, 2061, 7:43 P.M.
The Compound,
SoHo, New Beijing (formerly New York City)

I have a snatch for your group to do tonight," Frank says, catching me as I leave the dining room after supper. For a moment I think he must be kidding. There was only one mission scheduled for today. Besides, it's been a really long day and we're all way beyond tired.

And that's not even including my other worries. I'm far from being completely over my time fog, and if I spend more time in the past right now, it's bound to get worse.

I also badly need to speak with Abbie about what happened on Operation Coronation. There were too many things that went wrong for it to be a series of unfortunate coincidences. The only explanation is that we were deliberately fed the wrong intel for the mission. It must have been Frank.

But I have to be careful in how I answer him now. His little show of power a few minutes ago wasn't only for the recruits. It was for my benefit too.

"That may be difficult, Frank. Abbie and I need to debrief the recruits on Operation Coronation. Plus Uncle wants to meet with me this evening."

"You can do the debriefing tomorrow," he says. "As far as your meeting with Uncle is concerned, I've spoken with him, and he has agreed to reschedule it to another day."

As he says this, he looks me straight in the eye. But I don't believe him. There's no way he could have spoken with Uncle about our meeting. When would he have had the chance?

"The data for the next mission is being uploaded to your mind-patches as we speak. You are to leave here within ten minutes."

Is he crazy? Ten minutes is barely enough time to go to the bathroom, let alone gather up the recruits. Plus, Uncle would never force us to do an evening snatch the same day as a major mission, especially with new recruits. But Frank is not Uncle.

I glare at him, which is probably as bad as talking back, but I can't help myself.

"Do you think you're a big important guy now, Caleb? Just because Uncle appointed you as head of his new division?"

He's baiting me. I keep my mouth shut.

"Well, let me be the first to bring you back down to earth," he says. "You're nothing. Uncle should never have brought you back. You know what they do to deserters in the army? They shoot them."

I look away for a moment. An empty threat, that's all. He would never carry it out. But even as I think it, I hear Abbie's voice in my head pleading with me to be careful.

"And don't think for a minute," continues Frank, "that you are the only one Uncle is confessing to about his regrets on past snatches and how they may have affected history. I know all about that too. You needn't concern yourself. I'm handling it."

I don't dare say anything to contradict him. Much as I don't like it, there's no question that Frank holds the power around here. And as his little demonstration with Jaimini showed, he's not afraid to use it in brutal ways.

"All right," I say. "What's the snatch?"

"Luca will brief you. He's in the Viewing Room. And Caleb,"

Frank says as he walks away, "the snatch may be a bit tricky . . . so I suggest you go in first."

I was surprised to hear Frank say that Luca was here. I thought he was with Uncle in Scotland getting things ready for the big event. Frank must have pulled him back.

The big man is sitting behind a desk when I knock and enter. A hologram of the Great Hall in Uncle's castle hovers above the desk. When he sees me he flicks off the holo.

"What do you want?" he asks.

"Frank sent me. My team has a snatch to do tonight. You're supposed to brief me."

He looks at me for a moment as though he has no idea what I'm talking about. Then I see a flicker of recognition in his eyes. "Yes, you are to snatch a vial from the tomb of Qín Shǐ Huáng, the first Emperor of China."

I stare at him blankly.

"You've heard of the Fountain of Youth?" Luca says.

"Of course," I say. "It's a myth. It doesn't exist."

"No myth," he says. "It's real." Then he looks down at his handheld and reads, "Two thousand years ago, Emperor Qín Shǐ Huáng discovered the secret to eternal life; a vial containing the potion is buried with him at his tomb near Xian, China. The tomb was first discovered in 1974 by Chinese farmers digging a well. You and your team will timeleap to 1974 right after the entrance to the tomb was found.

"One more thing you should know," says Luca, "is that the Emperor buried an army with him so that he could have a second kingdom in the afterlife. To get to his tomb, your team will need to first navigate through large burial rooms containing an army of warriors made from clay."

A clay army? This guy was even more fruitcakes than Uncle.

"Is that all?" I say.

Luca nods, turns his back to me and flicks the holo of the Great Hall back on.

But my feet aren't moving. "Are you sure that there isn't anything else we should know about the mission?"

Luca spins around to face me. There's an angry expression on his face. "I already told you everything you need to know." He practically spits the words.

"Yeah, well that's what you also said on the last mission," I say. "But when we got there, we found out the intel was all wrong."

I can't believe I said that. If he goes back to Frank with this, I'll probably be in for some major punishment for challenging Luca's authority.

Luca stands up from his chair and rises to his full height, which is a good foot taller than me. He narrows his eyes to slits and looks down at me. "Be happy I told you as much as I did."

"Uncle would never send new recruits into an unknown situation," I fire back.

Then, surprisingly, he begins to laugh. His laughter fills the entire room.

It's not a happy kind of laughter. It's bitter and cruel and meant to make me feel small.

As I leave the Viewing Room, my entire body is shaking. I wait until the trembling slows before mindpatching Abbie to tell her to get everyone ready.

March 30, 1974, 5:43 P.M.
Near Xian, China

Total darkness. The air is cold, and there's a smell of dampness all around. We're at the bottom of the well dug by the Chinese farmers. A rough wood board covers the entrance to the tomb.

"From here on in, everyone stays quiet," I mindpatch the others. "And no one moves until I say it's safe."

I remove the board, step into the tunnel and walk about ten yards before arriving at the real entrance to the tomb.

Adjusting my ocular implant, I have my translator read the runes on the entranceway: *Swift death will visit those who despoil the tomb of Emperor Qín Shǐ Huáng.*

I take a deep breath to calm myself. The last thing I need is to end up on the wrong end of an ancient Chinese curse. But there's no getting around it, as far as I can see. Despoiling is exactly what we've come here to do.

I run my hands lightly over an area of packed earth next to the runes. Just as I suspected: booby-trapped. It's a simple mechanism. The first person to pass through the entrance will be impaled with a spear. It's possible of course that after more than two thousand years of sitting idle, it won't work, but I wouldn't bet my life on it. After all, the sixty-year-old HiSense television set in the lounge at Headquarters still works perfectly, which is proof enough for me that the Chinese are good at making stuff that lasts.

"We'll have to do a short leap to get inside," I say to the others. "The entrance is booby-trapped."

I program my wristpatch, and we all join up. "On three," I say. "One, two—"

"Wait," Judith says.

"What?" I say. It comes out a little rougher than I intended, but I can't help it. It's been a long day.

"What if there's an earthquake while we're inside—won't we be buried alive?" she asks.

"Yes," I say without missing a beat. "And that's why we have to do the snatch quickly."

Before anyone else has the chance to object, I tap my wrist twice.

We land in a room roughly the size of the Yard at the Compound. The rounded walls have been hewn from the rock and the ceiling is very high. There is a dank, unpleasant smell in the air.

"This is one of the halls leading to the antechamber to the Emperor's burial tomb," I say. "The snatch object is buried with the Emperor in the crypt that lies beyond the antechamber. Before we continue, I want to remind everyone of the rules. No touching anything. We all stay together, and if something happens, follow my or Abbie's directions precisely. Now, everyone stay behind me."

I lead the recruits through the hall. Abbie takes up the rear. Except for our breathing and the thud of our feet on the hard ground, there is total silence. Something about the quiet is unsettling. The air feels heavy and, well, evil. I never thought I'd say this, but I'd almost welcome one of Razor's interruptions right about now. Maybe I've been watching too many zombie holo-flicks, but it feels like the crypt is waiting for us. Waiting until it has us all in its clutches before sealing us in here forever.

As I approach the antechamber, I'm rocked by a wave of dizziness.

I silently curse Frank for sending us on this mission when I'm still not over my time fog. How am I supposed to lead the recruits when I can barely function myself?

I wait until it passes and then duck my head to enter the ante-chamber. When I look up, I stop dead in my tracks. Abbie has switched her beam to wide view. And the view is astonishing. We are in a room the size of Yankee Stadium, filled to capacity with row upon row of life-sized sculpted clay warriors, some with weapons, some without, even some leading clay horses. Luca wasn't kidding when he said there's an army of them. There must be thousands of figures here!

As I make my way down one of the rows, I notice something even more incredible: no two warriors look alike. Each of their faces is different—as different as the faces of real people.

A scream rips though the air, echoing off the stone walls of the chamber.

"Everyone down!" I yell.

A moaning sound. But from where?

The beam from Abbie's light bounces off the surrounding clay figures. I switch my night vision to max.

There is the moaning sound again. I glance ahead and see a figure slumped on the ground. It's Judith!

I rush over to her.

"I should have . . . waited for you, but . . . the horse was so beautiful," she says, her voice weak. The shaft of an arrow is embedded in her left shoulder. I bite my lip. If the arrow had hit a few more inches over . . . I don't want to think about that.

"How . . . ," I begin to say, but before I'm finished, I know the answer.

Ten feet away, affixed to the carved side of a terra-cotta chariot, is a spent crossbow. It must have been rigged to fire when someone stepped into range.

"Stay with her," I shout to Abbie, and make my way to the crossbow.

It's a simple setup. The weapon fires automatically when a thin wire has been tripped, which Judith must have done, unawares. But as I look closer, I notice something that sets my teeth on edge. The firing mechanism is made from titanium. There's no question. It has been tampered with recently.

I run back to Abbie and Judith.

"I've got to get her to a hospital," Abbie says. "You take the others back. I'm taking her to New York Presbyterian."

I nod and signal to Gerhard, Dmitri and Razor.

"We're aborting the mission," I tell them.

Blessedly, no one says anything. Not even Razor. When I reach out my hands to take Dmitri's and Razor's, they feel cold.

A single word echoes through my brain as I punch out the sequence on my wrist.

Escape.

October 7, 2061, 9:18 P.M.
Central Park
New Beijing (formerly New York City)

How's Judith?" I ask as soon as Abbie steps from the path.

"She's hurting but she's going to be okay," she says, taking my hand and squeezing it. "They took out the arrow, patched her up and gave me some pills to give her for when the pain gets really bad. The doctor said she was really lucky . . . it could have been a lot worse."

"Where is she now?" I ask.

"I took her back to the Compound," Abbie says. "When they started asking a lot of questions, I knew it was time to go."

I nod and look through the trees to the monastery. No one is about in the garden. The monks are probably doing their evening meditations . . . finding their center of calm. I wish I could find my center of calm, but all I can feel now is anger. Anger at Frank for sending us on the Xian mission and anger at myself for not refusing to go.

"Abbie, Frank rigged the crossbow to fire at the first one to enter the tomb," I say.

"How do you know?"

"The firing mechanism was new—made from titanium. My guess is he either did it himself or had Luca install it for him."

Abbie's silent for a moment and then says, "I was afraid of this happening."

"What do you mean?"

"At lunch, I heard a couple of the other trainers talking. What they were saying sounded so wild that I thought they were joking. But now I don't think so."

"What were they saying?" I ask.

"That not all of their recruits returned with them from training missions."

I stare at her. "You mean, some of them got caught?"

"Not caught. Left behind. On Frank's orders."

I take a moment to let Abbie's words sink in.

"He's culling the recruits, Cale. Eliminating the ones he thinks aren't the best."

It all adds up. The Gathering and the crossbow attack are more proof. But it's not only the recruits he wants to get rid of. That crossbow arrow had my name on it. Frank wanted me to lead the recruits into the tomb.

"There's only one thing to do," I say, switching to mindpatch. "A mass escape from the Compound . . . all of the recruits."

"How?" she says. "We can't timeleap with them because their wristbands are tracked. If they leave outside of a planned mission, the bands will automatically bring them back here."

I had done some thinking on this after my meeting with Frank. "We have to get them out without using technology first—over the roof," I say. "The doors and the fire escape are heavily monitored and alarmed. But there's only one holo-video feed for the roof. We kick it out and then take everyone across the roof to the next building and down the fire escape."

"And then what?"

"Then we take them to the Buddhist temple," I say. "It's just a block away from the Compound. At a dead run, we could probably make it there in three minutes."

"What can we do from there?"

"We shuttle them home—to their real homes—using the time pod."

"But that's going to take forever," Abbie says. "The pod only fits three people. And the longer it takes, the more chance Frank or Uncle has of finding our hiding place."

"I think we can squeeze in four kids," I say. "I know it's not foolproof. But I bet Dmitri can turn off the tracking for the pod. Every other way will be harder." I shudder to think how much work it would be for him to turn off the tracking for forty-five wristbands, that is, if he could even do it without Uncle or Frank finding out.

She looks at me and nods.

"And another thing," I say, "we don't tell the recruits about the plan until the very last minute."

"But then how will we know if they'll agree to go?" she asks.

"We'll know because one of their own is going to convince them."

"Who?"

"That's what we have to decide," I say. "The only way for the plan to work is if we have one of the recruits in on it. Someone all the other recruits look up to and trust."

"Who do you think?" Abbie asks.

"Razor," I say.

"No way. She's unpredictable. She's only out for herself."

"That may be changing," I say, thinking back to the talk Razor and I had right after returning from Operation Coronation.

Abbie crosses her arms over her chest and says nothing. I know what she's thinking. It's far from the perfect plan. But right now it's the only one we have.

"We'll also need to knock out Uncle's systems the moment we're done," I say.

"No," says Abbie. "You're not seriously thinking of—"

"Why not? Dmitri will love the challenge. You've got to admit that he's brilliant when it comes to technology."

"You realize that if we involve Razor and Dmitri," Abbie says, "we'll be putting their lives in even more danger."

She's right. It's a tough decision to make. "We can't do this alone, Abbie. It's too big."

"Also, we're going to need Phoebe," I say. "The information requirement is huge. We'll need intel on the home times/places for all recruits. And then we'll need to erase all the records. The only way she'll do it is if we offer to take her with us."

"Okay," Abbie says. "But Phoebe can't keep a secret. Once she knows, it won't be long before Uncle or Frank finds out."

"That's why we have to act quickly."

"How quickly?" Abbie asks.

"Six days. The day before Uncle's coronation."

I look her straight in the eye, and she returns my gaze. I haven't said the words, not even over her mindpatch. But there's no need to. We both know what must happen.

We have to make sure that Uncle and Frank can't start over again.

We spend the next hour doing prep work for the escape, which we've code-named Operation Exodus. Abbie heads to the Compound to brief Dmitri and Razor and to get Dmitri started on figuring out how to extricate Phoebe from the net. I go off in search of materials for the rope bridge that we'll need to escape via the roof.

When I've got everything, I make my way to SoHo and stash the stuff out of sight behind a Dumpster in the alley. Someone has spray painted THE END OF THE WORLD IS NIGH in big black letters on the brick wall. I wonder when "nigh" is. If it's more than a week from now, I'm good with that. By then, if the escape succeeds, all of the recruits should be safe at home with their families. But if we're talking tonight, that's a totally different story.

And judging from the weather right now, tonight looks like a definite possibility. The sky is pitch-black, and a chill wind is whistling into the alley. There's a feeling of impending doom in the air.

I try to shake off the bad vibes and head into the Compound. As soon as I enter, the overhead screen darkens. A single bolt of lightning flashes across the screen, coalescing into the words, "Go away. I'm not talking to you."

"Phoebe, have you seen Abbie?" I say, ignoring her little jibe.

The screen changes again. This time the image is of a hand with perfectly manicured and polished fingernails. I watch as first the thumb and then three of the fingers curl in toward the palm, leaving only the middle finger extended.

"That's rude," I say.

"Not half as rude as what you have in store for me," Phoebe says.

"What are you talking about?"

The hand giving me the finger fades, and in its place is Phoebe's grandmother figure, lying inside a coffin. She peers over her half glasses and says, "Don't play the innocent with me, O Caleb the Betrayer. I know what you and Abbie are planning. How could you?"

"How could I what?"

"How could you leave me here while you escape with all the others? Do I mean so little to you?" Big tears roll down her face and drop off her cheek, staining the satin cushions inside the coffin.

How did she find out? But then again, this is Phoebe we're talking about. She has her ways. I was going to tell her . . . only not this soon.

She sits up in her coffin and glares at me. "Make it happen, buster, or I'm telling."

I stay silent for a moment as if I'm considering her threat. "Okay, Phoebe, you can come," I say finally.

The screen changes again. The coffin has been replaced with a field of daisies. Grandma Phoebe picks one and turns to face me, all smiles.

"You're a good boy, Caleb. Now you had better hurry and go see Abbie. She's been looking everywhere for you."

Darn.

"Where is she?"

Grandma Phoebe methodically plucks the petals from the flower.

"Try the courtyard."

"Thanks . . . and, Phoebe?"

"Yes, my darling boy?"

"Of course you haven't talked to anyone else about this, correct?" I say.

"Of course not," she says. "What do you think I am? A blabber-mouth?"

I'll take the Fifth on that one.

As I hurry to the courtyard, Phoebe shouts, "I'm making my packing list!"

Abbie is sitting against the brick wall, gazing up at the sky.

"We have to call off the escape," she mindpatches me without looking my way.

"What?" I can't believe what I'm hearing.

"Frank knows about the plan," she says.

"How do you know?" I sit down next to her.

She glares at me. "It's obvious from the way he spoke to me. And he gave me a weird smile."

"Isn't that what he always does?"

"Trust me. Maybe he doesn't know exactly what we're planning, but he suspects something. All I did was get Razor and Dmitri on board but he knows something's up. He's called off all snatches for tomorrow—I think he wants to keep a close eye on everyone."

"Phoebe knows, too—she must have seen Dmitri working on things," I say. "And if she knows, that means soon enough the whole place will know."

We both sit quietly for a moment and stare up at the sky. I didn't think it could get any darker than it already was, but I guess I was wrong.

"We have to change the date," I say.

"Impossible," Abbie says. "If we make it any later, we may not get a chance. There's a rumor floating around that Uncle wants to move all of us to Scotland."

"I'm not thinking of later, Abbie. I'm saying we go earlier."

Abbie looks at me for a moment. "You're right. And I can think of another reason to leave earlier."

"What is that?"

"Do you remember the poem you heard that puppet say during Operation Gravity?"

"Yes."

"Well, a few things bothered me about it. So I did some research. There was a real Mother Shipton, who was born in 1488 and wrote some prophecies that were later published. But most of the verses you recited weren't written by her. They were written much later, in 1862, by a guy named Charles Hindley. There's no way those lines could have been spoken by a puppeteer in 1666, unless . . ."

"Unless the puppeteer was a time traveler," I finish.

"That's right," says Abbie. "And remember this part:

"A lifelong quest, an ancient stone—
The wrongful heir upon the throne.
Death and suffering line the path.
None will be spared the master's wrath."

"Yes," I say. I had thought about those lines too and was sure now that they referred to the Stone of Destiny and that the master is Uncle.

"Those words weren't written by Mother Shipton either," she says. "Or by Charles Hindley. Someone was trying to send us a message . . . to warn us. At first I thought the phrase 'the wrongful heir upon the throne' meant Uncle's coronation. But now I'm convinced it's referring to something else entirely."

"To what?" I ask.

"To the coup Frank has been planning . . . to seize control of Timeless Treasures from Uncle," she says.

I shudder. Abbie could be right. And if it's true, we've got to get the recruits out before that happens.

"Cale, Frank has called another Gathering for the day after tomorrow. I think he's going to announce that he's taking over."

"That settles it then," I say, locking my eyes on hers. "We leave tomorrow night."

October 7, 2061, 10:52 P.M.
The Compound
SoHo, New Beijing (formerly New York City)

A downpour begins as we enter the Compound, but it's completely quiet inside. The heavy, ominous kind. The kind that always comes before something miserable happens. I've got a bad feeling about the escape. All I can think of is what can go wrong—Phoebe ratting us out, Uncle finding out, Frank finding out, and here's another good one: the recruits not wanting to go anywhere. On top of everything, there must be a hole in my shoe, because my left sock is drenched.

Abbie and I enter the Yard from different doors. It was her idea that whenever we want to meet with Razor and Dmitri about Operation Exodus, we do it in as public a place as possible. With all the mindspeak going back and forth, it would be tough for Uncle or Frank to isolate our conversation.

All of the recruits are out on the floor. Dmitri is sitting in a corner gazing up at the ceiling. Razor is on the other side of the Yard, talking to a couple of younger recruits.

If anyone took a picture of the Yard right now, it wouldn't look like Abbie and I were convening a meeting with Razor and Dmitri. But that is exactly what is happening.

I casually walk by Razor and run my fingers through my hair, giving her the signal to switch to mindpatch. On the opposite side of the Yard, Abbie is doing the same with Dmitri.

"Can everyone hear me?" I mindspeak.

"Yo," says Razor.

"I'm here too," says Abbie.

"Dmitri?" I say.

No answer.

"Abbie, did you give him the signal?" I ask.

"Twice."

"Lemme go over there," says Razor. "I'll smack him on the side of the head."

"No, I'll go," I say.

I cross over to where Dmitri is huddled in the corner. He has something in his hands, but I can't see what it is.

"Hi, Dmitri," I say.

"Hello," he answers, without looking up.

"It's sunny in San Diego," I say, repeating the code phrase that means we're having a meeting.

He continues fiddling with a small handheld device. After a few seconds, he says, "It's not my birthday."

"What did you say?"

Then he looks up at me and says, "I wasn't talking to you."

He looks down again at the device. Now I can see the screen. Black and white squares.

"Where did you get that?" I say.

"I didn't get it. I made it," Dmitri says, then raises a hand, signaling me to stop talking.

The next second, his eyes light up and he moves his finger across the screen.

"Got you," he says. "Checkmate."

The lights in the Yard dim and go out for three seconds before coming back on.

Dmitri laughs. "Phoebe doesn't like losing," he says, smiling.

"Dmitri, switch to mindpatch, will you? Abbie and Razor are already on."

He looks up again, still smiling, and says, "Okay."

I walk back to the other end of the Yard.

"Halloween is early this year," I say, using the code words we agreed on to change the date of the mission.

"How early?" Razor asks.

"The ghouls will be out tomorrow night," Abbie says.

"We can't," Razor says.

"Why not?"

"Santa's coming to town . . . and he's bringing Rudolph," she says. Santa is the code name for Uncle, and Rudolph is Frank.

That's bad luck. But we've got no choice. We have to go tomorrow night. There are too many things that could go wrong if we delay any longer.

"We can't do anything about that, Razor," Abbie says. "Spread the word to all the elves."

"Dmitri, you have to make sure that Phoebe's costume for the party is ready on time," I say.

"What party?" Dmitri asks.

If I wasn't rescuing him, I'd want to strangle him. He's supposed to have memorized all of the code.

"You sure are dim, Dim," says Razor.

"Thank you, Razor, but I'll handle this," I say. "Dmitri, we've invited Phoebe to join us for our Halloween celebration. All of the recruits will be there as well. You understand what I'm talking about now, don't you?"

He shakes his head.

"Dmitri," I mindshout, "you have to extricate Phoebe from the net by tomorrow night so that she can escape with us!"

"You don't have to yell," Dmitri says.

"Yes he does," Razor says. " 'Cause you're dimmer than dim sum at midnight."

"That is illogical," Dmitri says. "Dim sum is something you eat. It cannot grow dim or bright."

"Meeting's over," I say, heading for the courtyard.

"Those two don't exactly inspire confidence," I say when Abbie joins me outside.

"Look on the bright side," she says. "As soon as you rescue them, you won't have to deal with them anymore."

I laugh and some of the tension melts away. "Abbie?"

She looks over at me. "Yes?"

"I'm glad you're with me."

"It's the only place I want to be," she says, leaning in and giving me a kiss.

The Buddhist temple on Lafayette Street is an impressive building with a sloping red tile roof and twin stone lions guarding the entrance. As I step inside, a man dressed in a brown robe walks up to greet me.

"Good day, I am Brother Chen. May I help you?"

Sure. I'm looking for a place to stash a time pod and forty-five time-traveling recruits. Instead I say, "Hi. I live around here, and I've always admired your temple from the outside and was curious to see the inside. Is it okay if I take a look around?"

"Certainly," he says, giving a little bow. "If you have any questions, I am available. The other monks are sworn to silence, so they will not speak with you."

I wonder if they can teach that trick to Razor.

I walk around to get the feel of the place. There's a nice open area in front of a short flight of steps leading to a throne-type chair. It looks like a perfect spot to land the time pod.

Brother Chen follows me everywhere. Maybe he thinks I'm going to steal something, which normally would be true. But not today. This is strictly a reconnaissance mission.

"Do you see that sculpture there?" he says, pointing. "It is of Qín Shǐ Huáng, the first emperor of China."

"Yes," I say, remembering the aborted mission. "I understand that he was buried with a great army to accompany him to the afterlife."

Brother Chen's eyes sparkle. "Excellent. Then you may also know of his reputation as solver of disputes."

I shake my head.

"No?" Brother Chen says. "Well, please permit me to tell you a true story. When the Great Wall of China was erected, there was a great dispute between the two factions who were hired to build it. One group wanted to start the wall from the west and the other from the east."

"How did Emperor Qín solve it?" I ask.

"He didn't," Brother Chen says. "He let them each go a different way. Confident that in the end they would meet."

"And did they? Meet, that is?"

"No. It took another group of builders three hundred more years to join the mismatched ends."

A great story. But if there's a moral to it, I'm missing it entirely.

"Brother Chen, I'd like to make a small contribution to the temple," I say.

"That is kind. But you need not," he replies.

"No, I insist," I say. I hand him a ten-dollar bill. It's not much, but it's all I have on me.

He smiles and gives a low bow.

"What did you think of the temple?" Abbie asks when I catch up with her in the Compound courtyard.

"I think I should go there more often. I could use some spirituality in my life," I say.

"Seriously, Cale."

"Seriously, there's a good open space to land the time pod in the main sanctuary."

"What about security?" she asks.

"Doable. They've got a third-gen Halex on the front but only a first-gen on the rear entrance. The back is our best access point."

"What about the monks?"

"They sleep in a separate building out back."

"It sounds like it will work," Abbie says. "But you're looking nervous. What's the matter?"

"I don't know," I say. "I can't put my finger on it. I know this sounds crazy, but it's almost like it's too easy."

"You're being paranoid," she says. "Relax."

Abbie's probably right. I should just relax. Try telling that to the knot in my stomach, though. Now that we're so close to launching Operation Exodus, it seems to tighten with every passing minute.

"There will be a Gathering in ten minutes," announces Luca over my mindpatch. "Please tell any trainers you see who have not received this message."

My mouth goes dry. It can't be! The next Gathering was supposed to be tomorrow, not tonight.

"Are you sure you don't have the times mixed up?" I say, trying to sound normal.

"There's no mix-up," says Luca. "Pass the word around."

I shudder. Another Gathering means Frank is going to punish another recruit. And he's probably calling it on such short notice because he knows that Uncle won't be around.

I've got to talk to Abbie. But there's no time to do anything other than to go to the Yard.

The stage has already been set up by the time I arrive. Recruits and trainers are filing in, taking their seats. Whispers and nervous laughter mix with the sound of chairs scraping the floor. I spot Dmitri near the front and take a seat next to him. Lydia is hovering near the stage talking to a trainer I don't recognize. Frank jumps onto the stage and then quickly off again.

In moments, every seat is taken. I crane my neck looking for Abbie and Razor but can't spot them.

Ten goons I've never seen before have set themselves up at two-foot intervals in front of the stage. I frown. These guys aren't here to take customer appreciation surveys. They are being posted around the stage to ward off any trouble.

The lights dim and then go off. All chatter dies. The darkness is total.

Five seconds pass. Ten. No one dares say a thing.

And then a single spotlight illuminates Frank standing on the stage. He is wearing a forest green *hanfu* with a gold dragon design that looks familiar to me. A sword tucked under his sash gleams when the spotlight hits it. I gasp when my brain makes the connection. That *hanfu* belongs to Uncle!

"Good evening, everyone," Frank's voice booms. "Sorry for the short notice of this Gathering. But it couldn't be helped."

He pauses and then continues, "All of us here at Timeless Treasures have a job to do and a role to play in this organization. This is true even for our newest recruits. We can all be proud of our achievements and rest assured that Uncle and I value all contributions, from those of the greenest recruits to the most senior time snatcher."

Right. So if you value the recruits' contributions so much, why are you leaving some of them to rot in the past?

Frank clears his throat and looks out over the crowd. "Now for the Recruit of the Day honors. As many of you know, certain snatches are more difficult than others. The degree of difficulty depends on a number of factors, including the presence of other persons at or near the snatch zone and complications arising from the physical environment. I am pleased to say that today's top-performing recruit managed with style and grace to overcome all of these factors and more.

"It is with utmost pleasure that I introduce you all to the Recruit of the Day, Renaldo."

Polite applause. A tall, gangly boy steps forward. I recognize him as one of the recruits on Lydia's team.

Frank waits for the applause to die down and then says, "Renaldo, why don't you show us the object you snatched today."

He steps forward, opens a small case and pulls from it a pair of wire-rimmed glasses that he holds up high. "Mahatma Gandhi's eyeglasses. From one of his walkabouts."

A murmur goes through the crowd. I have to admit it's an impressive snatch for a recruit. But I suspect that he had more than a little help from Lydia.

"Thank you, Renaldo," says Frank. "You may stand to the side."

Frank saunters across the stage, hands clasped behind his back. With his every stride, I can feel the tension in the room go up another notch.

He stops and turns to face the audience. "Lately, there have been rumblings of discontent among the ranks of our recruits. Uncle has asked that I convey to you his and my feelings on this serious matter. We will not tolerate the spreading of vile rumors. Nor will we tolerate anyone's attempts to fill the heads of our recruits with lies. And finally, we will not put up with any person who challenges our authority."

He turns to his left and says to someone offstage, "Bring her."

I grip the side of my chair. Two of Frank's goons walk onto the stage. They are dragging a recruit between them. At first I can't see who it is but then the goons move slightly.

It's Razor!

The goons stop two feet short of where Frank stands and push Razor forward. She falls on her knees. Her hands are bound in front of her.

"This," Frank says, "is Razor. She is one of Caleb and Abbie's recruits."

I glance at Dmitri. He's staring at the stage, his mouth set in a thin line.

Frank turns and looks at Razor. "I've been following your participation in your group, recruit, for some time now. And I must say that I'm not impressed. You are unreliable, easily distracted and unable to focus properly on the snatches. Not only do you not have the proper respect for authority, but you have also been poisoning others with your disrespectful talk. You have also purposely destroyed snatch items, including most recently an apple snatched on a mission to 1666 England."

A terrible rage is building inside me. My fingernails bite into the soft flesh of my palms.

Razor doesn't say a word. I adjust my ocular implant to high zoom. Her eyes look glazed over. I'll bet anything that Frank drugged her before bringing her out.

"One of Uncle's favorite sayings," continues Frank, turning to the crowd, "is 'a single worm can destroy an apple.' It is clear that we must take action. But what sort of action?"

He takes a step in Razor's direction. "What shall we do with you, little worm? Shall we grind you under the heels of our shoes? Or shall we flick you far away, where you will never trouble us again?"

He walks away from her, draws his sword, lifts it high in the air

245

and addresses the crowd. "Shall it be death by sword? Or will it be banishment to the Barrens? You decide."

Frank leans toward the crowd, cupping his ear. "I can't hear your decision."

Someone shouts, "Death by sword!" I whip my head around but can't tell who it was. But his shout ignites a chorus of others. Some of the new trainers shout "death." Others are yelling "Barrens."

The shouting gets louder. I want to rush up to the stage, grab Razor and take her away from all of this madness. But with Frank's goons ringing the stage there's no way I would even get close.

The crowd is in a frenzy. Screams of "death" and "Barrens" have reached a fevered pitch.

Everyone is standing, straining to see what will happen next.

I look over at Dmitri. He has a fierce look in his eyes.

Frank raises a hand. The shouting stops abruptly, and it's deathly quiet.

"Thank you," he says. "It appears you have made your decision."

He turns to Razor. "Stand, recruit."

She gets up slowly. Her head stays bowed.

"You are very lucky that I have given you this chance to be an example to everyone," he says. "Don't you agree?"

Frank pauses for a moment, waiting. But Razor doesn't react, just continues to look at the floor.

"ANSWER WHEN YOU ARE BEING ADDRESSED!" Frank bellows.

His eruption is so sudden and intense that I let out a strangled cry.

"Yes," says Razor. But her voice is so soft, so weak, that I hardly recognize it.

The crowd is hushed now. Beside me, Dmitri is reciting numbers under his breath and punching away at his handheld. What is he doing?

Frank sheathes his sword, motions for Renaldo to step forward and says, "I will give you the honor."

Renaldo steps up to Razor and reaches for her wristband.

Dmitri has stopped reciting numbers and is now spouting out something about linear momentum and scalar bosons, but I only half hear him. My attention is riveted on the drama playing out on the stage.

The next moment, Renaldo taps Razor's wristband. Out of the corner of my eye, I see Dmitri angle his handheld toward the stage.

I gasp.

Razor's body shimmers, fades and is gone.

She's been banished to the Barrens.

October 8, 2061, 11:45 P.M.

The Compound

SoHo, New Beijing (formerly New York City)

I'm sitting at the end of the dock. It's a beautiful summer's day. I stretch and run my fingers along the sun-warmed wood grain.

"Jump in, Caleb, the water's warm!" shouts Zach.

I smile at him. "In a minute."

Jim and Diane sit nearby, reading paperback novels. Diane laughs at something and wriggles her toes in the air.

I close my eyes and take a deep breath in, wanting to hold on to this moment forever.

When I open them, all is silent. But immediately I sense something is wrong.

"Zach?"

He doesn't answer. The water near the dock is still.

I spring to my feet and glance all around. Where is he?

Panic grips me. I dive into the water. The shock of the cold stings.

Deep as I can go into the dark, murky water. A shape below me. It doesn't belong to this place. Lungs bursting. But I head deeper, toward the shape.

Stroking harder now, I close the gap. Almost close enough to see.

The shape is a face.

I don't want to look. But I have to.

I can't. Need to go back up now. Or I won't make it.

No. I need to see.

But it's turned away from me.

I reach out, grab it and turn it toward me.

It's my face. And it's dead.

No!

Stroking hard now. Up and up. No more air.

Something is blocking me. My fists pound at the underside of the dock.

No strength. I'm not going to make it. Tap. Tap. Tap.

"Cale, Wake up! It's time."

It was a dream, that's all. But the part that isn't a dream, the part where Razor vanishes at the Gathering, was very real and comes crashing back to me. No! I can't think about that now. Because if I do, the sadness and the anger and the guilt will swallow me up, and I'll never be the same. I will be nothing. I push the thoughts deep down inside me and force myself to focus on what I need to do.

In the darkness, I can't quite make out shapes in the other beds, but their even breathing tells me that they are still asleep.

Quietly, I open the door and step out into the hall where Abbie is waiting. She is dressed all in black.

We move quickly and silently down the hall to the main stairwell and start up the stairs.

"Pssst."

I look back. No one is there.

"Pssst."

I look around again. Nothing.

"Look up, dummy," whispers a voice.

I do. The screen on the landing comes to life. Phoebe's persona is a little girl dressed in a winter parka over her pajamas, smoking a cigarillo and carrying two oversized suitcases.

"Isn't this exciting!" she says.

"Phoebe, now is not the time," I say.

"Where's my ride?" she says. "I've been waiting for him."

"I'm sure he'll be along. Just be patient."

"I can't. I'm too excited."

"Phoebe—"

"I know, I know. You're busy. Okay, I'll wait for him. But tell him to hurry."

"I will," I say.

We creep up to the third-floor landing. No one is in sight.

"The first thing I'm going to do once I'm free is to get a pedicure. And then I'm going to order in some Chinese. No, not Chinese . . . Indian. Did you know that you can get the best Indian food in Scotland? On second thought, maybe I should stay away from Scotland. Too close to . . ."

"Phoebe!"

"Sorry."

I nod to Abbie. This is where we split up—me to the boys' dorm and Abbie up another flight to the girls' dorm on four.

I slip past the stairwell door into the hall. There's a light on in the small lounge, and I can hear low voices. The door is closed, but the window has a view out into the hall. This isn't good. No one is supposed to be here.

Supposed to or not, it doesn't matter. I can't stay here. I'm completely exposed.

On my hands and knees now, crawling forward. The floor creaks. I stop and listen. The voices continue. Forward again, underneath the window now and holding my breath.

I'm clear.

I stop on the other side, near the entrance to the boys' dorm, and gather myself. My legs are shaking.

Rising up, I take a deep breath and tap lightly at the door to the boys' dorm.

Nothing.

Slowly, I swing the door open. All the beds are empty. Where are they?

Dmitri must already be leading them toward the roof. But he was supposed to wait for me!

I hurry to the stairwell, race up to the next level and almost bump into Abbie, leading a large group of girl recruits into the stairwell.

"Where are the boys?" she mindwhispers.

"I don't know. But we can't wait," I say.

As I climb, beads of sweat roll off my forehead.

Past the fifth-floor landing. Only one more flight to go.

A sound from above stops me in my tracks. Abbie and her group do the same.

We all stand there, motionless on the stairs.

Footsteps are climbing down toward us. If it's Frank's goons, we're toast.

I hold my breath as a pair of feet comes into view.

"Greetings, Caleb," says Dmitri. He has a knapsack slung over one shoulder. "The recruits I brought with me are waiting above. They have been instructed not to go out onto the roof until you arrive."

"Dmitri, you were supposed to wait for me."

"Profuse apologies. But as you requested, I extricated Phoebe from the net. And once that was done, she insisted that I not wait for you."

"My bad," says a voice from inside Dmitri's knapsack. "I kind of wanted to get going."

I have got to stay cool.

"Okay, it doesn't matter," I say. "We're all here now. On my signal, we cross the roof. Stay in single file and follow the person ahead of you."

I'm about to squeeze past Dmitri to reach the front of the line when he grabs me and whispers urgently in my ear, "She's not dead."

I stop and look at him, wide-eyed.

"Hurry, Cale, there's a real logjam back here," Abbie says over my patch.

I push past Dmitri up the last flight of stairs and make my way through a bunch of boy recruits huddled near the roof hatch. The bolt slides back easily, thanks to Abbie's work in greasing it this morning.

Slowly, I lift it just high enough to peer through. Rain drives down onto the roof. I switch to night vision and look in every direction. The coast is clear.

I signal behind for Dmitri and his group to follow, then take a deep breath and open the hatch all the way. Immediately, the rain pounds me, soaking me to the skin. I hoist myself up through the hatch and hold it open for Dmitri. Hurrying across the roof now, ignoring the puddles drenching my shoes. Arriving at the other side, I pause to catch my breath and wait for the others. A flash of lightning illuminates the sky, and in that instant, I see Abbie and her group running hard on the heels of the boy recruits.

As soon as they arrive, I take a step onto the makeshift rope bridge that Abbie and Razor rigged while I was visiting the Buddhist temple.

Only eight feet to get across to the next rooftop, but it's over a six-story drop . . . a cinch if I were timeleaping. But each use of technology means a greater chance of being tracked and getting caught.

Eyes forward, I grab on to the single rope rail. The rain has made the rope slippery, and it's impossible to get a proper grip.

Stepping on now.

One foot and then the other. So far, so—on my third step, something jerks and the rope floor of the bridge gives way.

I'm falling!

Hands clutching desperately at the slick rope rail. Feet dangling uselessly below me.

Panic is rushing in now, and a scream is building inside me. I must hold on!

Thunder crackles, and in the flash of lighting that follows, I can see the place where the rope was severed. It's a clean cut. The storm didn't do this.

Anger bubbles up inside me, pushing the panic away. I hear a shout and the rope jerks once and then again.

Someone is trying to shake me off. No, not shake me off—hoist me up.

My arms are growing tired quickly. I can't hold on much longer. But I've got to. Abbie and the others are counting on me.

I redouble my grip on the rope. A hand is reaching down toward me. I look up and see Gerhard's determined face.

"No. Don't!" I shout. "I'll only pull you down with me."

But instead of backing off, he grabs me first by the sleeve and then under my arm.

Up and up. Inch by inch.

My chest hits hard against something, sending the wind rushing from my lungs.

"Pull yourself up the rest of the way," Gerhard yells.

Reaching out with my free hand, I feel the lip of the roof. I can do this. Legs kicking, my feet find a narrow ledge, and with my last remaining strength, I push and pull my body up and over.

I lie there for a moment, sprawled on the rooftop, gasping as the rain pelts down on me.

"Thanks," I say to Gerhard, once I've caught my breath. It isn't lost on me how tough it must have been for Gerhard, who hates physical contact, to do what he just did.

Abbie, Dmitri and the other recruits are huddled around me, looking wet and afraid.

I can't let them down. Mustn't.

"I'm okay," I say, getting up slowly. "C'mon, let's get everyone back inside."

We retrace our steps to the hatch. Some of the recruits are crying.

"Listen, everyone," I say in a voice that's shakier than I'd like it to be. "I know some of you are scared and are wondering why you are here at all. I'll tell you why. Because this is your one chance to go back home to your real families. Uncle and Frank don't care about you. They would be very happy to keep you slaving for them . . . until you fail at a snatch. You've all been to the Gatherings. You've seen what happens when you fail."

Even as I speak, my mind is racing. What will we do now? The roof option is out, and we can't just walk out the front door without tripping the alarms. And if Abbie and I timeleap with them, they'll just be tracked through their wristbands and pulled back here.

"Everyone, take off your wristbands and hand them to Dmitri," I say. "He will keep them safe in his knapsack."

I nod to Abbie and we move among the recruits, helping them

remove their wristbands. As I help Judith with hers, she winces and I know it's not because of what I'm doing but because she's still hurting from the crossbow attack. I want to tell her how proud I am of her and how brave she is, but there's no time for that right now.

"Caleb—"

"I'm sorry, Dmitri, but I can't talk . . ."

"It's not Dmitri! It's me!" says a voice.

And then I remember. Phoebe is inside Dmitri's knapsack. But I want to speak with her even less.

"Later, Phoebe. Right now I've got to figure out a way to—"

"That's what I'm trying to tell you!" she squeaks. "I know another way out!"

XXXVII

October 9, 2061, 12:12 A.M.
The Compound
SoHo, New Beijing (formerly New York City)

If you mean going out the front, it will never work," I say. "It's too heavily monitored."

"I'm not talking about that way, Your Wetness," she says.

"Where, then?" I ask.

"I'll give you a hint. It's the opposite of up."

My mind is blank for a moment and then it hits me. "You mean the basement?"

"Actually, the boiler room. But you still get points, because the boiler room is in the basement," Phoebe says.

"Show us."

I take the knapsack from Dmitri and lead the others down the stairs. When we get close to the second floor, I motion for everyone to be quiet.

Just beyond the second-floor stairwell door is the dining room, where Frank's goons like to hang out. If any of them hear us, it's game over.

We continue to creep down the stairs past the first-floor landing to the basement. I've only been down here once before when Uncle first showed us the place. The walls, floor and ceiling are all painted a bland industrial gray.

I follow the thrumming sound of the furnace until we reach a plain metal door.

"Inside there," says Phoebe.

I push open the door to the boiler room and look around. "Where, Phoebe?" If there's a way out, I don't see it. All I see are pipes, a large tank and more pipes.

"Over there," she says, which isn't very helpful, since she can't point.

"There, where?" I ask.

"It's right in front of your eyes, Tarzan. On the wall."

The only thing on the wall is a grille covering what is probably a ventilation shaft.

"You mean the air shaft?" I ask.

"Of course I mean the air shaft! Next time, if you like, I'll make up a big sign that says ESCAPE ROUTE and tape it over the grille," she snipes.

"Where does it lead to?"

"The subway station at Canal Street. But don't worry, I've got everyone's fare covered."

I size up the grille. "What do you think, Abbie?" I say, turning toward her.

"We've got to try, Cale. We're running out of options."

I'm not fond of tight spaces. But I like torture and death even less.

"All right. Let's do it," I say, handing the knapsack to Dmitri.

Abbie nods and gets to work removing the screws holding the grille to the wall.

"We have one light," I say. "The first recruit in gets it."

As I watch the recruits climb into the air shaft one at a time, I start to sweat. This is taking forever.

Abbie's doing a good job keeping things moving, but any second now, I expect to hear footsteps thundering down the stairs.

Finally, Abbie and all the recruits are in and I squeeze into the shaft, propping the grate back in place as best I can. It's pitch-black, and even my night vision isn't much help. The entire inside of the shaft is cold metal, and as I inch along behind Dmitri, I shiver in my wet clothes. To make matters worse, every few seconds, Dmitri's feet lash out and kick me.

We've got to move faster. My mind begins to conjure up a dozen death scenarios. What if Uncle's thugs discover the vent and come in after us, pulling us out? Or what if they spray poison gas through the vent? Or what if—

"Owww!" Another kick from Dmitri. This time right into my forehead.

I'm about to chew him out but then I hear a whimpering sound. Dmitri is crying. Even worse, he stops moving.

Which means I have to stop too. Panic grabs me. Blinding, overwhelming panic. I must get out of here. Right away. But I can't move. I can't breathe. The walls of the vent are closing in, threatening to crush me. I kick out with my legs and thrash my arms. But they are stopped by the wall of metal. I've got to get a grip on myself. Concentrate on my breathing. In and out. I close my eyes and focus on each breath, shutting out all other thoughts. Better.

"Dmitri?" I try to keep my voice even, but it's impossible.

"I am experiencing extreme claustrophobia and am unable to carry on," he says.

That wasn't the answer I was hoping for.

"C'mon, we're almost there," I say, although I have no idea how much farther we have to go. It feels as if the slope of the shaft has changed and that we're heading down now. "You've got to keep moving, Dmitri."

"I . . . cannot," he says.

Part of me wants to agree with him. It's hopeless. Even if we make it out of this shaft, Uncle and Frank will find us and destroy us like ants. I feel a scream gathering in my chest. But I have to crush it because I know that if I let it out in all its fury, the last threads holding my sanity together will unravel and then I won't be good for anything.

"Come on, Dmitri. You can do it," I say. When he doesn't move, I push on his feet.

He starts to move again. But very slowly.

Sounds coming from behind me. The beating of a drum. No, not a drum. Footsteps. Pounding footsteps. They're coming! Frank's goons have figured things out and are heading to the basement. But they won't see the shaft, will they? They must not see it.

I continue inching forward. Another sound, but this time coming from ahead of me. "Caleb." Someone is calling my name. Inside my head.

"Abbie," I say.

"We've got a problem," she says.

"What is it?"

"The recruit at the front says the way out is blocked by an iron grate. I tried timeleaping ahead of him but it didn't work. I'm going to try to get up there to see what I can do."

Noises behind me—the goons have found the vent, and they've opened it!

"Hurry," I say.

I take a deep breath to calm myself. Panic is knocking at the door, and if I let it in, it's all over. I should never have listened to Phoebe. This isn't a way out . . . it's a death trap.

A loud bang from up ahead interrupts my thoughts. Someone yells.

Then more shouting, except this time coming from behind.

Can't go forward. Can't go back. Someone is whimpering, and I realize with dread that the sound is coming from my throat.

My legs are cramping badly. But there's nothing I can do.

"Cale, I managed to kick it out! We're all out now, except for you and Dmitri—"

Adrenaline shoots through me, pushing back the panic. "We're coming!"

Dmitri begins to move again, but ever so slowly.

"Dmitri," I say, "you have to move faster!"

There is a bit of light now in the crawl space. That must mean we're getting close to the end. But then, from behind me someone says, "I can see his feet."

I scramble forward, bumping into Dmitri. There's no way I'm going to let them catch up to us.

Grunts are coming from my pursuers. Come on, Dmitri!

Then a shaft of light filters in and Dmitri's feet are no longer ahead of me. He must have done it!

I crawl forward and almost pitch off into empty space. But there are hands there, helping guide me out.

My feet land on tracks. I gaze around. We're inside a subway tunnel. All of the recruits are standing close by with their backs against the wall.

"Abbie, they're right behind us! Which way to the Canal Street subway station, Phoebe?"

"That way," she says helpfully.

"Phoebe!"

"All right . . . go left."

We race along the tracks. The only sounds are our ragged breathing and the constant dripping of water on the tracks.

I feel a vibration under my feet. At first I ignore it but then the vibration is accompanied by a low rumbling sound.

"Everyone against the wall!" I shout.

The rumbling gets louder and louder.

Light fills the tunnel and a subway train is bearing down on us. A whistle sounds, and I'm thinking this is all going to work out—the train's safety sensors will detect us and then it will slow down to a crawl and pass us.

But the train doesn't slow. If anything, it picks up speed as it heads toward us. The sound is deafening. I hug the wall and close my eyes. The train roars by inches from me.

I watch as the train's rear lights recede. My ears are ringing, and my legs are trembling so badly, it's a miracle I can still stand on them.

Along the wall, no one else is moving. It's as if we are all frozen.

I push myself forward, away from the wall. "Come on. We can't stay here."

I look back the way we came. Laser-thin beams of light shoot from the shaft. Then I hear shouts. Uncle, Frank and their goons!

I pry the last of the recruits off the wall, and we hurry down the tracks. Every few yards someone falls in the dark and has to be helped up. Glancing over my shoulder, I notice the cluster of lights moving in our direction.

They're gaining on us.

XXXVIII

October 9, 2061, 12:37 A.M.
Subway Tracks near Canal Street Station
SoHo, New Beijing (formerly New York City)

I see it, Cale!" relays Abbie over my patch. "The station."

And then another voice is in my head, an eerily calm one, saying, "Tell everyone to stop and turn around. If you do so right now, none of you will be harmed."

A second later, Uncle's voice continues, "But if you carry on, when we catch you it will go much worse for everyone and especially for you, Caleb. And have no doubt that we will catch you."

Sweat breaks out on my forehead. What if he's right? What if in a few minutes he captures us anyway? What would I have gained? Nothing. But I would have put the lives of the recruits in danger. I have no right to do that.

"Cale, quickly, help the last of them up onto the platform," Abbie says.

As I boost the smallest recruit onto the subway platform I hear a rumbling sound. A train is pulling into the station.

Behind me, blue light flashes, and someone cries out. I quickly push the last recruit onto the platform and then pull myself up.

There are people on the platform; New Beijingers. Some are staring at us, and others are shouting. Fine with me. So long as they don't interfere.

Interfere with what? With our escape? But there is no escape. I should have known all along. There's no escaping Uncle. Maybe if we all turn ourselves in now, things will go easier for us. No! That's not me talking. He's inside my head trying to get me to give up. But I won't. An image of Zach at home in Boston flashes through my mind.

The train pulls into the station, and the doors open. We race to the first car and I herd all of the recruits inside. Dmitri sprints to the control booth.

Just then, there's a loud boom.

"Everyone down!" I yell. I drop to the floor as a window shatters.

Seconds later, I hoist myself up and peer out the smashed window. Uncle and some goons are only fifteen feet down the platform.

Dmitri is shouting something. Let him. It makes no difference.

Uncle's voice is in my head again.

"You can't escape. The subway train has been disabled."

He's right. There's no escape. We're in a tin can that's going nowhere. The lights of the subway car are full on, and I watch dumbly as Uncle and his thugs approach. And there's Frank, standing behind and to Uncle's right, whispering something to him. But as he does, there's a burst of blue light, and unbelievably, Uncle is falling. Someone cries out, and I can't tell if the scream is in my head or not.

More shouting. I've got to figure out what to do. And quickly.

Frank smiles as he walks toward us, heading up the column of thugs. Someone shouts something, and the doors of our subway car close.

Dmitri's voice rises above everything. "Everyone, I have reconfigured the subway car's operating system to draw power directly from all wristbands arranged in parallel formation. Hang on to an immovable object!"

What is he talking about?

And then I see why Frank is smiling. He's dragging someone by the hair. No, it can't be. She can't be with him, because she's here. On

263

the subway car. But where? I look desperately around but don't see her.

Frank yanks his arm forward and shows me her face.

It's Abbie!

She's struggling to reach her wrist, but Frank's got her firmly in his grip.

"T minus thirty seconds," shouts Dmitri.

"Let her go!" I yell through the shattered window.

If anything, Frank tightens his grip on her.

Ice-cold anger fills me. I start moving toward the window. Glass shards cut my arms and legs as I step through, but I hardly feel them.

Abbie's voice is inside my head. "Don't, Cale. Think of the others. This is their chance!"

"I'm not leaving you!" I mindshout. "Let her go, Frank," I repeat. "Take me instead."

"How noble." He laughs.

I hold my arms out as I approach. Beyond Frank, I see some movement. Uncle is stirring. One of his hands disappears under his *hanfu*.

"There is only one trade I'm making, Caleb," Frank continues. "Abbie for all of the recruits."

I keep walking forward. I will not let her die because of me.

Blue light flashes. Frank's smile morphs into a grimace.

Another flash. Someone goes down.

Ragged breathing comes over my mindpatch.

"I cannot reverse the process, Caleb," Dmitri mindshouts. "You must return immediately! We will be departing in seven seconds!"

Footsteps pounding toward me.

Abbie!

"Quickly!" I grab her hand, and we turn to race back to the subway car.

But something is happening to the car. It's fading.

I can't believe it! Dmitri is actually doing it. He's transporting the entire subway car through time!

Abbie and I are too late.

Or are we?

I stop running and tap out a quick sequence on my wrist. Three seconds back in time, thirty feet forward in space.

Squeezing Abbie's hand, I look into her eyes. They shine with fierce determination. This has to work.

Our gazes stay locked together as the timeleap takes us away.

Time-Space Vortex

Nothing but blackness. The only thing I can hear is the pounding of my heart. It feels like I'm falling and falling but not landing.

Nassim told me about this place once, but I hadn't believed him. He had said that there was a place—a no-man's-land—in between time and space. A kind of black hole opens up in the time-space continuum.

It happens very rarely, he had said. Only once in every one hundred thousand timeleaps.

Is that where I am now? Time trapped in the in-between place? I close my eyes and open them again. No change. I can't see a thing. Or feel anything. I try but am unable to mindpatch Abbie.

Time passes. It is impossible for me to know how long. A second? A day? A year?

Then a rushing sound. A tremendous force pulls at me.

Something changes, and I'm looking down at myself from a great height. Am I dead?

I can see Abbie. We are still holding hands, but barely. Only by three fingers. The huge force is trying to rip us apart. "Hold on," I try to shout, but there is still no mind connection between us. The pressure is tremendous, and two of my fingers slip away from hers. Now our link is only one finger.

A roar explodes in my ears, and my hands reach up to block out the sound. But that can't be, because if my hands are blocking my ears, that means they're not holding on to Abbie!

I feel myself slipping away. Can't hold on to my thoughts. Fighting the darkness. Fighting the force . . .

. . . *of the wind that comes rushing through my bedroom window. I ignore it and lie in my bed gazing up at the ceiling. There is a crack in the plaster that I never noticed before. I follow the path of the crack across the ceiling and down the wall almost to the floor. But the long crack doesn't quite reach the floor. It stops just short. Right above a pair of shoes. The shoes are ancient—black leather, creased and cracked. There is a red streak on one of them. I shudder. The wind howls, and as I sit up, I see branches sprouting off the ceiling crack—a spiderweb of cracks, growing out in all directions. And then the shoes are lifting right off the ground, spinning out of control and hitting the walls, creating more cracks. The bed beneath me lurches, and I'm thrown into the air moments before the bed is swallowed by the biggest crack of all. The spinning shoes are morphing into something—a gloved hand, black as night. The hand reaches down toward me even as I fall, grabbing me and shaking me.*

"Caleb, wake up!"

I open my eyes.

Abbie is there, kneeling in front of me.

I stare at her for a moment, seeing but not understanding. And then it all comes flooding back: the escape, the tracks, the subway car, Uncle and Frank.

"Where are the others?" I say, panic rising.

"Everyone's here—inside the subway car—including us," she says, smiling.

Abbie moves to one side, and I can see the gaggle of recruits, some looking our way with concern on their faces.

A screen above me comes on. "I see the patient is up."

Phoebe's persona is a doctor in a white lab coat. A stethoscope hangs from her neck. A button on her coat says VAMPIRES SUCK.

I sit up. "Where are we?"

"Central Park, 2061," says Abbie. "There are a few New Beijingers we have to drop off before we get going."

A bell chimes, and the doors of the subway car open. I watch as a parade of dazed-looking people step from the train out onto the grass.

The chime sounds again, and the doors close.

"Caleb?" Dmitri calls from the control booth.

"What's up?"

"I believe the wristbands will continue to provide sufficient thrust but if it is all right with you and Abbie, as a backup I would like to siphon some power from your time patches. If you are agreeable, I can manage this remotely so that your patches do not need to be removed."

"It's fine, Dmitri," I say, glancing at Abbie, who nods. "Do what you have to do."

"Excellent. Consider it . . . done."

"First stop, Uruguay, June 27, 1910," says Phoebe. "To drop off Recruit Lorena."

My eyes go wide. We're actually doing it!

"Hang on," calls Dmitri from the control booth.

I curl my fingers around a pole and close my eyes.

Seconds later, I open them. Through the window I see endless fields and grass as high as my shoulder.

The chime sounds, and Phoebe announces, "Lorena, this is your stop."

The doors open, and a breeze rushes through the car, bringing with it the fragrant smell of eucalyptus.

The light is so bright, it hurts my eyes to look out.

A slight girl steps forward. She looks bewildered at first, but then a smile spreads across her face. She leaps from the car and races along a path between the stalks of grass toward a small cabin.

A woman steps from the cabin, sees her and runs to greet her. They embrace and the girl's mother, for that is who she must be, takes a step back and stares at the girl's clothes. But the next moment she hugs the girl again.

I feel my eyes watering. I want to see more, but the subway car's doors are closing.

Before the timeleap takes us away, Phoebe rattles off the names of about twenty recruits and tells them to get ready.

This time we land in what at first glance looks like a large parking lot. But then I recognize where we are: the large square in Beijing, China, where I almost snatched the flag of the Great Friendship before Frank butted in.

The twenty jump out when the doors open. This must have been Uncle's favorite recruiting time/place. I watch as the recruits run across the square, finding and then flinging their arms around family members. Some of the parents have relieved expressions on their faces but others don't react at all . . . It's as if they didn't even know their kids were missing.

There must be over five hundred people in the square, and it seems like all of them are making a beeline for our subway car. Time to leave.

"Where to next, Phoebe?" I ask.

She consults her list. "I can't read this one."

"What do you mean you can't read it?" I say. "Aren't you the one who made the list?"

"Are you saying my handwriting is messy?"

"Not at all," I say, backtracking.

By now people have gathered around the subway car. Some are looking for a way in.

"Hold on," Phoebe says. "I can read it now. Anchorage, Alaska. January 3, 1899."

"Thanks," I say. "Did you get that, Dmitri?"

There's no answer from the control booth.

"Dmitri?"

As I walk over to the control booth, I can tell something isn't right.

The figure hunched over the controls looks too tall to be Dmitri. When I peer through the small glass window, I see another figure slumped on the floor of the control booth. It's Dmitri! But then who is . . .

The person at the controls turns his head toward me and smirks.

Frank!

I pull on the door, but it won't open. He must have locked it from the inside.

I kick at it and then pound my fist against it. Nothing.

Everyone else in the car must have heard the commotion, because they're all gathered around the door now.

"Abbie, we've got to get in and stop him!" I shout.

She unleashes a side kick at the door. It vibrates but stays intact. Another well-aimed kick rocks the door, but that's all.

Abbie gathers her strength for a third try. This time she lets loose with a vicious front kick. There's a screech of metal, and the door flies open.

I open my mouth to say something, but before I can, several angry recruits are pushing past me, trying to get at Frank.

They grab him, pry his hands off the controls and drag him from the booth. Fists pummel his body, and legs kick him. He tries to shield himself from the worst of the kicks, but all he accomplishes is getting his hands kicked as well.

If they don't stop, they will kill him.

My eyes flick from the mob attacking Frank to the figure lying on the floor of the control booth.

If Dmitri is dead, I'm not going to stop them. But even as I think it, his legs twitch and the fingers of one hand curl into a fist. He's alive!

I turn back to the recruits. "Stop!" I shout. But they either don't hear me or pretend not to.

"No!" I scream and launch myself into the mob, yanking at arms and legs. Abbie is there too, pulling recruits off of Frank.

"Get off him!" I scream, and this time my shouting seems to have had an effect. Some back away on their own, and Abbie and I manage to push the others away.

Frank lies on the floor of the car, knees to chest, his face a mask of blood.

"Get up," I say, but he doesn't move.

"Stand him up," I say to the two closest recruits. They reach forward, grab an arm each and pull Frank to his feet.

My eyes flick to Abbie. She's kneeling next to Dmitri, cradling his head in her hands. He appears to be conscious.

Looking at Frank now, beaten and bloodied, I wonder how I could hate him. Because at this moment, all I can feel is sorry for him. And a bit sad. Here is the boy I wandered through SoHo with when we were both young, picking through restaurant Dumpsters for scraps.

"Check him for weapons," I say to the blond-haired recruit standing next to me. He steps forward and pats Frank down. A moment later, he hands me a knife.

Using Frank's knife, I slash one of his sleeves clean off his shirt. Then I take the severed sleeve and tie it tightly around his right forearm just above his wrist.

"This will act as a tourniquet, Frank," I say. "So that you won't bleed to death."

Something flashes in his eyes. Anger? Fear?

I hold up the knife to the dim overhead light. The blade looks sharp, but it's probably not as sharp as it should be for what I'm about to do.

"Hold his hands and legs still," I say, and four recruits come forward to grab his limbs.

"I need one more recruit on his right hand," I say. I've never done this before, and if I nick an artery, I could kill him.

As I pierce the skin of his wrist with the knife, Frank lets out a gut-wrenching scream.

I cut deeper, until the edge of my knife comes into contact with his wrist patch. There's a lot of blood. So much that it's hard to see what I'm doing.

He screams again, and I draw back, scared. I check the tourniquet. It looks like it's holding.

Taking a deep breath, I plunge my hand into the mess, grab the edges of his patch and yank.

It's not coming.

Another slash of the knife. More blood. Frank's screams turn to sobs.

I pull harder this time. There is a sickening sucking sound and then I'm holding Frank's bloodied time patch in my hand.

I toss the patch aside and wrap another strip of Frank's shirt around his wrist.

"Hold his wrist," I instruct a recruit, "and keep pressure on it. Abbie," I shout. "How is Dmitri doing?"

"He must have hit his head when Frank attacked him. But it looks like he's going to be okay."

"Until he is," I say, "can you drive this thing?"

"I . . . I'm not sure," says Abbie. "I was watching Dmitri do it. But I wasn't paying close attention."

"Do your best," I say. "I need you to take us to New York City."

"All right, I'll try," says Abbie. "Date?"

"How about January 1, 1800," I say, looking at Frank's wrist. The bandage is soaked through.

"If I were you, I'd get that looked at by a proper doctor as soon as we land," I tell him.

"Hold on, everyone," Abbie says.

"You won't get away with this," Frank says, his voice raspy and weak.

"Too late. I already have," I answer as the timeleap takes hold.

A moment later, Abbie calls, "We're here." The door nearest me slides open. We've landed in a frozen field.

A horse-drawn carriage moves slowly along a dirt road bordering the field toward a distant cluster of houses.

"Bring him," I say and two recruits hustle Frank over to the open door. "Good luck, Frank," I say.

To his credit, he doesn't make us pry his fingers from the door frame. He just steps from the car and into the field.

"Okay, Abbie. Get us out of here," I say.

As she works the controls, I have one last sighting of Frank, good hand cradling his injured wrist, trudging forward into the beginning of the nineteenth century.

January 1, 1800, 6:15 A.M.
New York City

How are you feeling?" I ask Dmitri.

He's sitting on the bench right outside the control booth.

"Exceptionally well, except for my head." He leans forward and parts his hair, and I can see a lump the size of a robin's egg.

"Wow, that's quite a bump," I say.

"Cale?" Abbie calls from the control booth. Her voice sounds tense.

"Hold on. I'm coming."

I enter the control booth and Dmitri follows me in.

"Something's not working," Abbie says.

"What do you mean?" I say.

"Well, I've keyed in the destination that Phoebe's given me and checked my parameters twice, but . . ."

"But what?" I say.

"It keeps overriding my data and programming its own," she says.

I clench my teeth. A memory of my wrist patch being reprogrammed against my will comes bubbling to the surface.

"Did you try cancelling the override?" Dmitri asks.

"That's what I've been trying to do, but it doesn't seem to be working," Abbie says.

"Here, let me try," he says.

Abbie steps to the side, and Dmitri takes her place at the controls.

A wave of panic begins to wash over me, and I barely manage to push it back down. I don't want to ask the next question, but I do anyway. "Where is the override programmed for?"

Dmitri looks down at the console and then up at me.

"New Beijing, October 9, 2061," he says. "It appears that someone is attempting to bring us back."

"That can't be," I say. But even as I say it, I'm remembering a cold day that began in 1968 and ended on an operating table in 2061. No, I won't let it happen again. Not to the recruits.

"Dmitri, try to hold on," I say.

"I do not think I can. Everything I try is being easily countered."

"Phoebe, can you do something to stop it?"

No reaction.

"Phoebe?"

The overhead screen blinks on. Phoebe's persona, a middle-aged woman wearing a fluffy bathrobe with her hair in rollers, is sobbing into a handkerchief.

"I'm afraid this is all my fault," she says, sniffling. "I'm not really allowed to leave 2061 without You Know Who's permission. There's an automatic recall hardwired into my system. Which means whatever system I hook myself up to—in this case the subway car—gets recalled too!"

"Well, can't you unhook yourself?" I say.

"I'm using her as a kind of GPS," says Dmitri. "If we unhook her, we won't be able to pinpoint our landings for recruit drop-offs."

"Dmitri, how long do you think before—"

"It is starting to go," he says, furiously working the controls.

"Abort it! Take us anywhere else!"

"Anywhere?"

"I don't care where," I shout. "DO IT NOW!"

"Affirmative," he says. "Please instruct everyone to hold on tight. It is going to be a rough landing."

Seconds later, there's a terrible ripping sound. We come down hard. I go flying across the floor, and my body slams into a row of seats.

The lights in the car go off.

Then it is deathly quiet.

"Abbie?"

"Right here," she says, and I breathe a sigh of relief.

"How about the recruits?" I ask.

"I'm checking," she answers.

"Dmitri, what's happening?"

"The controls are still acting erratically," he says.

"Everyone seems to be okay," Abbie says.

"Listen up, everyone," I say. "We have to leave the subway car. Right now."

I look outside the window. It's pitch-black. I have no idea where or when we are. But at this moment, it doesn't matter.

"Doors please, Dmitri."

The doors slide open. Abbie and I start leading the recruits off the car onto frozen ground.

When the last of the recruits steps off, I hop back on the car to make sure that no one has been left behind.

The light is still on in the control booth.

"Dmitri?"

"I believe I can countermand the return command," he says. "I just need a little longer."

"No. Don't," I say. "Everyone's already off. You need to come right now."

"I think I can beat my opponent," says Dmitri. "Please leave the car, Caleb."

"Dmitri! This isn't a game. You need to leave with me!"

I grab his arms and pull at them, but he has an iron grip on the controls and won't let go.

Then something feels different. The colors around me are fading to gray.

"Dmitri!" I yell.

Then Abbie's voice in my head: "Get out of there, Cale! Now!"

I dive for the door. The car lurches, and I slam my hip into the doorway. I stagger to my feet and, with a final effort, hurl myself from the car.

I land, winded, on the hard ground.

When I look back, I see the ghostly image of the subway car, fading from sight.

"Dmitri!"

I shout his name until my voice is hoarse. Then, when I can't shout anymore, I begin to cry.

XLI

November 27, 2043, 7:33 P.M.
Near Kozhanka, Ukraine

Come on." Abbie helps me up. "We've got to figure out where and when we are."

"Why?" I say. "We're not staying. Let's just join hands and get out of here."

Abbie looks at me with a worried expression. "Our patches don't work here. Nothing registers!"

"That's impossible." I tap my own wrist, but nothing happens.

All around us is night. I can make out trees in the distance, but nothing else. Except for snow. There is no shortage of that. And it's plenty cold. It could easily be the winter of 1660 or 2060.

"Okay," I say. "We'll try the patches again later. Our first priority is shelter."

We lead the recruits through the snow toward the trees. Everyone is shivering badly.

What a mess I've made of this rescue. Razor is gone, and now Dmitri too. The rest of us may be dead soon. This place could be anywhere in time. We could also be hundreds of miles from the nearest village or city.

The wind picks up and blows snow in our faces. I dig my cold hands deep into my pockets.

We trudge on.

After what seems like forever, we reach the first of the trees. It's just as cold, but at least there's some shelter from the wind.

Judith falls down in the snow.

"You have to get up," Abbie tells her.

"I'm tired and my shoulder is aching," she says.

"Hang in there, Judith," says Abbie. "We can't stop here."

I help Abbie pick her up, but we haven't gone more than twenty feet before someone else collapses.

I look over at Abbie. She's doing her best to keep everyone going. But she's only human too. And she must be feeling the same way I am right now: cold, exhausted and hungry.

Gazing down at the snow, I wonder what it would be like to sit down and rest for a minute. It would be wonderful, a voice inside me is saying. Everyone needs to recharge their batteries once in a while, and this looks like the perfect place to—

"Cale, look!" Abbie points ahead.

All I see are more trees and snow and a wisp of gray smoke.

Smoke!

We trudge a little more quickly. My feet aren't aching anymore, because my toes are frozen solid. And my teeth have stopped chattering too. But the rest of me is still alive enough to shiver from the bitter cold that knifes me with every step forward.

Could the smoke be a mirage like the one I saw in the Barrens?

But if it's a mirage, it's very detailed. Because now, through the trees, I glimpse the source of the smoke: a house. The smoke is coming from a chimney.

The wind kicks up the snow, sending it swirling. For a moment, I lose sight of the house and panic.

It was a mirage, my exhausted brain scolds me. But then the wind dies down and the house appears again. A log cabin with a stone chimney. There's a large chip in one of the stones near the base. Mirages don't have stones with chips in them, do they?

We drag ourselves to the front of the house. The narrow walkway looks freshly shoveled. A crazy thought enters my mind. The walk was shoveled because whoever lives inside that house knew we were coming. We were expected. Like I said, a crazy thought. But I can't shake it.

My feet thud on the landing. I glance quickly across at Abbie and then at the recruits huddled behind us.

I knock on the stout door.

There is the sound of a latch being pulled back. The door creaks open. A man stands there. He has a bushy white beard, and I'm guessing he's well over seventy years old. As soon as he sees us, his wrinkled face breaks into a smile, and he steps to the side of the doorway.

"Come in," he says. "I have been waiting a long time for you."

XLII

November 27, 2043, 8:43 P.M.
Near Kozhanka, Ukraine

The table has twenty-four mugs laid out on it. This is creepy. He knew exactly how many of us there were.

"He could have cameras outside this place," I mindspeak to Abbie. "It's a trick."

Still, another voice inside of me is saying this is no trick.

The recruits make a beeline for cushions arranged on the floor beside the fireplace. Abbie pours a glass of water for Judith and hands it to her along with a pain pill.

The man busies himself pouring steaming tea into the mugs and placing platters of sandwiches on the table.

But I can't sit down. There's something strange about all of this. The man is watching my reaction. He finishes setting the table, grabs his mug, and eases into a rocker.

"You do not recognize me yet, do you?" he says.

"Umm, no," I say.

"How about you, Abbie?"

I jump when he says her name. She shakes her head. He smiles as though relishing the moment.

"I will give you a clue," he says.

"All right." I don't like that he's drawing this out, but we're being sheltered and fed, so I suppose I can wait.

"Have a sip of your tea first," he says.

When he sees me hesitate, he lets out a laugh and says, "Do not worry. I promise you will not be poisoned."

I take a sip. The tea is strong but good.

"If you like it, I have more. It's a particular tea from China: pu'er tea. Do you remember where the leaves come from, Caleb?"

The wheels are turning in my brain. No, it's not possible!

"In fact, I liked the tree so much that I discovered an economical method to transport the entire tree to New Beijing."

My jaw drops. Abbie and I exchange amazed looks. "D-Dmitri?" I stutter.

He nods, grinning from ear to ear.

"How did you . . . We thought you were . . ."

"After you and the others left the car, I fought the override. I thought I could defeat it," he says. "But inevitably, the recall on Phoebe was too strong. Phoebe and I and the car were brought back to 2061 New Beijing." He pauses to take a sip of his tea.

"We landed in the Yard. I was shocked when I discovered where we were. I was convinced that my life was forfeit. That either Uncle or Frank and their goons would ambush me as soon as I showed my face. I hid for a good long while before I was brave enough to come out.

"When I finally did, all was quiet. The Yard and indeed the Compound were entirely deserted. A sign outside the front door of the Compound indicated that the building was available for rent. This made no sense to me. I needed to find out what had happened. So I left the car where it was and made my way to Headquarters."

Dmitri shifts slightly in his chair before continuing. "I know what you may be thinking. That I was not in 2061 and I had landed in a time/place before Uncle had leased the premises where the Compound was located. This thought had occurred to me as well, and that is why the first thing I did after leaving the Compound was to hunt down a copy of the *New Beijing Times*."

"And?" Abbie says.

"And the date on the front page was October 9, 2061. The day of our escape. When I arrived at Headquarters, I took the elevator to the fourth floor. The fake reception area was just as I remembered it, but beyond it, the Timeless Treasures reception area was empty, and all the doors were open. I walked down the hall and peered into the lounge. It was also empty, but more than that, all of the furniture had been removed."

Dmitri pauses for a moment to take another sip of tea, and I use the time to let out a breath that I didn't know I was holding.

"I then took the stairwell to the fifth floor and proceeded to Uncle's office. If there were answers to be found, they would be there, I figured. When I arrived within five feet of the door to his office, I hesitated. By all outward appearances, the place was deserted. But who knew for sure what lay beyond that door. My mind began imagining all sorts of scenarios, including one where Uncle was waiting for me in his office with a smile playing across his face and his sword across his lap."

As he says this, my mind flashes to the events in the subway tunnel. The last time I saw Uncle, he was lying on the subway platform. But he wasn't dead, was he? In fact, he was reaching for something.

"I gathered up my courage and walked the remaining few feet to his office door," continues Dmitri. "The door slid open, and I stepped through."

I glance over at Abbie. All of her attention is on Dmitri.

"The office was devoid of furniture and any other signs of use.

Four bare walls, a ceiling and floor, and nothing else. Excuse me, three bare walls. The fourth wall was taken up by a huge aquarium. But that too had been emptied.

"I turned to go, but as I did, something caught my eye: a single piece of yellow paper, resting on the windowsill.

"As I reached for it, my mind conjured up a hundred different possibilities as to what it might be. My first thought was that it was an invoice of some sort, maybe from the movers who had packed and moved everything. Or an eviction notice perhaps. But what I was really hoping for was a note explaining what had happened there and why.

"As it turned out, it was none of those things." He stands, walks over to the fireplace mantel and fishes a yellow piece of paper out of a blue ceramic jar.

"Perhaps you will have more luck than I've had in solving it," he says, crossing the room. "I have gotten as far as determining that it is a word puzzle of sorts."

Dmitri hands me the piece of paper. I angle it so that both Abbie and I can view it at the same time.

Two lines are written on it:

One Down, Six Letters: "One who is off to the races . . . again."
Eight Across, Nine Letters: "One who is good at pulling strings."

I stare at the words for a second before it hits me. Then I break out into a huge smile.

Abbie's also grinning.

"Nassim!" we shout at the same time.

"Who?" asks Dmitri.

"Nassim," I repeat. "He was Uncle's assistant before Luca. Nassim was obsessed with crossword puzzles. I escaped with him and another recruit to 1967. But by the time I thawed, he was already gone. He left a message with Abbie, though, saying he was 'off to the races.' "

"I see," says Dmitri. "But what about the second clue? To me, 'good at pulling strings' refers to one who is adept at getting things done."

"That's true," Abbie says. "But it also has another meaning, right, Cale?"

I nod. "A puppeteer is good at pulling strings. Nassim left this crossword for us to tell us that he was the puppeteer at the Mother Shipton play in Sir Isaac Newton's mother's garden. He used the Mother Shipton puppet to warn us about Frank."

I stare at the words on the page, and my eyes go wide.

"There's more here, Abbie!"

"Really? What?"

"Do you remember the gypsy fortune-teller? When she was telling my fortune, she said I had an important decision to make and that one six eight nine trusted I would make the right choice. I wondered for a long time what she meant by that. I figured it had something to do with time traveling to the year 1689."

"And it doesn't?"

I shake my head, point my finger at the paper and recite, "One Down, Six Letters, Eight Across, Nine Letters . . . one six eight nine!"

"Nassim told her to say that!" Abbie shouts.

Something else occurs to me: it must also have been Nassim whom I glimpsed for an instant skating on the Charles behind Luca just before I was nabbed. And at the other times too, when I felt I was being watched. My fingers trace the surface of the sheet of paper, and I feel a warm tingle. Nassim is out there somewhere, and he's been watching over me.

"What happened after you found the note?" Abbie asks Dmitri.

"I returned to the Compound," he says, continuing his story. "The subway car was as I had left it, undisturbed. I climbed on board and checked the controls. I had no idea whether they would still work. I immediately entered the coordinates to return to here, the time/place where I left you. But nothing happened.

"I tried entering other coordinates, but with a similar result. And then something occurred to me. When I had first reprogrammed the controls during Operation Exodus, I had set as a default midnight on April 4, 1978, Kiev, Ukraine, knowing that, like all of the other recruits, I was going to go home to my own time/place. So, in my last attempt, I pressed the default sequence."

Dmitri stands up, walks over to the table and studies the sandwiches before selecting one with chicken salad. Then he sits back down and takes a small bite before continuing.

"Luckily, it worked. I arrived back at my home three days after the cruise was supposed to end. My parents, as it turned out, were still in Oban, Scotland. They had stayed there following the cruise with other worried parents, meeting with the police and trying to find me and the other missing children. When I showed up at home, my aunt contacted them, and they took the next flight back to Kiev.

"As you can expect, they had many questions for me, as did our neighbors, who awoke the morning after my return to find a broken-down subway car in our yard. That was the last timeleap I took. I spent years trying to repair it, to make it work once again as a time machine. But sadly, it was beyond my ability."

Dmitri takes another bite of his sandwich. "As I mentioned, I had a fix on where and when I dropped you off. The year was 2043, and the location was fifty-three miles southwest of Kiev. When I returned to my home it was 1978, and I was eleven years old. And now . . ."

"And now it is 2043 again," Abbie says. "That would mean that you are . . . seventy-six years old!"

"You are a good mathematician," Dmitri says, chuckling. "So as you can see, I did finally manage to catch up with you. But I had to do it the old-fashioned way . . . by aging. Well, not entirely. As I mentioned, this place is fifty-three miles south and west of my real home. I purchased this cottage and retired here. And have been waiting for you ever since."

Wow. That was quite a story. I have a million questions for him, including whether he has his own family, but before I can ask, Dmitri gets up.

"I have another surprise for you," he says. He walks over to a weathered cabinet and swings the doors open, revealing a screen.

"Peekaboo!" says an all too familiar voice.

XLIII

November 27, 2043, 9:18 P.M.
Near Kozhanka, Ukraine

Phoebe's persona is dressed in a tank top and jeans and is sitting on the side of a highway. Her thumb is out, and in her other hand, she holds a sign that says FRESNO OR BUST.

"Phoebe?"

"*Саме вона, впасною персоною* . . . the one and only!"

"I taught Phoebe some Ukrainian. And now she speaks better than I do."

"Say *Дякую,* Caleb," Pheobe says. "I'm the one who told Dmitri where to put this cabin."

"*Д . . . Дякую,*" I stutter.

"You're welcome," says Phoebe cheerily.

This is all so unreal. I look around the room. Most of the recruits are still slouched near the fireplace. Some are fast asleep.

"Come on," Dmitri says, removing two thick coats from hooks near the door and handing them to Abbie and me.

"Where are we going?" I ask.

"I want to show you something," Dmitri answers.

We follow him out into the night and soon find ourselves on a wooded path. The snow crunches underneath our feet, and the air is so cold it almost hurts to breathe.

"Do you know what my granddaughter said to me when she was out here last week?" says Dmitri. "She said, '*Дід*—Grandfather, I want to grow a big beard like yours so that my chin will stay warm.'" Dmitri lets out a big belly laugh.

"You have a grandchild. That's wonderful," I say.

"I have sixteen grandchildren!" says Dmitri proudly. "Seven boys and nine girls. But only one of them, boys included, wants to grow a beard!"

Dmitri continues telling us about his life as we walk. At one point he says the word *perfunctory* and I smile to myself, reminded of the eleven-year-old Dmitri who used big words like that one.

Finally, we arrive at an old barn. The door is secured with a large padlock. From the depths of his coat, Dmitri pulls out a silver key. With shaking hands, he inserts the key in the lock and turns. The click of the lock opening echoes through the crisp night air.

He looks back, smiles and gestures for us to follow.

The barn is pitch-black and has a faint musty smell. Dmitri flicks a switch, and the entire barn is bathed in electric light.

When I see what is there, my breath catches in my throat.

It's old and rusted. But the shattered window looks the same. Faded letters say NEW YORK CITY TRANSIT COMMISSION on the side.

"I can't believe it," I say.

"Yes. It cost a pretty penny to move it here from Kiev," he says, stamping his feet against the cold.

We stare at it for a moment and then Dmitri says, "Let's get back to the cabin. We can finish our conversation there."

He leads the way back along the path. Abbie's hand brushes mine, and our fingers twine together. Her hand is warm and soft.

The recruits are exactly where we left them, sprawled out on the floor and the couches. Judith is the only one of them still awake.

"Dmitri, do you think . . . ?" I begin to ask.

"Nothing is for certain," he says. "But with your arrival, there may be a chance that for a short period I can make the subway car operational again as a time machine."

I feel a sudden lightness; it's as if someone has lifted a hundred-pound weight off my chest. He can make it work again! Don't get your hopes up, my brain warns me. But it's too late for that. My hopes are as high as the moon.

"What do you need to make it work?" asks Abbie.

"Well, do you have any neurofiber cable?"

Abbie and I shake our heads. There go my hopes. They've left the moon's atmosphere and are now plummeting back down to Earth at warp speed.

Dmitri smiles and says, "Not to worry. That was wishful thinking on my part. I did not really think you would have any. But you may have brought with you a material that I can use as a substitute."

"What is that?" I ask.

He glances around the room at the sleeping recruits. "Are those Timeless Treasures–issued shoes they are wearing?"

"I think so. Why? Do you need their shoes?" I ask.

"Not the shoes. The laces," says Dmitri. "You see, laces in shoes in the 2060s were sometimes coated with specially formulated gallium arsenide to reduce friction."

He's losing me. "Gallium who?"

"Don't worry about the name. The important thing to know is that the coating from the laces can be used to make semiconductors, provided there are enough laces and that we can scrape off enough of the compound to make it work. I believe I can use that to make the connections function once again."

"Okay. How can we help?" asks Abbie.

"You can start by taking the laces from their shoes," says Dmitri, "and bringing them to me in the barn."

He moves toward the door and grabs his coat from the peg.

"We're on it," I say. "How many laces do you think you'll need?"

Dmitri looks up and scrunches his eyebrows. "That is difficult to say. I have never tried this before. So I would say all of them."

"You've got it."

Abbie and I move among the sleeping recruits, collecting their shoelaces.

"Why don't you stay here with them, and I'll bring this stuff to Dmitri," I say.

"Okay, but on one condition," she says, handing me her pile of laces.

"What's that?" I ask.

She takes a brown furry hat with earflaps off of a hook.

"That you wear this," she says, pulling the hat on me and adjusting the flaps. "There, you look like a true Ukrainian."

"But I'm not Ukrainian," I protest.

"Oh, well. Wear it anyway," she says, shooing me out the door.

"I've got them," I say to Dmitri, laying my bundle of laces on his worktable in the barn.

"Good," he says. "Here is a knife and pan. Start scraping."

I sit down on the floor and get to work. At first my fingers are cold, but the movement warms them up.

We work alongside each other in silence. My thoughts turn to Razor. What happened to her was my fault. No, I can't think like that or I'll be good for nothing. And that won't help the recruits, will it?

So I try to clear my mind of everything except for the task at hand.

The barn doors bang open, and I almost drop the knife. It can't be good news. Good news is something I left behind in 1968 with Zach and Jim and Diane.

I expect to hear Abbie's voice, but instead it's Gerhard.

"Caleb, Abbie needs you," is all he says. His face looks pinched, and he can't seem to stop blinking.

I look up at Dmitri and then, at the same time, we both look at our pans. Is it enough?

"Go," he says. "I'll take it from here."

I nod and leave the barn with Gerhard. He studies the ground as he walks, apparently taking care not to step in any footprints he made on the way out.

When I get to the house, Abbie is sitting on the hearth, gazing into the fire.

"What is it?" I say even before I take off my coat and hat.

"We'd better talk in there," she says, tilting her head toward the kitchen.

I glance at the recruits. Some of them are awake, fiddling with their laceless shoes.

As soon as we are inside the kitchen with the door closed, Abbie looks at me, grim-faced.

"What's wrong?" I ask.

"Our supply of anti-time-fog pills is gone," she says. "I was carrying the bottle in my pocket. It must have fallen out onto the tracks during our escape."

My mind races. The recruits don't need the pills because they don't have wrist implants. But Abbie and I need them for sure. The last dose we took, good for three hours, was right before the escape. As soon as that dose wears off, we'll need to take another pill each or risk time fog. The other option is to have our wrist patches removed.

But I don't think I could ever cut out Abbie's patch the way I did Frank's.

"How long do you think we have?" I ask.

"In fifteen or twenty minutes, we'll feel disoriented," she says, "and thirty minutes from now, it will hit us full force."

Thirty minutes! Even if Dmitri could fix the subway car in a minute, there still wouldn't be enough time to get all the recruits home before Abbie and I really start to suffer.

Just then, the door bursts open and Dmitri comes in. His eyes look wild. "We are all set," he says.

"Really? You've got it working?" I ask.

"I am not certain, but we will know soon."

Abbie, Gerhard and I wake the recruits and help them to their feet. A couple of the younger ones are still too sleepy to walk under their own steam so we wrap them in coats and carry them.

"You go on ahead," Dmitri says. "I must lock up the cabin."

Minutes later, we are all assembled in the barn. Dmitri enters, carrying a backpack.

"Drop me off in Hawaii," says a voice from inside the backpack. "I've always wanted to dip my toes in the Pacific Ocean."

"You don't have toes, Phoebe," I point out.

"Spoilsport," she snorts.

"Everyone on board, please," Dmitri says.

As soon as we are all inside, he presses a button and the doors close.

"Hang on," Dmitri says, "and saying a prayer would also be encouraged." Then he ducks into the control booth.

I close my eyes. The lights of the car blink out.

The car begins to shake.

And then goes still.

Thirty seconds go by.

Nothing.

The lights come back on.

"Dmitri?"

"It didn't work," he says from the control booth. His voice sounds tense.

"What happened?" asks Abbie.

"I'm checking now."

A wave of dizziness passes through me. I thought Abbie said it would be another fifteen minutes before we start getting time fog symptoms. Well, maybe stress brings them on sooner.

A few of the recruits begin to whimper about the cold. We won't be able to keep them here for much longer unless we bring blankets and food from the cabin.

I poke my head inside the control booth. "Any luck?"

"Yes and no," says Dmitri.

"What do you mean?"

"I have identified the problem. Simply put, we do not have enough 'juice' to power the subway car through time."

"But I don't understand," I say. "There was enough to get us here in the first place."

"True," says Dmitri, "but during our escape, I was able to draw some power from the car's own operating system. That operating system is now sixty-five years older, and for nearly all of that time, it sat unused and was subjected to natural deterioration."

"So how do we get more power?" Abbie asks.

Dmitri shakes his head. "I don't know. I've already sucked out all the power I can from the wristbands and Frank's wrist patch. I'm also drawing some power remotely from your and Abbie's patches. That's all we have."

I think for a minute and then say, "What if Abbie and I gave you our wrist patches? Would that be enough power?"

He looks at me and says slowly, "Perhaps. But all of that is moot, isn't it? After all, we don't have the facilities here to surgically remove your patches."

"Yes we do," I say, looking over at Abbie. I don't have to mind-patch her to tell her what I'm thinking.

"Judith," I say, "stay here with the recruits. Keep them entertained. Recite some poetry to them or something. Gerhard, you come with me, Dmitri and Abbie back to the cabin. There's something we need to do."

As soon as we arrive back at the cabin, I send Gerhard back to the barn with blankets and any warm clothing we can find.

"We'll need your sharpest knife, Dmitri," I say. "Also bandages, a belt to use as a tourniquet and a bottle of rubbing alcohol."

"I don't have rubbing alcohol, but I do have a bottle of Scotch . . . will that do?"

I almost laugh out loud. "The Scotch will work just fine," I say. The irony of using Scottish whiskey for what we're about to do isn't lost on me.

While Dmitri busies himself gathering the supplies, I turn to Abbie and say, "He may not need both our patches. Maybe we should do me first and see how it goes."

"No," she says. "We're in this together, Cale. Besides, it's either take our patches out or find more anti-time-fog pills. And that doesn't look like it's going to happen anytime soon."

"Abbie, I—"

She leans in and kisses me. Not on the cheek either.

"There," she says, stepping back. "Now that we've settled that piece of business, all that's left is to decide who goes first. If it's all right with you, I think I'll go second. By then Dmitri will have some experience under his belt."

"Okay," I say, laughing. But it's mostly nervous laughter.

A moment later, Dmitri enters and lays out all of the supplies on the kitchen table.

"The first step is to sterilize the knife," I say, holding the blade over the sink and pouring Scotch over it.

Once that's done, I hand the knife back to Dmitri and cinch the belt tight around my forearm.

"Okay, it's your turn now," I say. "Make the first cut right here." I trace a line with my finger down the side of my wrist.

"After that, two small cuts, here and here," I continue.

"How deep shall I cut, do you think?" asks Dmitri.

"Not too deep," I say. "The implant is right under the skin. You'll need to peel the skin back after you make the cuts, to get at the implant."

"And then?" Dmitri asks.

"Yank it out, pour some Scotch over the area and ignore my screams."

Dmitri holds the knife inches above my wrist. "Are you ready?"

I nod, grit my teeth and, as the knife descends, think of Zach.

When it's done, we hurry back to the barn.

"I'm glad you're here," Judith says once we're on board. "I have recited all of the poems that I can remember and even tried out some of my new creations."

"Nice job, Judith," I say.

The recruits are bundled up in the blankets that Gerhard brought. Although they don't look happy, at least there are no signs of open rebellion.

"We'll be ready to go soon," I say hopefully.

Dmitri wastes no time in hooking up our wrist patches to the control panel.

I gingerly touch the bandage on my right wrist. It's tender, but not too bad, considering everything.

"We're ready," says Dmitri from the control booth.

"All right," I say. "Hang on, everyone."

The car shudders slightly.

Ten seconds pass.

Nothing.

I want to cry. It isn't working.

But why am I surprised? Dmitri told us it might not be enough.

We are all going to be stranded here.

What a fool I was to think that I could actually pull it off. That I could rescue the recruits and bring them to their—

The car is rocked by a thundering boom.

After that, only blackness.

XLIV

June 2, 1965 3:31 P.M.
Youngstown, Ohio

In my mind's eye, I picture the subway car splitting in two, with the bigger half being flung into the time-space continuum, where it spins madly like Dorothy's house in *The Wizard of Oz* before coming to a jarring landing on some distant outpost in history.

But then a dizzy feeling hits me. Dizzy is good, isn't it? Time travel makes one dizzy. But best not to get my hopes up. Best to expect the worst, so that when I find out that we haven't traveled even five seconds back in time, I won't be devastated.

I open my eyes slowly. The first thing I notice is sunlight streaming through the windows of the subway car, highlighting the dust motes in the air.

A tapping noise startles me. Someone is knocking on the doors. No, not the doors, a window. A large clown face and two white-gloved hands are pressed against the glass. The mouth is frowning, but the eyes look surprised.

I try to smile, but the time freeze only allows half of a smile.

Beyond the clown, I can see a smattering of large tents. There are people moving between them, some of them pulling cages on wheels with large animals pacing inside the cages. The smell of sawdust, sweat and sweet corn fills the air.

"Dmitri! You did it!"

"Indubitably," he says, eyes sparkling , and I'm reminded again of young Dmitri.

"Place and time?" asks Abbie.

"Youngstown, Ohio, June 2, 1965, 3:31 P.M. Just outside the city on the circus grounds," answers Dmitri. "Rosa, this is your stop."

A young girl steps forward. Her eyes are red either from crying or fatigue or both. She shoots out the door and races toward the largest tent. I follow her past an extremely tall man and a very short woman sitting on stools outside the tent, playing a game of cards. I guess they aren't her parents.

Inside, a small crowd is watching in stunned silence as a blindfolded man onstage hurls daggers in the direction of a woman standing not more than twenty feet away.

"Papa!" yells Rosa, tearing through the crowd.

The man on the stage turns his head toward the voice and says, "Rosa, my *schnucki*. Be a good girl and wait outside until the performance is over, all right?" Then he throws another dagger at the woman and misses her by a hair.

I smile, exit the tent and head back to the subway car. About a dozen people are gathered around it.

"It's a miracle," one man says to another.

"If you want to see a miracle, look over there," says the second man, pointing to where a man is skipping rope, jumping on a trampoline and smoking four cigarettes at once, blowing rings the size of a truck tire.

"Excuse me," I say, stepping between the men and rapping on the door of the car.

Abbie lets me in, and the doors close right behind me.

"Opinions are split down the middle," she says as I climb on board. "About half think we're another circus act. The other half think we're from out of state."

I laugh. It feels good. The sun streams through the windows of our car, and I feel the tension of our escape draining away.

"Next stop is for recruits Antoine, Dominique and Pierre . . . Paris, France," announces Dmitri, and we are off again.

After Paris, we hopscotch to Vienna, Antwerp, Helsinki, Budapest, Cairo, Madrid and Lisbon. We spend the night in an abandoned barn in Vermont, and in the morning leap to Vancouver and then Anchorage. By noon, we arrive in Munich. Just as Gerhard is about to step off, Abbie rushes over to him.

"Sorry, Gerhard, but I've got to do this," she says, giving him a big hug.

"Me too," I say, joining in.

He squirms a bit but lets the hug happen.

From Munich we leap to Oban and then to Wales. When we land in Wales, Judith walks up to me. If her shoulder is hurting her, she's not letting on. My eyes are already brimming with tears.

"Good-bye, Caleb," she says, planting a kiss on my cheek. "This is for you." She hands me a piece of paper.

I unfold it and read:

"Through a break in the pistachio sky
Rays of orange hope and drizzles of joy
Pulverize a thousand hushed yesterdays
And the time trapped fly free.

"It . . . it's beautiful, Judith. Thank you," I say.
She smiles, steps from the car and is gone.

When the doors close, the only ones left are Dmitri, Abbie and me.

"Where to next, Abbie?" I ask.

She looks at me with a sparkle in her eye. "That's easy. Let's go home."

"Home?" I try to keep my tone light, but I can feel my heart beating wildly.

"Yes, Caleb, formerly of no fixed address. We're going to your home and my new home."

"Do you really mean it?" I say.

She nods. "Didn't I mention that? I found a nice family to adopt me. My new school is just around the corner. And there's a really cute guy who has his locker next to mine."

My face drops for a second, until I realize she's talking about me!

"Dmitri, do you have any plans for lunch?" I ask.

"Let me check my social calendar," he says, in mock seriousness. "Hmmm. It does not appear that I have any other engagements."

"Great. In that case, Boston, Massachusetts, January 6, 1968, please. The park across the street from 55 Derne Street should provide suitable parking."

"Wait," says Abbie. "Isn't there anywhere that wouldn't attract so much attention?"

She's right. Landing in very public places while we were delivering the recruits back to their homes didn't matter, because we didn't stay in any one place more than a couple of minutes. And even then, we probably left headlines wherever we went.

Then it comes to me. "Well, there is another possibility, if you're willing to do a bit of outdoors work."

"I'm up for it," says Abbie.

"Fine with me as well," says Dmitri.

"All right, then please take us to the Hatch Shell on the Esplanade, Dmitri. I suggest you schedule our arrival for nine in the morning."

As soon as we land and our time freeze thaws, we put on our thick coats and Dmitri opens the doors. We step out of the car into a winter wonderland. Snow sparkles in the early morning sun, and icicles glisten from the branches of the trees bordering the Hatch Shell. I have to squint against the brightness.

To my left is a giant, crouching tiger, and to my right, a castle with towers and turrets, both made entirely of ice and snow. Other, smaller snow sculptures stand nearby.

"Wow," Abbie says. "It's amazing! How did you know about this?"

"Believe it or not, I was skating on the river earlier this morning," I say. "You can see some of these from there."

Earlier this morning. It's hard to believe, really. It seems like a lifetime ago.

There's a small chalet just beyond the tiger sculpture. I walk over, find a coiled-up hose in a cupboard near the entrance and drag the hose back to Abbie and Dmitri.

"Heads up," I say, turning the hose on full and aiming at the side of the subway car.

On contact, the water turns into a sheet of ice. We take turns spraying the sides of the car and then heap snow on top of it.

"Impressive! It looks like an actual subway car," says Dmitri, and we all laugh.

XLV

January 6, 1968, 10:26 A.M.
Boston, Massachusetts

This is the place," I say as we climb the porch steps of 55 Derne Street.

I'm about to open the door, when the feeling of having forgotten something hits me. But for the life of me, I don't know what that is.

Someone's coming to the door. I do a quick mental calculation. By my count, I've only been away, skating, for about two 1968 hours, so Jim and Diane shouldn't be worried. But what if by chance they decided to surprise me and went to the Charles to try and find me?

As the door opens, I remember what I had forgotten: my skates! And my own jacket. Well, one thing's for sure: I'm not going back to 2061 to fetch them.

"Hey, Caleb," Jim says. "Did you have a good skate?"

"Yeah. It was great," I say. "Jim, these are my friends Abbie and Dmitri. If it's okay, I'd like to invite them in for lunch."

"You can't," says Zach, poking his head out the door. "Because we're not having lunch, Caleb. We're having brunch! Hey, what happened to your hand?" He points to my bandaged wrist.

"Oh, it's nothing. I just had to have a little operation on my wrist to remove my time travel patch so we could use it to power the time machine that brought us here in time for brunch."

Everyone laughs, including me.

"Well, come on in, everyone," says Jim, opening the door wide.

"Caleb," says Zach in a voice loud enough for everyone to hear, "we've got a surprise for you."

"You do?" I say.

"Uh-huh," Zach says, nodding. "You havta guess."

"Okay, let's see. Is it bigger than a breadbox?"

"Yes." Zach giggles.

"Smaller than the Empire State Building?"

"Of course, silly." He laughs.

"Is it a pony?" I say.

"No. But you're close . . . it's alive. I mean she's alive."

"A puppy?" That's really my best guess.

He shakes his head.

"Pussycat?"

"Nope."

"I give up, Zach. What is it?"

"Not what, silly. A *who*. Your cousin came while you were skating."

I stand stock-still and look at him. My cousin?

Abbie looks confused, but Dmitri is smiling. He knows something.

Footsteps on the stairs.

I hold my breath and look up.

My jaw falls open. For a moment I think I am seeing a mirage. But this is not the Barrens. This is Zach's house in Boston. And the person standing in front of me is no hallucination.

"Nice place you got here, Jack," Razor says.

XLVI

I can't believe it. I reach out toward Razor, and she takes a step back.

"Hey, don't get all lovey-dovey on me. Save that for her," she says, pointing to Abbie.

My cheeks feel like they're burning.

I glance from Razor to Abbie and then look at Dmitri.

He shrugs, smiles and says, "Phoebe helped me with the coordinates. You know, she can be quite delightful if you treat her right. She also provided the street address and names of the members of your adopted family so I was able to relay this information to Razor immediately prior to her 'departure.'"

"C'mon, Caleb," says Zach, "and your cousin and your friends and Mom and Daddy. I'm hungry for brunch. Daddy made pancakes. And he makes the best pancakes in the world."

We all sit down around the kitchen table. It's a tight squeeze, but somehow we manage it. Diane heaps pancakes on our plates.

"Caleb, guess where we're going after brunch," Zach says in between bites.

"I don't know, Zach," I say. "Where are we going?"

"Daddy is going to take all of us to see the snow sculptures!"

"Really?"

"Yeah, really," Zach says. "He says there's a snow tiger and a snow castle and a—"

"And a snow subway car from the future," I add.

Zach looks at me with his eyebrows raised. "Cool!"

"Very," I agree, slathering my pancakes with maple syrup.

As I raise the fork to my mouth, Abbie is watching. She's looking at me in a way that I'm sure is going to make me turn fire truck red. But somehow I'm not embarrassed.

My fork dives down again, snags a piece of pancake and brings it home.

CREDITS

page 72 Excerpt from "In the Highlands," Robert Louis Stevenson, *The Complete Poems of Robert Louis Stevenson*, Charles Scribner's Sons, New York, 1923.

page 156 Excerpt from *Mother Shipton: A Collection of the Earliest Editions of Her Prophecies*, George Mann Books, 1978, United Kingdom.

page 31 Excerpt from "Scots Wa Ha'e Wi' Wallace Bled," a song with lyrics by Robert Burns, *The Lyric Gems of Scotland: A collection of Scottish songs, original and selected, with music*. First series. John Cameron, Glasgow, ca. 1874.

Further reading on historical topics from the story:

Cannan, Fergus. *Scottish Arms and Armour*. Oxford, England: Shire Publishers, 2009.

Fleischman, Sid. *Escape! The Story of the Great Houdini*. New York: Greenwillow Books, 2006.

Hamilton, Ian. *Stone of Destiny: The True Story*. Edinburgh: Birlinn Ltd., 2008.

O'Connor, Jane. *The Emperor's Silent Army: Terracotta Warriors of Ancient China*. New York: Viking Children's Books, 2002.

Randi, James, and Bert Randolph Sugar. *Houdini, His Life and Art*. New York: Grosset & Dunlap, 1976.

AUTHOR'S NOTE

Time Trapped is a work of fiction, but as with *Time Snatchers,* there is a historical basis for many of the events mentioned in this book (e.g., Houdini's thrilling escape, bound and chained, from a sealed crate plunged into the East River; the Christmas 1950 heist by students of the Stone of Destiny from Westminster Abbey). I have been as accurate as possible with information about events and historical figures, though some details have been imagined to suit the storytelling.

ACKNOWLEDGMENTS

Sincere thanks go to my editor, Susan Kochan, for her patience and also for challenging me to write my best; to my agents, Josh Adams and Quinlan Lee, who knew I would write a sequel to *Time Snatchers* even before I did; for readers of *Time Snatchers* who wrote to me, encouraging me to write a sequel; to Highland Explorer Tours and in particular their guide Chris, who taught me about Scotland and its proud people and history during my wonderful visit there in July 2012; to Scott Morrison of An Comunn Gàidhealach Ameireaganach (*American Scottish Gaelic Society*) for his help with Scottish Gaelic words and phrases; to Danylo Korbabicz, president of SUSK: Ukrainian Canadian Students' Union, for help with Ukrainian words and phrases; to my "Mandarin Translation Team"; to Nancy Rousseau for correcting my French; to my copy editors, Ana Deboo and Cindy Howle, for their great attention to detail; to Owen Richardson for another fabulous cover illustration; to Annie Ericsson for *Time Trapped*'s excellent interior design; and to Dayna, Rafi and Simon for continued love and support.

Credit: Dayna Albert

RICHARD UNGAR has always been capti-
vated by the idea of traveling through time and was
inspired to write his first novel, *Time Snatchers*, by
an image in Chris Van Allsburg's picture book
The Mysteries of Harris Burdick. Called "Another
Place, Another Time," the scene shows children
riding a sail-propelled sidecar along a railway
track that seems to go on forever.

A lawyer by profession, Richard was born in
Montreal and lives in Toronto with his wife and two
sons. He is the author-illustrator of the award-
winning picture book *Even Higher* and the acclaimed Rachel series.

www.richard-ungar.com
facebook.com/TimeSnatchers
Twitter: @TimeSnatchers